The Lesser Evil

Time's Fickle Glass
Volume I

The Lesser Evil

TRISTAN STONE

This edition, 2019.
First published in the United Kingdom, 2015.

Cover Artwork by Andrew Dang

The right of Tristan Stone to be identified as author of this work has
been asserted by him in accordance with sections 77 and 78 of the
Copyright, Designs and Patents Act 1988.

Available from Amazon.com, Amazon.co.uk and other book
stores
Available on Kindle and other devices

www.tristanjstone.com

www .facebook.com/TimesFickleGlass
Twitter: @TristanJStone

To Laura

with all my love.

CONTENTS

Acknowledgments

ACKNOWLEDGMENTS

It has been a long journey to get this debut novel into print and I must, firstly, thank my parents for teaching me to read and write well before I set foot in school. The flashcards my mother made and the games my brother and I used to play making words come alive gave me a great fascination with words. Without my twin, playing endless games of the imagination with me, I would certainly not have loved inventing stories.

As the years have passed and I have put my pen to poetry and playwriting, I must thank those who have supported such ventures - particularly Michael, whose partnership and patronage brought *The Parachutist* and other characters to life on his stage.

In terms of the present work, I am particularly indebted to Bob Swindells, whose advice it was to write for Young Adults (between 14 and 114) and whose agent, Jennifer, kindly read an earlier draft.

I am also indebted to: Claire Daly, for painstakingly editing the very first draft and giving me such sage and frank advice; Matthew Munson, for the great encouragement you've given me over the years in getting something ready for publication, and Sara-Jayne Slack and her team at *Inspired Quill* for particular editorial advice.

To various students who have read excerpts and given me further advice - particularly the philosophers of Harris Westminster, without whose honest observations none of my readers would be able to follow chunks of dialogue. Friends, too various to mention, whose love and support over the years have made all endeavour possible; and my wife, Laura - not just for picking up my socks, giving me more time to write, but for listening to all my ramblings, always.

I am thoroughly delighted by the artwork from the pencils, brushes and mind of the talented ANDREW DANG and am indebted to his industrious commitment to bringing my Chronoverse to life for us all to see.

Donne's famous epigram, *no man is an island* was never truer than for writers in our present hour - as we stand on the shoulders of giants. My readers will, doubtless, guess my main sources of inspiration from the text but a few words of thanks to my predecessors must go to CS Lewis – whose Narnian Chronicles have been my companion since childhood; Gene Roddenberry – whose universe first sparked my fascination with time travel; Philip Pullman – who showed us that YA fiction can be literary; our greatest poets, and, always, the Bard. To anyone who ever introduced me to these marvellous architects of the castles of imagination – thank you.

Finally, to you, my reader – whom this is all for, and without whom, Christopher and Araminta would remain only ever in my mind's eye.

"Act only in accordance with that maxim through which you can at the same time will that it become a universal law."

– Kant, *Groundwork for the Metaphysics of Morals*

"Now, pleasure is in *itself* a good: nay, even setting aside immunity from pain, the only good: pain is in itself an evil; and, indeed, without exception, the only evil; or else the words good and evil have no meaning."

-    Bentham, *Principles of Morals and Legislation*

Part One

The world turns and THE WORLD CHANGES,
But one thing does not change.
In all of my years, one thing does not change,
However you disguise it, this thing does not change:
The perpetual struggle of Good and Evil.

TS Eliot - Choruses from The Rock

CHAPTER ONE

Time travel complicates most things, especially time; so I will have to tell you that it started, as these things often do, with a girl:

There was no reason we should have met really; she was in Year 10 and I was a year below her. She had things like GCSEs to concentrate on and I hadn't even chosen my Options yet. Also, she was from this totally loaded family – which explains her name – and I was just your average working-class teenager, living with his mum and sister. It was like Romeo and Juliet or something: total opposites.

My school, Westernford C of E, isn't exactly famous for its out-of-classroom learning experiences. I often think the place is a bit of a throw back to schools of the 1950s anyway – what with the brown uniforms, old fashioned bells and eccentric teachers. We didn't go on any trips in Year 7, one visit to a box factory in Year 8 and then a coach fifteen minutes down the road to this Tudor House in the October of Year 9.

I love October because it's usually not too wet or cold; the trees are all different colours; there's Half Term to look forward to at the end, and conkers to collect in the meantime. Except we're not allowed to play conkers any more because of health and safety (but we obviously do because the teachers don't care. I mean, it's not that they don't care but they just don't think we're going to die from hitting a conker).

I had been ill for the last couple of days with some flu or cold that I reckon I got from my sister, Kirsty, who had probably got it off some scabby boy she shouldn't have been kissing. She seems to have a new one every week. Mum doesn't seem to notice, as she's at work most of the time. Not that I'm saying she's wrong to be at work all the time – she has to so she can feed us – it's just that that probably explains why Kirsty gets away with a lot of what she gets away with.

Anyway, let's not talk about my sister. The point is, that I had been off school for a couple of days and so hadn't been told Araminta would be joining our trip.

So I'm sitting on the same old red-and-white *Black Orchid Travel* coach the school hires every year, halfway towards the back, on the right, by myself, failing to do a crossword, when my pen runs out, so I lean forward and call to Josh, two seats in front, to borrow his pen, except he can't hear me because he's plugged in to his iPod. Then, suddenly, this girl, sitting in the aisle opposite me and about three seats up, says:

"Here, use mine." At first I don't see her, just this sort of stick thing, poking out of the aisle. When I say *stick*, I mean, it looked like a sort of twig. I lean forward and see this hand, passing the stick/pen to me.

"Oh, thanks," I say. Then, the owner of the hand comes into view and I just sit there, gawping at this gorgeous girl with red hair and freckles. She smiles at me and then sort of nods her head and I realise that I haven't as yet taken the pen, and she leans back in her seat and looks out the window. She must be the only person besides myself who isn't listening to music. I'm not, because Mum can't afford to buy one for both of us so Kirsty and I share the ancient 4th gen Nano. Probably got it from a museum. Of course, when I say 'share,' I mean that she uses it and I steal the headphones on occasion to remind her I'm owed a turn (which I never get).

I turn the pen over in my hand. It's essentially a hollowed-out tree branch with a biro jammed up inside. Different.

"All right, do *not* move yet, thank you very much!" booms the voice of Mr Travis, our History teacher. Everyone groans and removes their earplugs and seat belts, sitting half up out of their seats, poised for the inevitable squashing to get off the coach.

"Listen to me. Listen carefully: *no one* but *no one* is to touch *anything* inside the house." Callum Taylor puts his hand up and I can see Mr Travis raise his eyes in expectation of a stupid question.

"Taylor?"

"What about the handrail on the stairs, sir? It should have a hand rail, surely?"

"Taylor?"

"Sir?"

"Your mum..." Everyone guffaws at this. Callum, opening his mouth to protest, is cut short by Mr Travis recovering his professionalism:

"Your mum, I am sure, Taylor, taught you some common sense. Kindly use it before you open your mouth to ask a question in the future." Callum looks down at the floor and mutters an abashed, "Sir."

Soon enough we are allowed off and push our way onto the narrow street in front of this old-looking, timber building. I must have gone past it hundreds of times but I don't recall noticing it before. Looking at it straight on I realise that it sort of bends. I cock my head in an attempt to straighten the house when I feel someone bash into me and, before I know it, I'm on the pavement. Seems that Big Dan decided to rugby tackle Callum in the queue and tripped up onto me. It's not a biggie but Mr Travis glares at me. Then, as I look up, I notice a slender, freckled hand reaching out. I look up and into Araminta's blue eyes. When I say 'look,' I probably stared because she raises an eyebrow and says:

"May I have my pen back, please?" It is then that I notice I had automatically taken her hand in mine, thinking she was offering to pull me up. I also seem to have attracted a crowd of leering spectators who will now deride me for the remainder of the visit.

"Oh, sorry," I bumble, "erm, yes, I err…sorry, I thought – " Araminta interrupts my digging-myself-into-a-hole by pulling me to my feet.

"Come *on*, Jones, we haven't got all day!"

"Sir!" I acknowledge, still staring into Araminta's eyes and then, checking myself and doing a quick dust down, I turn aside to enter the house.

Inside, there is a funny smell. It's not quite musty; in fact, what really strikes me is how *fresh* the scent is. It reminds me of a bakery. This of course makes me hungry, because I rushed out of the house without breakfast again. Mum is always telling me that it's "the most important meal of the day," but, to be honest, I'd rather forgo some cereal than have a Late Detention with Ms. Woolbeck. You'd understand if you met her; she has nasty breath and makes this really annoying clicking sound with her tongue.

We have been met by the Curator – a balding man in a tweed jacket and red cords that *really* don't go well together. He is lecturing us about the original infrastructure of the property or something and about how this guy, Edward something-or-other, invested some money into it because he believed there was something of value in the house. The idea of hidden treasure makes me curious but then he trails off into something else and my stomach rumbles loudly.

There is a definite draft in the house and most of us are shivering so we move a bit further in and he show us this old fireplace which has a fire going. Everyone is quite glad about that, although it seems a bit smoky.

"Now then, you might notice that this fireplace has been added to the property since the original build," says the Curator. Mr Travis nods affirmatively and the Curator continues: "Can anybody tell me *how* we know that?" Dead silence.

"Well, when was the house built?" Further awkward pause. "I did tell you earlier?"

"1520, sir." Luke, of course.

"Thank you, young man. 1520 is correct. So what clues do we have as to the relative age of the fireplace? I'll let you have a little think about that for a moment whilst I attend to another matter. Mr Travis –" and the two men disappear from the room for a few moments. It's a small room as it is and with more than a class load of kids it seems very crowded so I don't get a look in at first. However, almost everyone else seems fairly bored and, noticing the absence of staff in the room, my peers decide it's a perfect opportunity to update their Facebook and Twitter statuses, leaving me alone by the fireplace. It is beautiful, decorated with a mosaic depicting the story of the Garden of Eden up either panel, with the words, *Ye shall be as goddes* coming out the mouth of the serpent, who seems to be offering Eve a piece of fruit. Although, as I look closer at the fruit I notice that it's not an apple like it usually is. In fact, it doesn't even look like a fruit. More like an egg. It's odd. I want to get closer but the heat from the flames is pretty much unbearable.

"Well, anyone?" The others snap their phones back into the pockets and shrug their shoulders in vague "am-I-bovvered?"-ness. We're about to be told when I suddenly think of something.

"Is it because of the Bible verse?"

"Go on, boy."

"Well," I proceed, tentatively, "it's in English?"

"And?"

"And wasn't the Bible still in Latin in 1520?"

"Gold star. You're absolutely right. You're the first to get that one right. Well done. The carving is rather unusual in itself of course and the choice of text isn't exactly orthodox. Why use the serpent's words and not God's or Eve's? You see what I mean? Oh and, incidentally, who can tell me when the Great Bible was produced in English?" I shrink back into the shadows, not wanting to be branded a total teacher's pet, and brush up against Ryan who mimics the Curator and makes a sucking noise at me.

"Ooh, well done Christopher. Kissy-kiss. Teacher's pet!"

"Shut up Ryan." I catch a glare from Mr Travis and mutter an apology before following the others into the next room.

That night, over a late frozen-fish and chips supper, Mum asked me why I was so unusually quiet.

"Oh, nothing," I said and smiled. Kirsty must have known there was something different because she kicked me under the table and gave me a look.

"How was the trip?"

"Yeah, fine. Actually I got this question right that no one else did."

"Great. That's great, sweetie. Would you pass me the vinegar please?" I obliged and we sat in silence for the next five minutes until Kirsty got up and said, "Mum, I forgot to tell you I'm supposed to be buddying this new girl so is it cool if she comes over?"

"Oh, a new girl? Where's she from?"

"I dunno."

"Didn't you ask?"

"No, I only found out about it last period when Miss Humphreys asked me to, like, orienteer her. She been here, like, a few days but they didn't buddy her up yet." Kirsty stacked the plates and took them into the kitchen for me to wash up.

"What's her name?"

"Dunno!" called Kirsty from the kitchen. "Something posh."

"What did she say?"

"'Something posh,' I think, Mum. I'll wash up, shall I?" Mum nodded and I retreated into the kitchen, only to be interrogated by Kirsty:

"So what's with you?"

"What do you mean, what's with me? Nothing's *with* me."

"Yes there is – I can tell."

"Well, there's nothing *to* tell." I pushed past her and put on the rubber gloves.

"Chris has got a secret, Chris has got a secret!" chanted Kirsty.

"No I haven't got a secret; don't be ridiculous." Kirsty wasn't giving up.

"Look, if you *must* know, there was a girl today – a new girl – on the trip, who I thought was quite…different."

"New girl? On your trip?"

"Yeah. She um, she had red hair and freckles and she seemed a bit sort of different."

"Posh," said Kirsty.

"Sorry?"

"Posh. She comes across as being a bit sure of herself, doesn't she?"

"What do you mean?" I said, scraping off a bit of batter that had got stuck to Kirsty's plate.

"That's the girl I was meant to be, like, shadowing or buddying or whatever."

"It can't be!"

"Why not?"

"That would mean she's in your year but it was a Year 9 trip."

"No, I remember now, I was told she had gone on a trip today because she's doing this special research project on the Tudors or something. Well, that's what Miss Humphreys said."

I said nothing and turned the tap on instead to let it run hot.

"You like her, don't you? You *like* her."

"Don't be stupid. She's in Year 10."

"So? You still *like* her. I think it's sweet. I'll go tell Mum."

"No you *won't*!" I said and flicked water at her.

CHAPTER TWO

Araminta wasn't thrilled when her family had told her they would be moving house for the fifteenth time in as many years. It seemed that every time she had had a chance to settle down and make friends, they were taken away from her. Consequently, Araminta had learned to maintain a certain distance from people: it was less painful to part that way.

This latest house was, at least, comfortable. More than comfortable, in fact – it had the character and size of an old manor house.

"It's a little ostentatious, don't you think, darling?" said Araminta's mother to her husband, Dr Stirling, when they first arrived.

"I like it," said Araminta, "and there'll be lots of inspiration for your writing, Mother." Katherine Stirling smiled at her daughter and hoped that she would forgive her parents for such an interrupted upbringing. The house, it was true, was certainly inspiring and, if she were honest with herself, Katherine had felt a little claustrophobic in their last London apartment.

"So, what's your first week been like, then?" asked Dr Stirling over their Sunday roast.

"It's been fine, thank you."

"I'm sorry it's not exactly Eton, darling," said Katherine as she passed the horseradish sauce to her daughter.

"Well I'm not a boy, am I, so I couldn't go there, could I? Anyway, it's absolutely fine. Really," said Araminta, reassuringly, then muttered something about it being a throwback to the 1950s.

"Have you managed to make any –?" started Dr Stirling.

"Any *friends*? Well there are friendly people there but I don't know if we're even likely to be staying here long; so is it even worth my while trying to pursue a friendship that's doomed to a premature death?" Both her parents took their forks out of their mouths and looked at their daughter intently.

"I'm sorry, I didn't mean it like that. I mean, I wasn't meaning to blame or accuse you or anything; it's just that it so often happens to me that I go to all these efforts to fit in with people and then, when I finally have people I care about, or who care about me, we have to move away."

"I know, darling, but I think this time – " and here, Dr Stirling trailed off to seek approval from his wife, who pushed her horn rimmed glasses up her nose and nodded.

"I think that this time," he continued, "we can be confident that we won't need to leave any suitcases packed." Araminta looked at her mother and then her father.

"You mean you – ?"

"Your Father thinks he has found it."

"Here?"

"Well, you see, I finally solved the keyword."

"Father, that's *amazing!*"

"Only taken four years." Here, Dr Stirling leaned across the table and took his daughter's hand: "I'm so sorry I haven't been much of a father those four years. And before that even."

"Don't be silly, Father – "

"No. I'm not. I know you've had your interests but you must have been so lonely, being an only child and having to move away from any friends you've made all the time."

"I didn't say it for that."

"We know, sweetheart," said Katherine, softly.

"Anyway, I think things are going to change around here, pretty soon. I must be close now and, once it's all over, we can finally start living the lives we've pretended to have for so long."

Araminta knew better than to ask for more particulars about her father's work. He had always told her as much as he thought she needed to know and he might have kept her completely in the dark, so Araminta respected the boundaries of her permitted knowledge. However, her mother was quite sensible to Araminta's feelings and so she changed the subject:

"So; any *boys*?"

"At Westernford?! I don't think so!"

"Don't judge by appearances, Araminta," said Dr Stirling, raising his eyebrow in admonishment.

"Well, it's a good job most people do, with us, isn't it?" Araminta rebutted quickly, stuffing a carrot in her mouth.

"Touché, sweetheart. But, come on, is there no one?"

"Well," said Araminta slowly, "there was this *one* boy – on the trip last week?" Her parents nodded for her to continue. "Well I didn't *like* him or anything, it's just that he seemed a bit, I don't know, *different* from the others?"

"Different how? Has he got three arms?"

"Mother! No. It's just that he seemed pretty intelligent. There was this really interesting carving on a fireplace and he totally got that it didn't fit with the rest of the house."

"What do you mean?" said Dr Stirling, sharply. Araminta tried to describe the carving as accurately as possible to her father, who was becoming increasingly business-like in his questions.

"Try to remember, Araminta, this is extremely important."

"Sorry, Father, I wasn't right up close to it."

"But you say the fruit shown in the carving wasn't like an apple?"

"No. Definitely not." At that, Dr Stirling got up out of his seat as if somebody had fired a pistol at him, and dived into the next room to retrieve a large, leather bound book. He threw it down on the dining room table with a triumphant thud and said,

"There!"

"Where?" asked Araminta, confused at the blank page that had been set before her.

"Huh? Oh, sorry," said Dr Stirling, thumbing through the pages until he found what he was looking for – a sketch of an oval object, not unlike an egg, with Greek letters etched into its side.

"Oh my gosh, that's *it*!" exclaimed Araminta.

"Now, are you sure?"

"Yes. I'm absolutely certain. Hundred per cent."

Dr Stirling closed the book and looked at his wife.

"You know what this means?" he said and paused dramatically. "This means we are very, *very* close."

CHAPTER THREE

I don't know if you have an elder sister or not but I don't recommend it. Sometimes I wonder if it's the age thing, or if it's because she's a girl, or just because she's my sibling; although I do have mates who have sisters and they're not quite as annoying as Kirsty. Take this for example:

I was sitting, comfortably, in the lounge, when I heard her scream my name from upstairs:

"Christopher! Where are my headphones?"

"*Your* headphones?"

"Yes! The ones I bought last week."

"I don't know." Kirsty appeared at the door and switched off the TV with her universal remote. She's such a child.

"Hey, I was watching that!"

"What?"

"The programme."

"No you weren't, Chris – you were playing on your phone."

"Wasn't."

"Err…yes you were. Anyway. Headphones. Now!"
She held out her hand. To be fair I *was* playing on my
phone because I was trying to beat Josh's high score.

"Look, I haven't even seen them. Hang on, do you
mean the pink ones?"

"Yes." Kirsty gave me a filthy look.

"I haven't touched them! I haven't! I *do* know what
happened to them though." There was an awkward silence
and Kirsty switched on the TV.

"Happy now?"

"Thank you."

I had been watching the News. Well, not watching.
Most of it's pretty boring. Politics and economics and stuff
I don't really understand. Out of the corner of my eye, I
saw the word MURDER, though, so I turned up the
volume. I read on my paper round a week ago that they'd
found a body in a skip about a dozen miles up the road
from us. Apparently it looked like a professional kill and
there had been a domino piece near the body. Now it
seemed there was a second victim.

"So?"

"Kirsty, this might be important!"

"My headphones – where are they?"

"Oh, Mum found them. They went through the wash."

"Great!"

"Serves you right for hogging the iPod all the time."

"Yeah cause last time you had it – "

"You mean the *one* time I had it – "

"You erased all my music and synced it with your own
rubbish."

This is true. But mostly because she'd filled its memory
with the latest noise from the X Factor factory.

"Mozart isn't rubbish, Kirsty."

"I was talking about that weird hip-hop stuff."

"The *Rap Canterbury Tales?* They're great! Educational
and fun."

"Shut up Chris, don't be so sad."

"Where are you going, anyway?"

"Going for an ice cream."

"It's freezing cold!" Without saying another word, Kirsty walked out of the room and, five minutes later, I heard the front door slam shut.

I usually spent my Saturdays with friends or catching up on homework. Sam was visiting his mum this weekend and Josh and Tom had gone to Thorpe Park so I was left on my own with the choice of writing up the visit to the Tudor House or watching repeats of rubbish shows on TV. I could have done some piano practice but I wasn't especially in the mood for that either. I'm not very good but I always wanted to be in a band so I had lessons from quite a young age and can play to a passable standard. I was probably going to choose GCSE Music as one of my Options.

The homework didn't take too long. I did try to do some research about the fireplace carving but couldn't come up with anything. I found a few different things about the Bible verse and then started reading Philip Pullman's take on it in *His Dark Materials*.

Just as I sat down to the piano to do some song writing while my mum and sister were out of the house, I heard a key in the lock. I listened out for the usual, "hi*ya*" from Mum but there wasn't one so, figuring it must be Kirsty, I ducked out of the dining/music room and made for the staircase.

"Oh, heya," said a girl's voice. I turned round slowly, with my left hand still on the banister and was surprised to see Araminta standing in my hall, next to Kirsty.

"Hi."

"So you must be Kirsty's brother."

"Yep." I realised I should probably say something more and so added, "Chris. My name's Chris."

"It's nice to meet you, Chris," she said, offering me her hand which I took. "I'm Araminta."

"Araminta. I don't know any Aramintas. What does it mean?"

"I think it was made up for a book or something."

"Oh." Kirsty was obviously not impressed.

"Bugger off upstairs, Christopher, there's a good boy."

"I was just about to do some piano practice actually."

"No you weren't, you had your hand on the banister," said Kirsty.

"You play piano?" asked Araminta. She sounded interested so I said, "Yes. Well, just a bit. Do you?"

"I used to. I play the 'cello."

"That's great."

"Yeah. Whatever. Araminta, would you like a drink?"

"Please."

"Right, come this way." Pushing past me, Kirsty mouthed *bugger off* and I went into the front room to play some scales when I saw Mum arrive home with a car full of shopping.

"You're home early," I said as I carried the bags in.

"Yes." She looked tired. Her hair – long over due a visit to the salon – was getting a bit greasy. She looked like she hadn't slept properly for days. And she'd been biting her thumb again.

"Where's your sister?"

"Oh, she has Araminta round."

"Who?"

"The girl she has to buddy?"

"Right. She did say."

We carried the shopping into the kitchen silently and Kirsty introduced her to Araminta, who immediately offered to help with the unpacking ritual. Possibly my least favourite chore. I always hope Mum will have picked up some chocolately bargain and am usually disappointed.

Araminta accepted the offer to stay to dinner and we all sat down to a Bolognese an hour later. Araminta was a pretty deft hand in the kitchen, although she did suggest

adding cinnamon to the sauce which was vetoed.
Apparently it's what they do in Norway, where she lived for a couple of years.

"So, you've stayed in some interesting places, Araminta," said Mum as we were eating.

"Yes. I was in South Africa for the last two years."

"Wow, that's amazing!" said Kirsty, "I've always wanted to go to Africa!"

"Was it very different to here?"

"Well, I suppose the thing is that I've not spent much time in England at all so it's difficult to draw comparisons."

"But how are you liking it so far?" I said.

"It's fine." She smiled and added some parmesan to her Bolognese.

"So what do your folks do?" Mum asked. She uses the word 'folks' when she doesn't know someone because she hates it when people assume that we have both parents at home and there are loads of people in my year group who don't live with either of their real parents.

"Well, Mother is a writer and Fath–"

"A writer? That's amazing!" I said, rather too emphatically, spitting my sauce out. "I always wanted to be a writer. What does she write?"

"Um, mainly historical fiction."

"Would I have heard of her?" asked Mum.

"You might have. Katherine Stirling?" Clearly none of us had heard of her so there was a bit of an awkward pause where we all just looked ignorant.

"It's all right, she isn't, like, really famous anyway."

"And your dad? I interrupted you earlier, sorry."

"Oh, that's ok," said Araminta, smiling at me, "so Father is an academic – a theologian. He's been researching something for the Divinity Faculty at Cambridge."

"That's funny, I've just been re-reading *Northern Lights* and there are lots of theologians in that," I said cheerfully – and then realised that all the theologians are the baddies in

His Dark Materials so I tried to say that I wasn't trying to say that Araminta's dad was a villain but then I just got tongue tied so Kirsty kicked my shins and said,

"Shut up, Stupid!" which might have been helpful, or not. Fortunately, Mum helped me out by changing the subject:

"So, does your father have to commute much?"

"Well, I think he only needs to go up to the University about twice a week; and it was going to be too expensive living in Cambridge, anyway."

"Fair enough," said Kirsty.

"So, what do you make of the school?" I asked.

"Well, it is not the worst place in the world is it?"

"Very diplomatic, Araminta," said Mum.

"Don't think just because you went on a trip, that's usual. It's only the second one I've been on in three years!"

"Is that Tudor House open to the public?" asked Araminta in a business-like fashion.

"I'm not sure," said Mum. "Well, it must be. I'm sure you can find out on the internet or something?"

"Why, did you want to go back?"

Araminta didn't get to answer my question because her mobile rang at that precise moment. Excusing herself from the table to take the call, I caught Kirsty giving me looks and tried to prevent further merciless teasing by reminding her of her broken headphones.

"Mum?" I said, "I *was* right in thinking that Kirsty's headphones were caught in the wash wasn't I?"

"Yes, I'm afraid to say so, sweetheart." Kirsty gave Mum a glare.

"I'm always telling you to check your pockets before you put anything in the wash. I'm sorry I don't have the time to do that for you. Not with trying to hold down two jobs to support you. And before you ask me, you'll have to wait till Saturday to get those replacement headphones. I just don't have the cash at the moment. Sorry."

"That's okay Mum; of course. Thank you," muttered Kirsty. The 'thank you' clearly being an afterthought. I knew what she'd do next - she'd offer to wash up to wheedle her way into Mum's good books and to give Araminta the false impression that she's a human being and a good daughter and make me look like a lazy son. Then, later that evening, she'd have a 'girl' talk with Mum about how some scabby boy broke her heart and how she isn't pretty and is worried no one will ever marry her and compliment Mum's cooking and then, just as she's turning Mum's light out, she'll relent, instruct Kirsty to go to her cash box and take out a fiver:

"Will that be enough?" she'll ask.

"Oh, Mum, I couldn't!" Kirsty will feign in protest.

"It's OK, I want you to have it. Not much point in having an iPlayer if you can't use it, is there?"

"iPod, Mum. But thank you." Kirsty will let her voice quaver at just the last moment, indicating that £5 really isn't enough and Mum will tell her to take £15 in case and give her the change. Which she'll forget about.

"Don't tell Chris," Mum will say, knowing she can't afford to give me any money and thinking, mistakenly, that I'll be jealous. I won't be. I'm not that kind of person. I really don't care if Mum spends the occasional bit of money extra on my sister. It's the way Kirsty works around Mum that I don't like. Besides, I have my own money from my paper round.

Whilst all this was going round in my head, Araminta came back to the table and apologised. It seemed her parents were anxious to have her back home as it was dark.

"Of course!" said Mum, "I'm so sorry to have worried your parents. I'll give you a lift right away."

"I'm sorry. I hope you don't think me rude, Mrs Jones. It was lovely of you to invite me to stay and you make a wonderful Bolognese!"

"That's because I don't put cinnamon in it. Are you two coming for the ride?" Mum asked. Before I could open my mouth to say yes, Kirsty said:

"Oh no, Mummy. We'll stay and wash up, won't we, Chris?" She only calls her 'Mummy' when she's hatching a diabolical plan. So that scuppered it for me.

"Thanks, sweetheart. Oh and Chris, would you do the bins please? It's Recycling tomorrow."

I nodded my assent and, having retrieved her yellow raincoat (which looks like the one Gromit wears) from the rack, Araminta went to the front door.

"Well, I expect I'll see you. Around." I muttered, feebly.

"Don't be stupid, Chris; Araminta wouldn't be seen dead in your social circle! Lovely to have you round. I'll see you tomorrow in English first period," said Kirsty and deliberately gave Araminta a hug in front of me.

And that was it. The front door slammed, I didn't get to see the "incredible Georgian property" the Stirlings lived in, (as Mum described it on her return journey) and, as you'll have guessed, I ended up doing the washing up, too.

CHAPTER FOUR

It was a week or so later when Araminta came home to find the library completely turned out, with books strewn absolutely everywhere. At first, she was worried they had been burgled but there was no sign of forced entry, and then she heard her father speaking on the phone to somebody:

"Yes, I think I have it; at last!"

"Father?" Araminta called out, cautiously.

"Yes, Sweetheart, in here! Come in."

Araminta followed the sound of her father's voice and entered his Study. As ever, it was something of a mausoleum to the fruitless labours of academia: stuffy bits of yellowing paper with handwritten notes filled endless volumes, bound with bits of string in folders made from brown card. His favourite Mont Blanc pen in the ink well of a mahogany desk, the turntable on the sideboard playing Bach. Everything was as it had been throughout her childhood. Houses changed but there was always a Study. The addition of a computer in this one, and a rather hideous painting of a crow which had been left by the landlord hung on the wall opposite the bay window where her Father stood, hand on hip. He turned around, noticing his daughter and smiled.

"Before you say anything, I know; it's a terrible mess," he said.

"I thought we'd been robbed!"

"It worries me that I wouldn't notice if we had! Do sit down." Araminta looked around for a clean chair in vain and her father darted forward to remove a pile of papers off the Chesterfield carver in the corner.

"I need you to do me a favour." When Dr Stirling asked his daughter for 'favours', they were generally unfavourable and involved some sort of nefarious activity which wasn't strictly legal. The first time was when Araminta was barely four years old and her father asked her to pick-pocket an old man for a scrap of paper he had been carrying. At the time, Araminta supposed it was a sort of game but she began to realise, over time, that there were certain moral lines her father didn't mind crossing, as long as he didn't have to risk being caught himself. Araminta might have thought this selfish, except she supposed that her father's work must be truly important (for he never asked her to steal money or anything of financial value; it was always some form of reconnaissance and, more often than not, she was to put back what she had taken). Moreover, Araminta understood that if she were caught, a child was more likely to get off with a caution or slap on the wrists; besides which, Araminta took pride in the fact that she never *had* been caught and this alter-ego indulged her imagination.

"What is it, Father?" she asked.

He had taken his glasses off and was sucking the left arm at the bit that curled round behind his ear. It was a habit whenever deep in thought.

"Well, you know that Tudor House you visited? I've been doing some research and I think it is highly likely that there is something in that house."

"What?"

"I can't tell you precisely; partly because I'm not sure myself and partly because I'm not ready to tell you all I know; but suffice it to say that whatever it is, or might lead us to, is potentially very dangerous and must be destroyed at all costs." Araminta knew when her father was being serious and when not to probe further so she simply asked:

"How will I know where to find it or when I have?"

"Easy: Look for something that doesn't belong there. And, sweetheart? Be careful. I don't think we're the only people who are onto this. Which also means, I'm afraid, time is of the essence."

CHAPTER FIVE

It was a Tuesday morning and I had just been trading insults with Big Dan in the East Wing corridor, when I saw Araminta struggling with her locker. Plucking up my courage, I asked if she needed a hand.

"Hi Chris. No, it's fine. Thanks. I just have too much stuff in here!" I thought it was my imagination at first but she seemed to be hiding her face a little.

"Jones!" bellowed Mr Travis, making Araminta look up in surprise.

"Less fraternising with the ladies, more hurrying to lessons!" I smiled sheepishly at Araminta and then noticed the black eye she was sporting.

"Are you all right?" I whispered.

"Fine. I tripped."

"Oh. Looks nasty. Hope it doesn't hurt?"

"It's better than it looks."

"I didn't mean it looks nasty. I mean, you have really nice eyes. I just meant – "

"Jones!" bellowed Mr Travis again. "Time waits for no man. Least of all History."

I reluctantly slumped off to my lesson, looking over my shoulder to see if she was all right.

Mr Travis might seem like a bit of Sergeant Major but, actually, he's a really decent teacher and I always enjoy his lessons. I'm not sure many of my friends, do, as he tends to do more old-fashioned chalk-and-talk style delivery but he is always prepared to take questions and can answer nearly anything anyone throws at him.

I managed to find a seat next to Josh and got out my book and pen.

"Oi, Mate, lend us a pen?" whispered Josh.

"Sorry, Dude, I've only got one."

"Problem, Jones?" said Mr Travis.

"No, sir."

"Good. Then how about answering my question?"

"What question, sir?"

"The question you weren't listening to. Martin?" Mr Travis didn't need to relinquish his gaze on me to know that Luke Martin was possibly dying of raised-hand syndrome.

"The significance of the Great Bible, published in 1539, was that it allowed the man in the street – well, the *literate* man in the street – to read the Bible for himself, instead of relying on priests to tell him what it said and then, conjugate him like Marx – "

"You mean, *subjugate*, boy! You conjugate *verbs*. Like in French," said Mr Travis, wearily.

At this point, Ryan Chetwind, who had been swinging back on his chair, threw a paperclip at Luke's head and said:

"'Ere, this ain't Religious! You religious, sir?" I should explain that, for some reason at my school (even though it is a C of E comp), RS is called 'Religious' by the student body. Mr Travis, patrolling the classroom, bent down to pick up the paper clip.

"I'm an historian."

"What does that mean, sir?" said Ryan.

"It means, Chetwind, that I find the historical claims of Western religions, such as Christianity, difficult to measure against its supernatural claims. To deny that the man Jesus – or Yeshua as he would have been called – existed is foolish. Who he was is for the theologians to fight out."

Worried that we would soon have to turn to some page in the textbook and do copying or, worse, answer questions, Ryan piped up:

"Sir, can I have my paper clip back, please?"

Mr Travis, who had returned to his desk and was now fiddling with the small piece of metal, rubbing it between his thumb and forefinger quietly said, "Yes, I expect you can." Silence. Josh coughed, in a vain attempt to hide his laughter.

"Or perhaps not. At least, not quite the same paperclip." Mr Travis then turned around and walked back to the front of the classroom. Most of us shifted our seats in confusion.

"You see," announced Mr Travis, "this paperclip no longer exists in the same way that it did five minutes ago. I've bent it." Josh couldn't help but snigger at this.

"You're confused," Mr Travis continued; "all right." Here, he turned to the board and drew a crude oblong in three dimensions. Luke, of course, being Luke, copied it down instantly.

"How many dimensions does this object have?" asked Mr Travis, eagerly anticipating someone to fall into his trap.

"Three sir! Height, Length and Breadth!" shouted out Luke.

"No; stupid boy." Luke let out a whimper.

"Two?" asked Josh, tentatively.

"Are you asking or answering me? At least have the courage of your convictions! Why two?"

"Um, cause you've drawn it on a flat surface, so it doesn't actually exist in three dimensions." I could tell from the inflection in his voice that Josh was desperately trying not to raise pitch at the end and sound like another question.

29

"Yes it *does* have a third dimension. It's just not that deep. So. No one else?" Mr Travis searched the classroom with his flashing eyes.

"Four," I muttered under my breath.

"Who said that?" Everyone turned to look at me. Well, not everyone; there's Boston who only ever stares out the window into the Sixth Form Common Room (which is fair enough except Lucy Fox will *never* look his way. Or mine).

"I hope you weren't just guessing arbitrary numbers, Jones?"

"No sir. I was; um. I was thinking of time." Josh puffed out his cheeks and exhaled a slow, *you're-absolutely-stir-crazy-and-there's-nothing-I-can-do-to-protect-you-except-visit-you-in-the-nut-house* sigh, shaking his head, and most everyone else laughed except Mr Travis who waited and then cleared his throat.

"Time! The fourth dimension. As HG Wells reminds us in the beginning of *The Time Machine*, 'you cannot have an instantaneous cube'. Everything that exists in three dimensions - that is, everything that has height, length and depth, also exists in time. There was a point at which the paper clip was not, and there is a point at which it shall not be. All things known to exist in the universe are finite. That means they have a beginning and an end. Moreover, they change. The particles that make up this paperclip are changing all the time. And when I say 'all the time' you might be confused because time is simply the time that objects take to exist and the time time takes. But don't worry your puny little minds with trying to fathom that. Simply realise that everything has a beginning and an end. Nothing will last as it is, now. All fades into the annals of history. Which is why we are historians." He looked around the room and cleared his throat in correction: "Why *I* am an historian, and *you* are cretins. Now, turn to page twenty."

Most of us groaned. Josh whispered, "Quick, ask him something!" across the row at me but before I could have a chance to form a question on my lips, Mr Travis had remembered something and was off again, enthusing about paper clips and a school project in America that had collected six million of them to see what an incredibly large number of Jews were murdered in the Holocaust. To illustrate just how extreme the Nazis were, he made us all stand up and, one by one, according to different criteria (Jewish ancestry, race, disabilities etc) we were all sat down (with the exception of Gemma, whose Aryan looks would have saved her, according to Mr Travis).

"Yes, if Hitler had had his way, this might have been the only moron in the set;" continued Mr Travis. "Somewhat ironic for someone trying to create a master race. But therein you have the difficulty: Hitler's main problem was his ideology - which is to say, his values and beliefs. And it's difficult to know where he got them and who is to blame for them. In a way, he was only following on from Friedrich Nietzsche, who wrote in his 1895 book, *The Anti-Christ*, that 'the weak and botched shall perish...and one should help them to it'. One might argue that he was merely a social-Darwinist and that the *real* culprit for this line of thinking was the guy who used to be on our ten quid notes. Charles Darwin. Origin of Species. 1859. Natural Selection - the strong survive, the weak die. You see, everything is history: politics, religion, literature. Now run along to Geography and tell Mrs Winkler that her subject is as useless to you as a pair of reading glasses is to a blind man in a coal mine." Silence. "Off! Off!"

Geography was, it's true, particularly dull. Mostly because Mrs Winkler was about as exciting as finding out your parents are away for the weekend, only to leave you in the care of your least favourite uncle, whose idea of 'fun' is looking through countless albums of stamps. I was definitely going to opt for History at GCSE.

The afternoon went pretty slowly until, at the end of it, I bumped into Araminta. Literally. I was just coming round the corridor, fiddling with a packet of gum that Josh was offering me and then *wham!* I nearly had her flying.

"Oh my gosh, I'm so sorry!" I said, before I even realised whose personal space it was I'd invaded.

"No worries," she said, kindly. Fortunately, Josh is a good enough friend to take a hint and he slunk off quickly, out of sight.

"Have you had a good day? Before I bumped into you, obviously?!"

"Yes, thanks," she said, quietly.

"Your eye all right? Sorry, not...not meaning to pry." Araminta said nothing for a few seconds and then seemed to eye me up and down.

"Chris, I can *trust* you, can't I?"

My heart started beating faster and I managed to blurt out: "Of course!"

"Only…" Araminta teased and then seemed to think better of taking me into her confidence.

"What is it?"

"Not here. Meet me by the tree on the top field in fifteen minutes. Once most people have gone home."

"All right," I said and looked down at my watch. When I looked back up, she was gone.

The next quarter of an hour was spent in an agonising limbo in between trying to sort my unruly hair out in the loo (which never seems to do as it's told, despite the gel) and worrying that Araminta had some terrible secret to tell me about child abuse which I wouldn't be able to cope with. I needn't have worried. After some beating about the proverbial bush, she told me that the real reason that she had got the black eye was because she had been trying to break in to the Tudor House the night before last. Whilst *why?* was the most logical question, I was aware that it was what she would, most likely, be expecting me to ask (and want to avoid), so I simply said:

"What went wrong?" Definitely the right question. We were sitting at the base of the Silver Birch Tree that grew on the top field. It was the only one of its kind in the school and seemed completely out of place.

"I lost my balance and fell off the window ledge," she said, unashamedly. "I think it's because I was juggling too much in my hands. I should have also used some rope."

"It sounds like a two man job!" I said.

"What?"

"Person, I mean. Two person." Typical of a posh, nerdy kid to insist on *inclusive* language.

"Quite. So, you wanna help me?"

A stupid question with a dangerous answer. I should know by now that if a good looking girl wants me to do something, there is bound to be more in it for them than for me, and it usually doesn't go according to plan. But then, what else am I going to do? Say no? Of course not. Fortune favours the bold. Of course, so does Juvenile Detention.

CHAPTER SIX

I've always wanted to do something reckless, stupid and slightly illegal, ever since the day in Junior School (not long after my Dad left), our choir practice was interrupted by police sirens. We all looked up to see Rhys Coleman grinning wildly on the courtyard roof, being chased by four police officers. We simply stared as he was thrown to the ground, handcuffed and dragged off, still grinning. Standing with Araminta in the dead of night now, though, gave me the shivers. I didn't want to be carted off by the police.

She had it all planned down to the last detail: We had arranged to meet at 04:00 hours. This was an easy time for us to sneak out of our respective houses and particularly for me, as I would be getting up two hours later for my paper round anyway. I'd been instructed to wear something black, but the only thing I could find was a pair of dark blue jeans and an ill-fitting T-Shirt with *Back To The Future* on it.

Everything seemed to go smoothly. First of all, Araminta shinned up a tree next to the house and I successfully threw her the rope. (I say successfully – it took four attempts). The next task was to swing from the tree onto the window ledge. I wouldn't have liked to do that myself. It was pretty dangerous. Fortunately, Araminta hadn't eaten quite as many hamburgers as I have and she managed it easily enough. My heart was pounding. The house was situated in a quiet street, tucked out of sight from the main town. Every time the wind rustled through the trees, or I heard a rubbish bin being thrown onto its side by a hungry fox, I nearly jumped out of my skin. Luckily for us, it was a new moon that night, which gave us a cloak of darkness under which to operate our dastardly scheme. But it meant that we needed a torch and nothing says *burglar* like a big shiny torch on full beam pointed into a house in the middle of the night. I was beginning to see why Araminta needed my help: In order to gain access to the window, it was necessary to lean back – whilst retaining balance on the ledge – to jemmy the casement. There was, apparently, a small hook inside the window which was slightly faulty – something Araminta had discovered whilst on our History trip. I don't know whether I was more surprised that she was casing the joint during a school trip, or that she found the time to do it, avoiding the beady eyes of Mr Travis.

"How's it going?" I whispered, looking around me nervously.

"Shh! I'm trying to concentrate!"

"Sorry." A gust of wind blew an empty can along the street and startled me. I flashed the torch to my left and heard Araminta curse.

"Sorry!" I said. There was a lot of clicking and tapping sounds and then,

"Aweh!" (I had to ask what that means. Araminta picked it up in Africa. It sort of means *yay!* but also "hello"; which is confusing. It was one of her phrases).

"Right," she said, "I'll climb in and come and open the door for you. Standby." I just stood there, like an idiot, thinking I was finally in a spy film or an episode of *Star Trek* when something unexpected happened. We hadn't anticipated a burglar alarm. This was particularly stupid of us but it wasn't visible from the outside.

"What now?" I whispered in panic as I heard the monotone beep warning us we had only seconds to input the correct code. Araminta must not have heard me because I was left gawping up at the empty window. It occurred to me to run for my life and abandon Araminta to her fate: after all, it wouldn't be *my* finger prints on the outside wall. However, whether out of fear, chivalry or the knowledge that she would never speak to me again, I held my ground. A moment later, the front door opened.

"I think I've found the access panel!" Araminta said as I stepped inside.

"Great but what's the code?" I said. Both of us paused to think.

"OK; now the curator guy seemed pretty bland. I mean, he was wearing red cords for starters – he probably doesn't get out much!"

"So?" I said, ever conscious that, at any moment, Westernford's finest police offers would burst through the door, all guns blazing. (Possibly not *burst*, actually, being a listed building. Also without the guns. It's not America).

"So. I reckon the code is an obvious one – he clearly doesn't have much imagination."

"What makes you think he set it?" I said. Araminta had, indeed, found the panel to input the code and we were staring at it in the cold light of the torch.

"If only we had an ultra-violet light," I said.

"We don't need one. Look!" Araminta pointed to the number 1 on the pad; there was a faint stain of mustard.

"Like on his tweed jacket," said Araminta; "so the first number is probably 1." The beeps were getting faster. We had about five seconds. *Beep; beep; beep.* Without hesitation, heart thudding, I punched in the first thing I could think of and winced. The milliseconds that followed seemed an eternity.

"1520. Good call, Chris."

"Thanks. See, it does pay to listen to the tour!" Then I added, "Well, team effort anyway."

Araminta got up from her crouched position and made sure the front door was shut properly.

"Right. To business."

"Business? You mean you didn't just want to break into some old house for the thrill?"

"Not exactly." I didn't know why Araminta was being so coy: we were clearly in this together, whatever *this* was.

"What are you – what are *we* looking for?" I said, still whispering.

"We don't need to whisper, Chris. And let's turn on a light."

"What?! Are you crazy?"

"Look, now that we're inside, if anyone looks over the road or anything and sees a torch being flashed around, they'll assume someone's broken in but if we just put on the lights like normal people, they'll assume it's all kosher, right?" I nodded; her logic was pretty sound.

Araminta explained that her father seemed to think we would find something out of place in the house - perhaps an object or a piece of parchment. I pointed out how vague that was but we agreed that the fireplace would be the best place to start as it had been a more recent addition to the house. Araminta confided that it was when she described the pattern to her father that his suspicions had been aroused. We had to crouch down to examine it properly. Araminta pulled out her phone and took pictures.

The workmanship alone was faultless. The titles in the mosaics were small and interwoven with meticulous care.

"Isn't it unusual in itself to have a mosaic and not a carving?" I asked.

"I don't know. Maybe."

The left panel began the story, with Adam and Eve standing hand-in-hand, unashamed and surrounded by

37

animals. As the scene continued, Eve stood alone at the bottom of the great tree, looking up. The serpent, who was depicted as more of a dragon, draped a silver tail around the branches of the tree. The inscription started from the dragon's mouth and stretched across the centre of the fireplace, bridging the gap between the two panels. The right hand panel then showed Eve offering Adam the fruit. Below this, a simple green fig leaf separated the final tableau, showing a flaming sword stood in the place of the tree. Adam and Eve's ashamed, horrified faces disappeared out of sight.

"I've never really understood the fascination with the Fall," I said.

"What do you mean?"

"Well, wasn't it supposed to be, like, really *bad*? I mean, why not put something more positive up?"

"What, like the Crucifixion?"

"Good point." I had been hoping there was a secret panel stuffed up the chimney but, despite my best efforts at feeling around, there was nothing there.

"Here, let me try. No offence, but I think my arms are thinner." Araminta and I exchanged places and she wriggled into an uncomfortable position, with her back to the grate, left hand stuffed up the chimney. Suddenly she let out a scream.

"What? Araminta!?" Araminta withdrew her hand, laughing.

"Sorry," she said, "I couldn't resist. Guess you've never seen *Roman Holiday*?"

"What's that?"

"An old black and white film with Gregory Peck and Audrey Hepburn?"

"No. Then again I was born in this millennium...and I'm not a geek," I said.

"No, of course not, Chris. Geeks are cool...whereas you're just a nerd who plays the piano."

I had been leaning on the left panel, trying to direct the light of the torch up the chimney and, as Araminta came out of the grate, I tripped and whacked the torch into the edge of the Fruit on the right hand panel, chipping a bit off.

"Oops."

"'Oops'? Chris! Now you've really done it! The whole point of bringing you along was to minimise damage. Now the Curator will probably dust the place for fingerprints!"

"All right, Steve!" (For some reason I can't remember, Josh and I always call each other 'Steve' in these situations) "I'll just put it back." Unfortunately, this proved rather more difficult than I had anticipated. I could see that Araminta was becoming more impatient and then she tried to snatch the little piece of marble out of my hand which, instead, slipped into the grating and was lost forever. Araminta gave me a look and I shrugged my shoulders. Putting my finger in the gap I had left I said, sheepishly, "There, it doesn't look so bad!"

My finger seemed to slip. At first I thought that I had broken off yet more of the mosaic but I soon realised that the marble itself was moving.

"Araminta, look!" The pieces were definitely sliding – like one of those puzzles you get where you have to rearrange the tiles to make a picture, except, in this case, there was no obvious picture to make.

"Here, let me see!" I stepped aside and let Araminta have a go. I would say we must have tried every combination possible but that is unlikely, as there were hundreds of small pieces to move. At length, whether by chance, skill or miracle, Araminta seemed to have clicked the mosaic into a secret position and we were rewarded with the sound of turning cogs and a creaking emanating from the fireplace. As both of us stooped down, I was hit in the face by something which seemed to fly out of nowhere and nearly had my eye out.

"Ow!"

"Chris, look!" There was a small piece of paper on the floor.

"It must have come out of the fireplace." I let Araminta pick it up and peered over her shoulder as she unfolded it. It wasn't paper, it was a sort of parchment material. The writing was a little faded, in a brown ink, which made it tricky to decipher but eventually we were able to make out what it said:

> *Between the time the cradle maker points*
> *(If time is measured by the steps we tread*
> *Or what we stand for, and against); the joint*
> *Circumferences of all our hopes and dread*
> *Become the globe we must traverse to find*
> *The sacred twin of this dear sanctuary.*
> *And there, where once a martyr was enshrined,*
> *Look: Look on your past and future. Learn*
> *That all is vanity. The House of he*
> *Who had destroyed this house (you must return)*
> *Some secrets better hid, if gods ye be.*
>   *For even priests sometimes plot ill, for good.*
>   *Then verses rearranged are understood.*

We read it over a few times and then, as if I were coming out of a trance, I caught sight of my watch. It was coming up to six.

"We'd better go." I said.

"Go? Chris! This is *amazing!* Did Christopher Columbus just turn on his heel and go back to Europe once he found America? We can't go now!

"Look, Christopher Columbus didn't have to go do a paper round. Which I do – in about ten minutes. Besides, people will be getting up now. We can talk about this at school."

"Fine."

We carefully brushed down the mantel to get rid of our prints and tried to rearrange the tiles as best we could. Araminta remembered to close the window upstairs and we crept out, into the street, and parted company, silently.

CHAPTER SEVEN

Araminta was usually an obedient daughter. The only time she remembered disobeying her father was when they were living in Sydney. She was seven and they had gone to the zoo for the day. Ignoring her father's wishes, Araminta decided she wanted to stroke the kangaroos. The kangaroos did not reciprocate Araminta's feelings. In the few seconds that it took for her father to turn his back on the enclosure, she was inside it. Araminta learned two things that day: firstly, kangaroos stand on their tails to kick-box their opponents and, secondly: the reason her parents gave their instructions was to protect her. If ever Araminta was in doubt of this second truth, she touched the scar on her left elbow to remind her.

That being said, it was not completely deliberate disobedience that made Araminta keep the parchment to herself upon her return home from the Tudor House. She was surprised to find her mother sitting in the kitchen in her dressing gown when she snuck back into the house; for although her father, naturally, knew all about her little escapade, Araminta's mother had always been kept completely oblivious of the 'favours' her daughter carried out on her husband's behalf.

"What are you doing up so early?!" Araminta was about to make a feeble lie about having just woken up but, dressed as she was, it was obvious she had been out.

"Oh, didn't I tell you? I went to help Chris with his paper round."

"Chris? Who's Chris?" said her mother.

"Christopher Jones. I *did* mention it. He was going to show me the ropes so I can apply for a job next week."

"Young lady," her mother said, sternly, "there has certainly been no mention of this at all. Otherwise your father and I would have discussed it." At this she stood up and added, kindly, "I mean, what do you want with a rotten paper round? If your allowance isn't enough, then you ought to speak to your father." Araminta saw her opportunity here to change the subject, so she did:

"Speaking of Father, where is he?"

"Oh, the University needed him to go in to cover a sick colleague. I expect he'll be gone a few days. I got up to see him off."

Araminta gave her mother a kiss and went upstairs. Carefully taking out the piece of parchment, Araminta sat on her bed and unfolded it. Next, she made two copies of the text in her best handwriting and tore the next two pages from her journal (in case anyone used that trick with the pencil to see what she had been writing). Araminta knew it would be dangerous to type the poem up – once something enters the digital world, it is far too easily copied and accessible to third parties. Araminta lifted up the loose floorboard she had discovered in her first week at the house and stuffed the parchment in the rusty tin box she kept there, making sure no-one had moved it and sprinkling sawdust back on top to track any opportunist burglar.

Once satisfied, Araminta studied her copy of the poem until it was time to shower, re-dress, and leave for school.

CHAPTER EIGHT

"The first thing we have to do is translate it," I announced to Araminta, stupidly.

"Why? It's not Middle English, Chris!" It was lunchtime and we were sat under the Birch on top of the mound. Araminta is one of those people who don't care what others think of her or who they see her with. I don't tend to either but it couldn't hurt my reputation being seen with the new Year 10 girl, could it? Mind you, to be fair, I was genuinely intrigued about our find and determined to beat the riddle if I could.

"I think we need an English scholar," I said.

"Father will figure it out soon enough," said Araminta.

"Your father?" I said in surprise.

"Yes. Look, I'd rather not say anymore. Besides, we have a few days till he's back to try and crack this on our own!"

"OK." We read through our copies silently and I looked out across the field. The rest of the school was neatly segregated into its usual groups. I expect you have them at your school: the die-hard football fans who only get up in the morning to kick around a ball at break and lunch;

they don't even eat and are always the last into class with mud and grass stains down their school shirts. Next, you have the popular girls, all sat on the benches, doing make up and reading celebrity gossip magazines. Over in the corner by the basketball courts are the Emo girls who are also doing make-up (white, black or red) and reading (Goth) magazines, chatting about how stupid the popular girls are.

The skaters hang out near the smokers where the teachers can't be bothered to ask them to stop practising their stunts on the broken steps and railings and the smokers are only harming themselves. The Year 7s play bulldog on the mound and some of the in-betweeners hang out near the Tree. It's kind of understood to be a first-come-first-served thing so no one would approach us. (I'm forgetting to mention all the couples and the loners and the geeks who stay indoors, or the musos who are in bands and choirs, of course, but the list is pretty endless. You get the picture).

"I think we should approach this like any poem in English. Y'know, first try to get the big picture and then work through each line. Or something?" I said, after some time. Araminta agreed and we each offered our view on what the main idea of the poem was.

"Well it's kind of religious," I offered.

"That's not the theme, that's the imagery," said Araminta. I was beginning to get the impression that she was starting to regret inviting me along at all. I opened my mouth to point out that until she decided to let me in on the whole secret I was bound to be a bit clueless, but thought better of it and said, instead,

"Do you think it's a kind of map?" Really, I had no idea, but it seemed likely, given the secrecy and the fact that Araminta had been rather desperate to find it. Clearly it was a means to an end and not valuable in itself.

"Well, obviously it's a clue, Chris! That's why we're studying it. We need to know where it'll take us next!"

"Next?"

"Haven't you read anything, Chris?" I was beginning to feel like a slightly thick and annoying sidekick.

"I thought the whole clues to other clues to other clues thing was just a cliché?"

"Sometimes clichés are cliches because they're true," said Araminta. That seemed to make sense.

"All right. So; 'cradle maker.' Who makes cradles? Carpenters?" I offered.

"Carpenters. Possibly. It's a bit vague though. I mean this refers to one in particular."

"Right, So – "

"And," Araminta continued over me, "it's safe to assume that whoever wrote this had some future date in mind. I mean, who leaves clues to treasure or to another clue if that clue might move or change?"

"Right. Makes sense," I muttered. It sort of made sense but Araminta was talking faster than I could think.

"OK, so we're looking for something where there's a cradle maker that doesn't move. Now it could be metaphorical. It could be local or, I suppose, it could be a famous landmark."

"A statue," I said, slowly, "I reckon it's a statue pointing to something."

"Yes! That's good. Well done!" said Araminta, trying not to sound too much like a teacher.

Realising it was time for lessons, we agreed to spend the afternoon researching famous cradle makers and any statues of them and meet back at the tree after school. I was secretly hoping I'd get ahead on this but as I had double Physics with Mr Chase (who has about five eyes in the back of his bald head) and Araminta had ICT, I wasn't going to beat myself up about it if she worked out the clue first.

"Isaac Newton!" We chorused together when we rendezvoused. As luck would have it, Mr Chase decided to give us a lesson on laws of motion, which he demonstrated with a model of Newton's Cradle. I'd seen one plenty of times before but forgotten about it completely. Mr Chase is pretty boring though and we were only allowed to watch as he lifted one of the metal spheres up and let go, setting the chain of motion in...well, motion. Araminta, meanwhile, had turned to our friend Google for the answer. Apparently it took her half an hour of searching images of cradles to come across the vital clue.

"All right. So. What next?" I asked, making a mental note to be more assertive in future or Araminta would just run the show.

"Well," she said, "I found about six statues or busts of Newton. Mainly in England. One in India."

"Oh. I hope it's not that one!" I said.

"I don't think so – he's not standing in it."

"What makes you think Newton's standing?"

"Well," said Araminta, "the bit about 'steps.' Mmm, maybe you're right. But how else are we going to narrow it down?"

Araminta had helpfully printed off pictures of the statues and monuments in question. We discounted the bust in the 'Temple of the British Worthies' and hoped it wasn't the one in India. We thought it extremely unlikely that the riddle was referring to the statue outside the British Library because it's so modern.

"Actually, there's a point," I said.

"What?"

"Have we been really stupid?"

"Stupid, how?" asked Araminta.

"Well, these statues are far newer than that fireplace. I mean, Newton wasn't even born in 1540 anyway!" This made us pause for a moment but Araminta rightly pointed out that, just because the fireplace was from 1540 (or thereabouts), it didn't mean that the parchment was from that time period too.

"I mean the spelling is much more modern anyway. It's clearly been done in the style of a Shakespearean sonnet and it's probably much later," reasoned Araminta. "No, I reckon it belonged to that Edward guy who re-did the house. Or someone just before him."

"Right," I said, and we continued with our process of elimination.

We had whittled the options down to:

1. a statue of Newton at Oxford Natural History Museum by Munro, mid 19th Century
2. a statue of Newton in Trinity College Chapel, Cambridge by Louis Francois Roubiliac in 1755.
3. Newton's memorial in Westminster Abbey.

We thought the earlier dates were more likely candidates and something about the "sanctuary" made us think that the Chapel or Abbey were really what we were looking for.

Here, our opinions divided. Looking at the picture of the monument in the Abbey, I noticed there was a sort of globe on the top.

"The poem says 'the globe we must traverse!'" I insisted.

"Yes, but I'm not sure if that isn't a different sort of clue."

"Well, why not check them both out?" I said, "after all, London is less than an hour from Cambridge."

"True."

"Hang on," I said, remembering something, "doesn't your Dad work in Cambridge?"

"Yes, Father works at the Divinity Faculty at the moment."

"Araminta?"

"Yes?"

"You should really stop calling him 'Father', y'know? It's not very cool." I wished I hadn't said that. Firstly, I think it hurt her feelings; secondly, I really think she had no idea about British culture; thirdly, it made me sound obnoxious and judgmental (which is the fastest way of putting off a girl); and fourthly, I mean, does it matter what she calls her parents? I hear Ryan calls his Dad by his first name.

"What would you know? You don't have a father anyway!" snapped Araminta in defence. As soon as the words were out, I could tell she regretted saying them and I knew she didn't really mean it.

"I'm sorry, Chris. That was awful of me. I – "

"I shouldn't have said what I did, either. Sorry. Let's forget about it."

"You can't forget things, Christopher. You can forgive but you can't forget." Her use of my full name marked the loss of something between us. Something I wanted to get back.

"Hey, you were probably right. I do envy your home life, you know," I said.

"Well you know what they say about grass?"

"Grass?"

"Always greener on the other side."

"Well it is a lot greener over there," I said, pointing to the bottom field which doesn't get used very much because no one can be bothered to traipse over that far.

At that moment, my phone rang. It was Kirsty, demanding I return home immediately.

"Sorry, Araminta." I said, "Got to fly."

"Tempus fugit," said Araminta, wistfully.

"What?"

"Time Flies."

"Oh. Right. Well I don't fly, so I'd better run instead. Um, I'll see you tomorrow?" Barely waiting for an answer I turned on my heel and slipped ungracefully down the mound.

"I'm all right!" I called out and started jogging home, thinking I should add Latin to my list of things to learn if I wanted to keep up with Araminta.

CHAPTER NINE

The journey to Cambridge wasn't one I wish to repeat in a hurry: the bus broke down after ten miles and we had to get off by the side of the road and wait for about two hours. We were about to abandon the mission, when a burly bloke in a silly yellow hat and check trousers bounded up and told us that a replacement coach had arrived. You certainly learn one or two things about girls when you have to wait with them for something to happen. Mostly, it seems it was my fault that the bus had broken down; or, if it wasn't my fault, it was certainly my responsibility to get it fixed. In this respect, Araminta was beginning to act a lot more like Kirsty and a lot less like somebody I wanted to be spending two hours on the side of the road with. I suggested playing cards or looking at the poem again but she decided that cards were boring and that we shouldn't take out the poem in public.

We finally got to Cambridge about lunch time. I'd packed a sandwich but had already scoffed it on the bus. I had a few toffees in my pocket, which had gone slightly sticky, so I suggested getting a KFC or something.

"We're not here to eat, Christopher!" said Araminta sharply. I think the heat had got to her.

"*You* might not be, but I'm starving!"

"We'll get something on the way back. We should make our way to the statue in case they close the Chapel or something," she said. I couldn't really argue with her so muttered something under my breath about women and followed her down the road.

"Have you been here before?" I asked, as Araminta picked up the pace.

"No." I had to get her out of her sullen mood somehow.

"Then how –?"

"Oh do stop being such a bore, Christopher!"

"Sorry!" I said, sarcastically.

"I've got an app, if you must know," she said and showed me her phone. "We're the blue dot and the red thing is the Chapel. So we keep going down this road and then make a left into Market Square, all right?"

"Fine."

Perhaps it was the air or the bustle of the City which relaxed Araminta, because by the time we reached the entrance to Trinity College, she was back to her usual self.

"Sorry about that," she said, "I just don't like travelling. Always get a bit sick and stressed."

"Sure. Anyway, we're here now, so what shall we do?"

"Go in?"

"Right!"

I was beginning to get the sense that Araminta didn't like not being in charge, or control. Perhaps it's because she's an only child.

It being term time, I suppose, there were more students milling about. Of course we looked too young to be members of the University, but, somehow, we managed to slip in past the Porters without having to pay the entrance fee.

"Wow!" was all I could think of to say. It was how I had imagined Hogwarts to be, only ten times better.

"Come on," said Araminta, "let's find the Chapel."

The statue of Newton was actually in the Antechapel. He stood, larger than I had imagined and younger.

"He looks a little uncertain," I said.

"His clothes look so real. I just can't imagine having the skill to look at a bit of marble and chip away at it to make something so beautiful."

Despite it being a weekend, there weren't that many visitors. (I guess most were probably having KFC or something nicer for lunch; as that's what most civilised people do: they eat). The majority of them walked right past the statue and into the Chapel.

"Right, let's put our thinking caps on. What does the poem say again?" I asked.

Araminta had committed the lines to memory:

"'Between the time the cradle maker points

(If time is measured by the steps we tread

 Or what we stand for, and against); the joint

 Circumferences of all our hopes and dread

 Become the globe we must traverse to find

 The sacred twin of this dear sanctuary.'"

"Yeah," I said, "That's great. Except I didn't catch it. Just say the first bit again?" Araminta patiently repeated the first line as I walked around the base of the statue.

"Time...Time...I don't see a clock here, do you?"

"No." We stood back a little and paused to think. Araminta turned to look out, as if she were Newton, in the hope that we'd been missing something.

"Chris!" she said in an urgent whisper.

"What?"

"Shh. Don't turn round. There's a man, staring at us."

"Where?" I asked.

"At your six."

"What?"

"Six o'clock! Seven now...eight...oh, he's gone."
Araminta turned back round to me and, suddenly, the
penny dropped.

"That's it! Araminta, you're a genius!"

"What? What did I say?"

"It's his feet – look, they're pointing like a clock face!"

We looked at the base of the statue. Newton was
standing, feet apart at, "about ten-to-two I reckon," said
Araminta, tilting her head to the right.

"Right," I agreed. "Hey, that fits with the whole, 'if time
is measured by the steps we tread' thing!"

"Exactly!" The bit about hope and dread flummoxed us
a bit.

"But I think the next bit, about the globe is saying we
have to go somewhere," said Araminta. As we were
puzzling it over, the Chaplain came over and told us there
was a service about to start and we should come into the
Chapel, if we'd like.

"I think he meant to add 'or clear off,'" I said.

"I agree. We should probably go."

"But we haven't solved it yet!"

"Well there's nothing here. It's such a public place
anyway, we couldn't be expected to really *find* anything that
couldn't be plainly seen."

"Right," I said, unconvinced. "Hey, do you think it's
like a bearing? You know, that we should sort of take the
direction of his feet as a map bearing, or compass point, or
something?"

"Brilliant! Chris, have you got a compass?"

"No. Don't you have an app for it or something?"

"Yes. I don't always think it works though." The
Chaplain was walking towards us again, smiling. Araminta
fumbled with her phone and we scuttled out of the
Antechapel, nearly tripping up over a bald man who was
loitering on the step.

"Excuse me," I said. I swore I heard him mutter my name.

CHAPTER TEN

Armed with a map and Araminta's fluctuating compass readings, we tried to sketch a likely path out from the statue.

"Let's just think about this logically," she said as we sat on the coach back home.

"Chapels face East. The statue was at the West end, looking East and his feet, at ten-to-two were sort of pointing – "

"South East," I interrupted.

"Right. So, let's draw a line roughly South East of the Chapel and see what we come up with."

Unfortunately, the answer was water.

"Going straight South East just makes you end up in the North Sea. It's hopeless. We got the wrong clue. We probably went to the wrong place. Bet it was Westminster Abbey all along." I said, trying not to sound as smug as I felt.

"Look, don't be so precise about the angle, Chris! We said *roughly* South-East, so let's just widen the search radius a bit."

"OK." The coach was a little bumpy and the map we'd bought at the tourist shop wasn't brilliant but we both agreed anywhere south and east of Cambridge was worth considering. It was just then that I looked out of the coach window as we passed a sign welcoming us to: *Godmanchester. Twinned with Wertheim, Salon de Provence and Szentendre.*

"Araminta!" I said, excitedly, prodding her in the ribs.

"What?"

"Look! Twins! Maybe it means town twinning?"

"I don't think so. Didn't town-twinning start after the War? Also, I think we should focus more on the Chapel and less on Cambridge itself." Trust her to know that.

"OK then, Smarty Pants, what's the 'sacred twin' of Trinity Chapel?" I might have got a sharp remark or a sharper poke, had it not been for the fact that Araminta thought I was on to something.

"What did you say?"

"Sorry. I didn't mean to call you Smar–"

"Shh! I'm trying to think!" Araminta thinks quickly, thank goodness, as I was literally holding my breath.

"Got it!"

"What? What is it?" I asked, still feeling like Watson to her Holmes.

"Well, all this time I was thinking of it as the Chapel at Trinity College but, just now, you called it 'Trinity Chapel.'"

"Right."

"Right – which made me think: there must be a Trinity Chapel somewhere else in the South East of England!"

"*Right!*"

We high-fived each other and said nothing for the rest of the journey. We were certainly closer - I could feel it. Of course, what we were closer *to*, I couldn't have possibly begun to imagine. Which is probably a good thing.

CHAPTER ELEVEN

Araminta generally enjoyed a free reign at the weekends. Some might have called her parents Bohemian; still others might have ventured so much as to say they tended towards the neglectful, but the truth of the matter was, that the Stirlings had brought their daughter up with enough common sense and imagination to look after and amuse herself.

Many of Katherine's friends didn't appreciate that writing is a full time occupation. When Katherine wasn't locked away in her study, typing furiously, she was doing research at some library or other. Meal times were, however, sacrosanct; so, whilst Araminta had not needed to ask permission to go out for the day, she did have to explain why she was forty minutes late home for dinner.

"I'm really sorry, Mother. It's just that – "

"Yes?"

Araminta had just walked in to the wonderful smell of her mother's beef casserole and tried to sneak upstairs unnoticed. She was now standing in the kitchen, being interrogated by a fierce pair of green eyes peering over horn-rimmed glasses.

"Well, it's just that I –" began Araminta again, touching her left elbow. She wasn't very good at this.

"Don't be hard on the child, Darling; I expect she's had a bit of an adventure and simply lost track of time," said Dr Stirling, as he made his way downstairs and into the kitchen.

"Father, you're home!"

"Yes. I only arrived a half hour ago myself."

"Except your father had the courtesy to call ahead," said Katherine; she was clearly not in a forgiving mood.

"Shall we just enjoy our dinner and we can tell each other about our days?" said Dr Stirling. Araminta smiled; although she was dreading having to make up a lie about the whole day.

Katherine served the dinner onto some warm plates and Araminta set the table with candles before they sat down together and tucked in.

"How's the book going, Mother?"

"Dreadful. I've had a block on this chapter for a week now. I knew it was a mistake to write about something so modern as the 1930s. It's really not my period; I don't think I'm doing justice to the era or the characters at all." Katherine took her glasses off and rubbed her tired eyes. "But, it's what the publisher wants, so…"

Dr Stirling took his wife's hand, kindly and reassured her.

"So, sweetheart, what kept you entertained all day and evening?" he said to his daughter.

This was Araminta's cue to give a long spiel about going to Kirsty or Gemma's house, watching crummy Rom-Coms all day and experimenting with makeup but she found it hard to lie to those piercing green eyes.

"Well, actually, I was doing a bit of research on this History project."

"Alone?" asked Dr Stirling, pointedly.

"No. Um, with Christopher Jones?"

"Ah, you've mentioned him before. So what's going on between you?" Araminta's mother was always trying to find out about her private life.

"Nothing!" blurted out Araminta, a little defensively.

"'The lady protests too much...'" joked Dr Stirling.

"I mean, nothing like *that*. Anyway he's in the year below me. We're just...working on this project together."

Araminta managed to deflect a question about keeping company with younger boys.

"Well," said Katherine, helping herself to some more carrots, "perhaps you should invite him over for dinner next week?"

"Oh, no, I don't think –"

"I insist. After all, if he's the reason you were late tonight, it's the least he can do to atone."

Araminta smiled and nodded her assent before successfully diverting attention to her father.

"My day?" said Dr Stirling in answer to his daughter's question. "Well, it was certainly interesting."

Realising that would be all that was said on the matter, Katherine changed the subject.

"The other reason I was worried, sweetheart, was that there's been another of those Domino murders."

"What did you say?" said Dr Stirling, a little sharply.

"Well, that's what they're calling them, isn't it?" said Katherine.

"Is it? Sorry I haven't watched the news for a day or so," said Dr Stirling.

Katherine explained that there had been three murders up and down the breadth of the country. All that seemed to link them was that a Domino had been placed on each of the victim's chests. It had several police forces baffled. The numbers on the Dominos were unique to each case and none of the detectives working on the various cases had recently formed a task force. Still, without anything else connecting the victims, the chances of catching the killer – or predicting the next victim – were remote.

Having heard enough, Dr Stirling remarked that such talk was, "hardly dinner conversation" and they shifted down into small talk and all was forgiven, if not forgotten.

Araminta washed and dried, allowing her parents to return to their respective studies. She had just finished putting away the last glass when her phone vibrated with a text message:

Come to my Study now. Father x

For a few moments, Araminta stood in silence, listening to the metronome ticking of the grandfather clock in the far corner. She looked about, nervously; the crow's beady eyes seemed to be boring into her soul.

"Well, what do you have for me?" said Dr Stirling, from behind his desk. He was in interrogation mode. Araminta never liked this sort of thing; she always had the impression that her father knew rather more than he was letting on. She was right to trust her instincts.

"I found something. In the Tudor House. Like you said."

"*I?*"

Araminta looked at the floor, the crow, and back at her Father and realised she would have to tell him everything.

Once she had finished her testimony, Dr Stirling stood up and walked over to his daughter. Araminta very nearly flinched. She had never had cause to be frightened of her father but she did find him imposing – especially when he was in the middle of one of his mysterious schemes. Dr Stirling put his hands on Araminta's shoulders and stooped slightly to look level into her blue eyes.

"Well done, Minty. Well done." Releasing her from his embrace, Dr Stirling invited her to sit.

"Sorry, you've been standing all this time!" he said. "I'm so glad you're safe and...you've done so well."

"Safe? Why wouldn't I be safe?" she asked.

"I'm afraid," he continued, ignoring this interjection, "that I'm going to have to ask you for a little more."

"More?"

"Yes."

He got up and went to the door, checking it was shut tightly.

"Now, what I'm about to say must go no further. You must not even tell Christopher Jones. At least, not for the moment. But I want you both to continue with the... 'research' for me. You see, people are watching and I can't investigate myself. Two teenagers will be less conspicuous. Anything you do find, report to me. Tell your mother nothing. She mustn't worry."

"Worry?! Should *I* be worried?"

Saying nothing, Dr Stirling went over to the picture of the crow, removed it from its place on the wall and opened the safe that lay behind it.

"Here's some money in case you need it," he said. "Now, listen extremely carefully."

CHAPTER TWELVE

I'd spent most of Sunday waiting for Kirsty to get off Facebook so I could do some research on the computer. I was hoping Araminta might have called me but I was obviously out-of-sight-out-of-mind. I was worried that she had found the next clue all by herself (or, worse, with someone else) and that, having served my purpose, I was redundant.

I needn't have worried. As it happens, I was actually one step ahead of her when we met on Monday.

"Canterbury!" I said, triumphantly, pointing to the map I had circled with all sorts of annotations (most, crossed out. For some reason I could never get the hang of using a protractor).

"Sorry?"

"Canterbury," I repeated. "Specifically, Canterbury Cathedral. It has a chapel inside called Trinity Chapel – so, *twin* – and it's pretty much directly southeast of Cambridge."

"Are you sure?"

"Pretty sure," I said, feeling less sure now.

"Anything else to support your case?" said Araminta, raising her right eyebrow. It was the first time I took note of her doing it but it seems she did so whenever she found something I did slightly annoying, or not matching up to her high standards of detective work. She was to do it a lot more. I suppose I'm a little less cautious. On this occasion, however, my stab-in-the-dark guess was more than Araminta had and so, after what seemed like an interminable pause, she said,

"All right. Let's go to Canterbury."

"Go?! It's a hundred miles away! More!"

"It won't take that long. It's not the middle ages, Chris."

"When, Saturday?"

"No," said Araminta to herself, "that's too late. Let's go tomorrow!"

"Tomorrow? Are you crazy? Have you forgotten we have school?"

"Come on, Chris, it'll be fun!"

"It'll be stupid. How are we going to get away with that one?"

Araminta said she'd think about it and we agreed to meet after school.

Thinking the whole enterprise was in the realms of fantasy, I didn't really give it much thought for the rest of the day. Josh asked how my weekend was and got suspicious when I didn't give him an account of my movements.

"You've been a bit distant recently, mate. It wouldn't have anything to do with that girl I saw you with, would it?"

"What? When did you see me?"

"The other day by the lockers. You know – you gave me the wink and I had to bail?"

"Oh. Yeah. Sorry about that." Josh was clearly expecting a little more so I simply said that I had been

63

spending a bit of time with Araminta, helping her with some History stuff.

"See, I knew I should have paid more attention in class!" said Josh.

"Jones! Perhaps you'd care to share your forthcoming nuptials with your confederates?" Mr Travis had crept up behind us.

"Sorry?" I said, bewildered.

"Apology accepted. As long as you can tell me what Newton has to do with my lesson."

"Newton, sir?" My heart thudded; for a moment I was half convinced that Mr Travis was the magician behind the curtain and knew everything. He was wearing his green Harris tweed jacket today and that usually meant we were in for a lecture and a particularly difficult homework essay. As he leaned over my desk I could smell the remnants of Old Spice on his clean shaven chin. That and the Brill Cream really made me think he had been frozen in the 1950s and thawed out in some post Cold War experiment.

"Yes, boy. You seem to have taken out your Physics text book and not your homework?"

"Oh!" I said, relieved. Mr Travis was not joking. He hardly ever joked about that sort of thing.

"Well," I faltered. "Newton's about motion, right? Like his cradle? You know, set one thing in motion and everything follows. Every reaction has an equal and opposite reaction. It's like in History. One thing leads to another like a chain reaction and, y'know, we don't like know what the consequences are going to be, but when we study history we can see the motion being passed along like the balls in the cradle?"

Mr Travis bore down his fiery gaze upon me as the class erupted in guffaws.

"Vague, Jones. Vague and woolly. As woolly as a woolly mammoth, whose grandmother knitted a woolly jumper for Christmas and whose political persuasion tends towards the worst form of woolly liberalism. But, you're not wrong. Put your name down for History GCSE and we'll make a scholar out of you yet." Mr Travis returned to his desk and Ryan flicked a rubber at my ear. You can't win.

Araminta's plan involved a lot of lying and the collusion of her father. I was to tell Mum I'd be eating at Araminta's after school tomorrow and would be picked up by her parents straight after the bell. Meanwhile, Araminta's dad had, apparently, agreed to phone up the school first thing, saying they'd invited me round to dinner the *previous* night and both Araminta and I had contracted food poisoning. For some reason, Araminta's mum had to be kept out of the loop. In the morning I would leave for school as usual and meet Araminta at the station where we'd take a series of trains to Canterbury. Mum would leave for work at 06.00, so the only problem was Kirsty. I don't travel in with her anymore but I thought she'd notice I wasn't in school. Fortunately, as she hates me being at "her" school, she does tend to avoid me like the plague.

"Only thing is that Josh might call home," I said.

"Well, tell him not to."

"Right."

In the end I had to just tell Josh I was going to bunk off tomorrow with Araminta.

"Dude, that's crazy! You'll get in so much trouble!"

"That's why I've got a best friend," I said. It took Josh a while to weigh up what he could get out of this, but he obviously thought a 'favour' would be worth at least a fiver, or doing his homework (again).

"OK," he said, flashing his braces in a wide smile. "But I want to hear all the juicy little details when I see you Wednesday. And if there aren't any, make them up!"

"All right." And that was it: the game was afoot.

CHAPTER THIRTEEN

The butterflies in my stomach only lasted till London. Araminta's dad was obviously much cooler than mine had ever been and I said as much as we made our way to St. Pancras.

"You'd be surprised," was all Araminta would say. At a quiet part in the journey she asked if I was still in contact with my Dad.

"Not so much," I said. "I remember the day he left. He stood in our kitchen and said to Mum, 'Do I *have* to see the children?' Right in front of me and Kirsty."

"That's horrid. I'm so sorry." Her hand went out instinctively to touch mine but she withdrew it.

"It's pretty ingrained on the old memory, y'know," I said. "He moved away to the West country anyway and he's been bad at keeping in touch. Can't remember the last Birthday card he sent."

"How do you feel about that?"

"How do you think I feel? Sorry, that's not a fair question. I think I'm a bit confused. He's been gone for as long as he was there, now. Well, from my perspective.

Less actually. I was seven when he left so I probably only remember about four years of him being at home."

"What does Kirsty make of it?"

"She hates him." That's all she ever says. (Well, it's not *all*, but I couldn't repeat what she usually calls him).

The train down to Canterbury was pretty fast. Neither of us had visited the City before so we were both looking forward to a bit of sightseeing. I wasn't really expecting the Cathedral to be so big. I mean I know it's Canterbury Cathedral, but most cathedrals I'd been to (the one, actually) were a lot smaller. I did think it was bad we had to pay to get in.

"Isn't it God's house?" I said, in a vain attempt to get in free.

"Yeah, but we pay the bills," said the woman on the barrier, chewing gum.

"That's funny," said Araminta.

"It's not my joke," she said, blowing a bubble. "I don't believe in God. We just have that line cause so many people complain."

We managed to tack onto a guided tour, which turned out to be the best thing we could have possibly done, as the old biddy who pottered around with the aid of a walking stick was actually incredibly knowledgeable (if a little deaf).

"I'm so glad you young-uns are into your history," she said to us. "Most people these days seem to think it's not at all relevant."

"Oh, no," I said, "we're *very* interested." We had been joined by a middle aged couple with cameras round their necks who kept fidgeting and a Korean man in his sixties who clearly didn't speak English, but smiled and nodded a lot.

"This," said the Guide, "is the Trinity Chapel."

The Korean gentleman was so impressed by the ceiling that he almost fell over a candle that had been left in the middle of the floor.

"That's dangerous!" said the woman with the camera round her neck. "It's just asking for trouble. Why have you got a dirty great big candle in the middle of the floor?"

"I'm glad you asked that," said the Guide. "It's there for St. Thomas a Becket. He was murdered in this Cathedral."

"I thought that churches and things were, like, sanctuaries?" I said: "Didn't people claim sanctuary?"

"Yes, of course," said the Guide. "But you can't very well stop people breaking the law, can you? You can only have the law in place. You can tell people not to park on double yellow lines, smoke on train stations or truant from school, but you can't force them." Worried she was on to us, I kept my mouth shut and dropped back a little.

"Chris!" exclaimed Araminta suddenly, in excitement.

"What?"

"That's it. The martyr! I bet it's that Thomas guy!" Before I could stop her, Araminta was asking if there was a shrine to Becket, besides the candle.

"Yes, dear, there is. We'll get to that later. Although it's not where it originally was. The reason we have the candle here is because this is where he was initially enshrined."

That was it! I exchanged a knowing glance with Araminta and pressed the Guide to show us the exact spot.

"We have to look from this exact spot," I said. "I'm sure that's what it means: 'there, where once a martyr was enshrined, Look. Look on your past and future.'"

We looked but nothing immediately leapt out at us.

"Come on, dearies, we have to see the rest of the Nave yet!" our Guide said, cheerily, checking a Nurse's watch that was hanging from her blouse. Anxious that we might miss the vital clue, I grabbed the Guide's grey cardigan.

"Oh, sorry, I didn't mean to grab you. I, um... Just wondered. What's that?" I pointed in the vague direction that I thought the poem was telling us to look at.

"Oh, that? That is the Corona Chapel. It's a sort of tribute to modern saints and martyrs: Martin Luther King Junior, Kolbe, Bonhoeffer and the like."

"MLK I've heard of, obviously, but not Coal-bur and Bon-whoever," I said, sounding very unintelligent.

"Well," said the Guide, "Maximillian Kolbe was a priest held in a concentration camp for political reasons. When two Jews escaped the camp, the Nazis rounded up ten Jews whom they chose to starve to death. One man started crying and Kolbe volunteered to take his place. It took almost two weeks for him to die but he did so with a smile and a prayer on his lips. Bonhoeffer, also a priest, was executed in 1943 for a botched attempt to assassinate Hitler."

"Wow," I said, rather slowly and stupidly.

The Guide smiled at us and looked at her watch again.

"I'm very sorry, but I must leave you here if you don't mind? I have a large party who have booked a tour."

We thanked her and watched her cross the Chapel and make her way to the West Door. The couple walked on behind her and the Korean smiled at us and gave a little bow before going over to inspect the stained glass windows. When we were alone, Araminta ran her fingers through her hair and sat down on the cold stone floor.

"Well, Chris, that really wasn't much good at all. Talk about dead end."

"I know. I really thought we had it with the whole enshrined martyr thing."

I crouched down beside her and thought of putting a hand on her shoulder but didn't. We stared at the candle together and said nothing. The hushed din of tourists and pilgrims became as mesmeric as the flame in front of our eyes. It might have been a minute or an hour before Araminta spoke again:

"Well, I guess it's back to the drawing board for us."

"Guess so." I muttered in reply. Araminta stood up and we meekly made for the exit.

And that was it. We said virtually nothing to each other on the journey home; only to point out the hilarious sight of a woman wearing a grey leopard-print dress, struggling with a trolley of grey leopard-print luggage across the platform from us.

It wasn't too late when we got back, so Araminta invited me back for tea.

"Otherwise," she said, "your mum will wonder why you've come home so early; y'know, she might worry you broke our Ming Vase or something."

"You have a minging vase?"

Araminta just raised her eyebrow and I got the impression I had said something stupid again.

I was sort of expecting this twenty bedroom mansion from what Kirsty and Mum had said, but it was less posh than all that. Still pretty posh though: everyone had their own study and there was a library and a *billiard* room, a dining room, a music room, a sitting room and a 'cinema'.

"Wow! You could hide the population of a small Middle Eastern country in here!"

"Chris, were you born racist, or did you just learn it?"

"Racist? I wasn't being racist. I was – "

I was cut off as I nearly ploughed into Dr Stirling's chest, which seemed to have come out of nowhere to halt my path through the third floor hallway.

"Oh, excuse me, um, Mr Stirling."

I looked up at this bear of a man. No, 'bear' makes him sound fat, which he wasn't. He was just *very* big – tall and grey, like an owl or something. Wise but with a sharp beak. And a thick head of wiry hair.

"It's Doctor, actually."

"Oh. Sorry. *Dr* Stirling."

70

He smiled and took a step back, clapped his hands together and said:

"So you must be the young Master Jones my daughter has been waxing lyrical about?"

"Um, she has? I mean. Yes...Yes, I'm Christopher." We shook hands. A warm, firm grip. Certainly more paws than talons.

Mrs Stirling, I found much less foreboding. In fact, she seemed just a little on the dotty side. What she was, however, was a wonderful chef and we were soon sat down to a risotto.

"So, Sweetheart, how was the trip?" said Mrs Stirling. I nearly choked on a bit of chicken.

"Good. Good, thanks. Wasn't it, Chris?"

"Absolutely. First rate." I said, in my best posh voice, reserved for parents of my middle class friends.

"Did you learn anything?" asked Dr Stirling.

"Oh, always. Always learning, sir," I muttered, stupidly.

"Do you always jabber like a babboon, Mr Jones?" he said.

"I...I, err..."

"Joseph, give the lad a break!" said Mrs. Stirling.

"Well," said Araminta. "We had a good Guide round the Cathedral but I'm not sure we got everything out of it. You know, I expect there's always more to see. In fact, having a Guide can sometimes hinder you. It might be better next time to just have a look round ourselves."

"Next time?" asked Mrs Stirling. I got the impression that each of us knew a little more, and a little less than the person we were sitting next to. Except Dr Stirling, who seemed pretty omniscient.

"You mean you'll have to repeat the trip? But that doesn't make sense, Sweetheart!"

"Oh no, Mother. I just meant, if the school repeats the trip – I might recommend they don't have the Guided

Tour. Or, at least, have some time for the students to explore the Cathedral for themselves."

"I see. So, Christopher, tell me about your family. What do your parents do?" said Mrs Stirling, in that way that adults do when they can't think what to say but don't want to patronise you by asking how school is going.

"Mother – " began Araminta.

"Don't interrupt, Sweetheart."

"Chris' parents are –"

"Divorced. They're divorced," I said, quickly. "It's fine. I mean it happened about seven years ago. My Dad just decided he didn't want us anymore and upped and left and Mum has been struggling to support us ever since. Me and my sister, Kirsty, that is. I don't really know what she does. A couple of jobs. I think they're boring. She doesn't talk about it much."

Mrs Stirling pushed her glasses up her nose and we carried on eating.

After dinner, Mrs Stirling showed me her books. She'd written dozens and they lined two shelves of the first mahogany bookcase in their library.

"Don't pretend you've heard of them," she said.

"No. I'm sorry, I haven't," I said, "but then I'm a bit of a Palestine."

"Philistine, dear."

"Right, that's what I said. I *am* interested in history though. We've got a very good teacher at school. And I'm really getting into the Tudors. Have you written anything set then?"

"Yes, my third novel, *To Take A Crown* was set in the Tudor period. Should you like to read it?"

"Absolutely!" I said, enthusiastically.

"Good boy. I pride myself on being being to read people and that was genuine enthusiasm, I can tell." She smiled and then added: "Well, either that or I'm losing my touch! Or you're a very good actor."

"I'm not."

"Well, we can't all be Shakespeare, can we?"

She took down a copy of her book, scrawled a brief dedication in it and handed it to me. She held on to it fast as I went to take it from her and she said, peering over her glasses at me:

"Mind, I'll quiz you on it, Christopher."

"Thanks. I'll...um...I'll do my best," I promised.

CHAPTER FOURTEEN

Besides a mildly amusing anecdote involving Kirsty, a kebab and a carton of orange juice, nothing of consequence happened until Friday, when a chance remark made by Josh over a school lunch of bacon rolls, chips and salad, made me think again:

"I mean it's like that dude Mr Travis was banging on about."

"Which dude?" I said.

"Oh that's right; you weren't there. You were with lover girl!" he said, making a kissing noise with his lips.

"Shut up, Josh. It was nothing like that; I told you."

"Still, she must sort of *like* you!"

"What about the dead dude from History?" I pressed.

"It's just these Domino murders. You know everyone says it's bad, but what if they were bad people?" said Josh, shovelling a chip into his mouth and getting a bit of potato stuck in his upper brace.

"Wasn't one of them a twenty year old student?" I said.

"Well, yeah but, y'know he might have been a sleaze ball."

"So that makes it all right to kill someone, does it Josh? Now you're sounding like Hitler!"

"I am *not* sounding like" – here, Josh lowered his voice, as we were sat in the canteen near the German exchange students that had come over from Bonn last week – "Hitler. All I'm saying is that, sometimes, it might be right to do the wrong thing, in order to do the right thing. Like that dude in History."

"Yeah, well that's really vague, isn't it, mate? Well done. Bloody hell! I hope your homework's better than this, or Mr Travis won't let you do History next year and I'll have to sit next to Stacey," I said.

"Or Luke," added Josh.

"Right. Oh, no! Please – not Luke!"

"It's all right. I'll make the team." Josh smiled and stuffed a runaway tomato into his mouth.

"Well you can start by remembering this dude's name!" I said.

"Why? It isn't important."

"No. It is. I was away, remember, so you'd better get me up to speed before fourth period or I'll have an after school detention, won't I?"

"No you won't. It's Friday – he has to give your Mum a day's notice, remember?" said Josh, cheerfully.

"Mr Travis doesn't live by those rules though, does he? And you know what my Mum's like."

"Good point." Josh dived into his rucksack and took out his History exercise book and passed it over.

"Here. Don't spill ketchup on it whatever you do!"

I took the book and thumbed through to the last entry. Josh's handwriting was atrocious and I could barely make out the title.

"What does this even say? Bonch? Cough? I can't read your idiot writing!"

"Give it me." Josh squinted in an attempt to read his own writing.

75

"Oh, yeah. 'Bonhoeffer.' Diedrich Bonhoeffer."

"Wait a minute, I've heard of him!" I said, a bit too excitedly, remembering the Corona Chapel in the Cathedral.

"Right. So he was, like, this priest who tried to assassinate Hitler and got executed."

"Shh!!" I said, "don't mention the war!" I motioned my head towards the German exchange students and we giggled.

"Yeah. So, you gonna eat those chips or what?" said Josh, eyeing up my plate.

"What?"

"The chips, Chris."

"No. You have them." To be honest, the canteen chips are a bit dry and I'm too fat anyway. I shunted them in Josh's direction and muttered a "see ya," leaving the table as quickly as I could (without it looking like I was rushing), bolted out of the canteen and ran over to the Birch Tree, hoping to find Araminta sat under it. She wasn't, unfortunately – it was being occupied by some Year 11s who just gave me The Finger, so I couldn't even ask if they'd seen her. It was already 13:26 so, with the four minutes left of Lunch, I scrawled a note and tried to stuff it in her locker before making it to History (on time for a change).

Three lessons a week for History is a bit heavy in Year 9 but as we only got two in Years 7 and 8 I think they try and change it around. We *are* supposed to be a Humanities Specialist School.

I waited a good twenty minutes for Araminta after school and was about to give up on her when I suddenly noticed her ambling towards me with a green satchel on her left shoulder. It went well with her red hair and I thought of telling her as much but, as usual, faltered and simply waved at her.

"So, what have you got?" she said.

"You're not going to like this," I said. "Or maybe you will. It's kind of funny actually, when you think about it."

"What? Spit it out, Christopher!"

"I think we have to go back."

Araminta raised her eyebrow again. Whether in frustration or intrigue I wasn't sure.

When we looked at it again, it seemed pretty obvious, really. I don't know why we hadn't worked it out before but, there you go. Once you know how the magic is done it doesn't seem like magic anymore (which is why it's best not to know).

"It all seems to point back to 1540," I said. "That was the date Henry VIII tore down Thomas a Beckett's shrine and abolished the monasteries."

"Right. I'm not getting the link here." said Araminta. I was enjoying being in the know for a change but tried not to rub it in too much.

"Well that fireplace was dated 1540, right?"

"Or after," she said, pointedly.

"Right. Or after. Anyway, the point is that, 'the house of he who had destroyed this house' is the Tudor House. You see? Henry Tudor. The first house being spoken about is the Trinity Chapel in the Cathedral that used to house St. Thomas' remains."

Araminta considered this for a moment but thought it was all a bit too nebulous and she took some convincing. I tried to argue that the instructions were for us to return to where we were before and that we would find a better clue hidden somewhere in the fireplace, as it had cited the biblical quotation from the fireplace in the poem. Once I finished my speech I sat down and waited for her answer.

"I just don't think it would be that. It seems too simple. And why should it be here? Doesn't it all seem a bit...I don't know, convenient?" said Araminta, defeatedly. It did, I couldn't deny it.

"Well, have you got a better plan?" I said, knowing full well she hadn't. "Besides, it's only convenient because we live here. I mean if it ended up that we had to go to Basingstoke or Peru or something, it wouldn't be convenient to us but it would for the people who live there. It's like saying no-one wins the lottery but, obviously, *some* people do; sometimes."

There wasn't much Araminta could say to that.

"All right, Chris. But we have to plan this properly. And I think we should try to work out what the last part of the poem means before we break in again."

"Deal," I said, and we shook hands.

CHAPTER FIFTEEN

I spent a lot of the weekend in the public Library. I hadn't been in there since my first week of Year 7, when I lost my library card, forgot to return a book and then found Kirsty had spilt something sticky on it, so I didn't dare try to borrow anything, but I figured they wouldn't know me by sight (I'd grown a bit since) so it was probably safe to do some research there.

Josh and I had planned to take his Dad's kayak out for a trip, but it started raining heavily in the early hours and didn't look like it was going to let up, so I suggested we take a rain-check for next weekend. I was aware that Josh felt I was becoming distant and I didn't want to lose my best friend but, on the other hand, whatever Araminta and I were about to discover was, potentially, the most significant thing to happen to me since finding out about Father Christmas.

Late Saturday afternoon, I was struck with the idea of looking at the letters of Bonhoeffer: if he was the "priest" mentioned in the thirteenth line of the poem, I thought it was only probable that the "letters rearranged" were his. Apparently he wrote quite a lot. Westernford Library wasn't very well resourced and I was going to have to order the book in especially from another town.

"It should be here within the month," the librarian said. She was probably in her mid-forties with a large, friendly smile and a button nose.

"A *month*?!"

"You're in a hurry?" she said.

"Yeah. It's for a project, you see. Bit of a time limit on it." That was true, at least.

The Librarian flashed her brown eyes at me and said, "Well, you might check out the Oxfam shop in the High Street. They have a good religious section. Failing that, there's a Christian book shop in Kingsbridge."

"Will Oxfam still be open?" I asked. The Librarian turned round to look at the large Art Deco clock behind her.

"Yes. You've got about thirty minutes, I think." I thanked her and darted out, running through the rain down the High Street.

I never used to like Charity shops. They are usually full of old people, skanky clothes and VHS tapes of *Star Trek* that no one wants anymore. They all have those horrid carpets and you feel like you can't talk in them. That being said, Mum often used to bring clothes home from them which I used to wear quite happily.

The Librarian was right – there was certainly a large collection of religious books there, besides all the bibles: CS Lewis, St. Augustine, a bloke called Bede and then Calvin. No Bonhoeffer.

"Can I help you at all?" asked the Assistant. He wasn't as old as their usual volunteers: probably about fifty, with a shock of grey hair swept back. He looked like a badger. I usually hate it when assistants ask if you want help. They're usually saying it because they are worried you're going to nick something or they just want you out of the way so they can attend to customers with more surplus income. The curse of being a teenager.

"Um, I was after some Bonhoeffer," I said.

"Bonhoeffer?!" The badger-man looked me up and down and raised an eyebrow. He probably thought I was being a smart Alec.

"Yes," I said, trying to reassure him, "his letters?" This seemed to satisfy him; clearing his throat and adjusting his black corduroy jacket, he said:

"Well, it just so happens that Father McCormac passed away last month and left us his entire library. I'll have a look out the back for you." With that, he disappeared behind a curtain at the rear of the shop, as I tried not to giggle at the stereotypical name.

I was pleasantly surprised to see that Oxfam had entered the world of DVDs. Of course they were pretty rubbishy ones, but at least they weren't video cassettes. Maybe one day they even have Bluray? (not that we have a Bluray player at home). I was just reading the back of the box of *Somewhere In Time* when Badger-Man returned, with a paperback in hand.

"*Letters and Papers From Prison!*" he said, triumphantly.

"Wow! Excellent. How much do I owe you?" I asked.

"Nothing; if you promise to look after it."

"Well, that's awfully generous of you," I said. (I added the 'awfully' because I thought it might make me sound a bit more grown up. Or slightly posh at the least).

"I think Father McCormac would have liked you to have it." I thanked him again, put the book in my coat pocket and ran home as fast as I could through the downpour.

It was an interesting read. The man was clearly torn between his sense of Christian ethic and *duty*. He started by saying something about time being precious and then that, "the great masquerade of evil has played havoc with all our ethical concepts." I can't pretend that I understood it all and I had found nothing to solve the last line of the poem. I was so engrossed in the book that I didn't notice Kirsty come into the lounge and snatch it out of my hand.

"What are you doing? I was reading that!" I said.

"You were reading some, like, convict's letters? Always thought you were weird."

I resisted the temptation to get into a debate and simply asked, again, for Kirsty to return the book.

"Not until you tell me what you've done with my iPod," she said.

"Look, I haven't seen the iPod."

"Oh, so you admit it's mine?"

"What? Oh, look here —" I lunged for the book but Kirsty held it over my head. (She has very long arms). Soon we were wrestling and there was no way I was going to win so I tickled her stomach (which she hates) and then she kicked me somewhere I'd prefer not to mention (Kirsty never fought fair) and I fell off the settee and knocked my glass of Coke over.

"Well done, Chris."

"Well done *me*? It was *you* who kicked me!"

"Mum'll go ape if that leaves a stain. Better clean it up," she said in her 'grown up' voice. I went into the kitchen to get the cloth and Kirsty plonked herself down on the settee and switched on the TV and channel hopped.

"Rubbish. I wish Mum would get Sky!" she said to herself and made her way upstairs as I came back into the lounge and started to scrub the carpet.

"Oh, Chris! Turn off the TV for us!" she ordered from her bedroom. I reached for the remote and then remembered I'd better use the switch, or I'd get another lecture from Mum about the electricity bill. Just at that moment, I heard something important:

"All right Norman, let's hear your six."

"Mosaic," said a thin Asian man in a green jumper.

"Mosaic. Well done. And, Debbie, what's your five letter word?"

"Scone," said a kindly looking brunette wearing a grey woollen cardigan.

"Scone, thank you. And anything from our Dictionary Corner?"

I stood, riveted to the set as the penny dropped.

CHAPTER SIXTEEN

"*Countdown*? That's your big break through?" said Araminta when I told her what I'd discovered.

"Yes! Well, no, not the programme, I mean the whole thing with the anagrams."

"You mean the letters?" asked Araminta.

"Yes. You see, all weekend I'd been thinking about that last line in the poem and then it occurred to me that I wasn't being literal enough. And the fact that the contestant said 'mosaic' – well, it was just the perfect wake up call."

"So, what you're saying is that we need to break back into the house and play around with the mosaic to form an anagram of that Bible verse and hope something happens?"

"Right," I said, trying to sound as confident and rational as possible.

"Chris, do you have any idea how many thousands of possible anagrams you could make out of the letters of *YE SHALL BE AS GODDES*?"

"No. Do you?"

"No. But there must be literally thousands. It would take us a century to try them all. That's once we'd even worked it out," she said.

"Well, haven't you got an app for it?" I said, cheekily. Araminta was not impressed.

"I suppose there might be something on a computer somewhere that can help. Meantime, I don't think there's any point in breaking back into the House and moving things around willy nilly until we're sure. Or at least have a better idea. And I'm still not convinced anyway."

I was a little taken aback, to be honest; I thought she'd have been pleased and given me a proverbial pat on the back, but I felt more like I was being told off for something. Perhaps she was just a bit jealous because I'd come up with the solution.

Araminta must have had a change of heart as she posted a list of phrases in my locker which I found at the end of Friday with *Shortlist x* scribbled on a green post-it note. I smiled and stuffed the wad of paper into my rucksack.

Trawling through that list was like one of the labours of Hercules – an impossible sea of alliterated phrases which made no sense at all. There was no way to sift through them. Not one stood out. I dreaded to think what the long list was like.

"It's no good," I said when we met the following day by the Tree. "I was staring at them for hours but none of them leaped out."

"I know," she said, chewing the end of her hair in the right corner of her mouth. "I think we'll have to try a different algorithm or something. It found over 88000, you know."

"Maybe." I picked at a blade of grass to make a whistle out of it. Over my left shoulder I could hear a couple of Year 8s arguing about which had the better phone:

"Yeah but, like, when do you ever write anything by hand anymore? It's all about the qwerty keyboard," said one.

"I just like being able to take notes," said the other.

They were both those sort of girls who straighten their hair for half an hour before school and spend their lives snapchatting or Facebooking and generally talking about snapchat, Facebook or hair straightening. But the first girl's remark suddenly made me think of something.

"Hey, Minty!" I said, jabbing Araminta in the arm.

"What did you call me?"

"Um, I don't know."

"Minty. You called me Minty."

"Did I?" I said, unconvincingly.

"Yeah."

"Oh. Sorry?"

"No, it's fine, I quite like it. My...Dad calls me that sometimes." It was the first time she had called him that and I could tell it felt a little awkward for her to say.

"Oh, good; so, anyway, I think I've thought of something," I said.

Araminta drew her knees up to her chin and said, wearily: "Go on, then."

Remembering that it was always best to butter up a girl (or anyone) whose work, method or appearance you're about to criticise, I said,

"Well, I mean it was great that you got that list together. And...and thanks a lot for that. But I'm just wondering if we shouldn't have used the internet at all."

"How do you mean?"

"Well, whoever wrote this did it a long time ago, without the aid of computers and algorithms and things, so maybe we should just try to replicate that and do some anagrams ourselves and try the first three or something that we come up with?"

"Well, it's worth a try I suppose," Araminta conceded. "Let's try to do three each before the end of school and meet here at four."

It seemed as good a plan as any.

Of course the best laid plans of mice and men often go wrong, don't they?

"It's schemes."

"Sorry?"

"Schemes," Araminta said when we met up later. "The quotation you're looking for is 'the best laid *schemes* of mice and men gang aft agly; and leave us naught but grief and pain for promised joy.'"

"Right. Cheerful girl, aren't you?"

"We're doing the book *Of Mice And Men* in English so we had to do the poem first. I expect you'll do it next year." I don't know if that was her idea of reminding me that I was younger than her and I should, therefore, do as she said, but I chose to ignore it and compare anagrams. Most of them were terrible but we picked our two favourites each:

YES HE SOLD A GAS BLADE

GOLDE BED HEALS SAYS

BLEED OLD GAS HE SAYS

SHE GOES BY ALL DEAD

I liked the last one best. Minty wasn't sure about me putting an 'e' on the end of gold but I argued it sounded more old fashioned.

"We'll try these four tomorrow morning" she said. "That is, if it doesn't take too long to shift the tiles to form the right pattern."

"And don't forget we'll have to try to remember which pieces we moved in sequence so we can put it back to 'YE SHALL BE AS GODDES' at the end. And we don't really want to be caught playing tile swap when the Curator comes to open up!" I added.

"Yes, I thought of that. How about I film us rearranging the tiles so we can do it all backwards at the end? I'll borrow Mother's iPad - it's got a big screen," she said.

"Oh. Cool."

"Zero-four-hundred?"

"Zero-four-hundred," I agreed and gave her a salute.

CHAPTER SEVENTEEN

You really don't want to hear the same story of us breaking into the Tudor House again, do you? Right, I'll cut to the chase then. Just imagine watching a film on 32x fast-forward and follow Minty up the tree, through the window, disabling the alarm, letting me in through the front door and setting up in the back room by the fireplace.

The mosaic tiles actually moved fairly easily and I'd been practising those tile-shift games I had in my old toy cupboard so it actually only took us about fifteen minutes per anagram.

If you're thinking, 'it's always the last one you try' well, that's obvious, isn't it? Because after that you don't try any more. But in this case it wasn't even the last one. We went with Minty's choice; mine; hers and ended with my, "Bleed old gas he says." The whole thing was a clear disappointment and we sat down on the floor staring at the fireplace wishing we'd brought a flask of coffee and a Jammie Dodger (or at least I did).

"What's the time?" asked Araminta.

"Um, five fifteen," I said, checking my watch.

"Guess we'd better put it all back and go then."

"Yep." I said. Neither of us moved; we were clearly both bitterly disappointed and not quite ready to give up and go home, having come so far for nothing. I shivered, involuntarily.

"You cold?" asked Araminta.

"No," I said, "it's strangely warm in here. Just one of those shivers that suddenly goes right through you."

Araminta stood up suddenly.

"What, did you hear something?" I asked. I was immediately 'sshhh!'ed as Minty went over to the fireplace and then to the window.

"Of course!" she said.

"Oh. Yeah. 'Of *course!*'" I repeated sarcastically. "Look, Sherlock, can you stop assuming I'm a mind reader?"

"Oh, sorry. I forgot you're male. Central heating, Chris. The house has *central heating!*"

"Oh!" I said, pretending I understood what she was driving at. The idea of a Tudor house having central heating was pretty weird but then so was a burglar alarm. I still didn't understand.

"What if the anagram is like a direction?" said Araminta.

"Bleed old gas?"

"Bleed old gas." said Minty, affirmatively.

"No, I'm sorry," I said after an awkward pause, "I have no idea what that means."

"Haven't you ever bled the radiators?" she said.

"No."

"Well, start looking for a little key," she instructed.

You'd probably think it more realistic if I told you that we couldn't find the key and had to pack up, go home and return the next morning with a radiator key, but the truth is that the Curator was predictably boring and we found it in the little cupboard where the burglar alarm was.

"I suppose I'd better do it, if you've never tried," said Araminta, crossly. I was going to protest that she was treating me like a girl but thought better of it and watched as she spurted hot, oily water all over her shoes.

Nothing happened. Not at first. Then we heard a slight creaking sound. It was horrible actually: iron being scraped over stone or something and it was impossible to tell where it was coming from, except it felt like there was an earthquake and the iPad that Minty had propped up on the window sill fell off, onto the floor.

"Chris! The fireplace!"

I looked over to where the fireplace was – or rather, *had been* – and saw, instead, a great gaping hole with a cloud of dust pouring out.

"Now that's more like it!" I said.

Switching her torch on, Araminta stepped inside the opening and disappeared inside the cavity.

"Wait for me!" I called after her and, taking a breath, followed her.

CHAPTER EIGHTEEN

I don't think either of us was expecting it to be such a vast area. We nearly tripped on some stone steps which formed a spiral staircase down to a crypt. Of course there was no electricity there so we had to make do with the torch. Incredible how cold torch-light is. There were some candles on the walls but neither of us had a lighter or matches, so we kept close together and tried to make a systematic sweep of the place.

"This must go underneath the whole house," I said.

The flooring felt worn and it was certainly damp. A stone sarcophagus lay in the centre of the room, bearing an inscription we couldn't quite make out.

"I don't like dead people," whispered Minty.

"I can't say as I've met any myself," I said, trying to lighten the mood.

"What was that?"

We stood rigid and listened. There was a faint, slow, dripping sound coming from somewhere.

"Here, give me the torch!" I said, grabbing it before Minty could protest. I flashed around the corners of the crypt. I couldn't see any sign of water but I did notice a small alcove, high up in the far right corner.

"Look – what's that?" I said, pointing.

Minty took the torch back off me and walked over to the alcove. Standing on tiptoes she peered into the recess.

"I think there's something in it but I'm too short."

I was probably about four inches taller than her but even then, it was slightly out of my reach, so I suggested giving Minty a leg up, but she almost fell backwards.

"It's all right, I might be a girl, but I can take your weight you know!" We swapped and I managed to get eye level with the alcove, holding the torch in my mouth. This was a particularly stupid thing to do, as exclaiming my excitement made the torch drop out of my mouth onto the floor, closely followed by myself.

"Ow!" I said.

The torch had gone out and it took a few moments of groping about in the pitch dark to find where it had rolled to.

"Well?" said Minty.

"Well there seems to be a sort of box-thing wedged in there."

"What sort of box-thing?"

"I don't know, do I? You weren't supporting me very well!"

"Well, you're fatter than you look," she said.

"Thanks. Hey, I've just had a thought – haven't you got that piece of rope you used to climb into the window?"

"Yes; it's back in the room with the fireplace."

"Well, get it!" I said.

We had completely forgotten about the time in all our excitement. Being a Saturday, it wasn't so imperative that I make it to the Newsagent's before 07.30 but it was well past six already and the house was a mess.

It took us several attempts to hook a lasso around one of the iron candle holders above but we succeeded eventually and after a few tugs to test its load-bearing abilities, Minty started climbing up it. I've never been good at shinning up ropes. I used to hate it at Junior school because I would always slide down it and burn my hands. Fortunately, she was pretty good at it.

"All right, you're level now! Try swinging a bit to the left!"

By some Olympic feat of gymnastics, she succeeded in grabbing hold of the alcove but still couldn't find a purchase for her legs.

Finally, I had a brainwave and suggested Minty stand on my shoulders (she wasn't afraid of heights). Again, this took a bit of practice but it was, without a doubt, the best plan we'd had.

"OK, I can reach it easily now. I'm going to try pulling whatever it is out. Just stand absolutely still, Chris!"

She wasn't so light herself and the pressure of her feet on my shoulders was starting to really hurt.

"Aweh!" she exclaimed.

Coming down wasn't so elegant, but neither of us (quite) fell over, so I guess that was a bonus. Minty was holding a box. There was nothing remarkable about it – just an old, wooden, rectangular shaped box.

"Does it open?" I asked.

"Of course it opens. No one's going to go to the trouble of stuffing an empty box in an incredibly difficult-to-reach cubby hole, are they?"

There wasn't a lock on it so we set it down on top of the sarcophagus and opened it together.

Inside was one of the most beautiful objects I had ever seen. It was egg-shaped and made of some sort of metal I supposed was white gold (except it was actually white, not silver in colour). Around its flat base was lettering in a language I didn't recognise but thought might be Greek.

"It's heavy, isn't it?" I said, passing it to Minty.

The next thing she did took me completely by surprise: quite calmly, she set the Egg down on top of the sarcophagus and reached into her coat pocket.

"What are you doing?!" I screamed. She had taken out a small hammer and was about to strike the Egg with it when I grabbed it.

"Put it back, Chris," she said, calmly.

"Put *it* back?! Put the hammer back, Minty!"

"Chris. I'm not going to tell you again." She tightened her grip on the hammer and, for a moment, I was half afraid she was going to hit me with it.

"Araminta! You've gone mad! All this – all this work, all the clues! Why are you trying to hit it?"

"Look I haven't got time to explain but Father said that I would find some Artefact eventually and that I had to destroy it. Apparently if I aim a blow at the right point – "

Assessing the situation I thought it best to make a run for it and made my way to the exit as quickly as possible with torch and Egg in hand.

"Look, it's dangerous! Chris!"

"Why? Why is it dangerous?"

Neither of us had noticed the sound of water getting steadily louder and faster.

Then we noticed it all right: Minty lunged forward at me as we were both swept off our feet by a sudden tidal wave that seemed to come out of nowhere and hit us right in the face.

I don't know if you've ever been to a water park? There aren't that many in England but I remember going to one when I was about eight. There were these slides and you had a mat and went down inside them and suddenly found yourself in a pool of water. Well, it was nothing like that. This was more like being slapped hard in the face by Big Dan whilst someone else takes the ground out from underneath you and, as you're winded, you realise you're wet and try to push your way up to the surface. And all this in the dark – the torch had fallen out of my hand and was sinking.

Don't ask me where the water came from, incidentally. That was pretty much the last thing on my mind (alongside the score on my History test and Kirsty's new boyfriend). What I wanted to know was why the room was filling up so quickly, and why I couldn't breathe. Also, what had happened to the exit?

It seems that the moment Minty had retrieved the box, a lever had caused a great piece of stone to slide over the entrance to the crypt, sealing us in, whilst it flooded with water. Very quickly.

I've never really been a swimmer.

My head was bobbing up and down as I was gurgling.

They say your life flashes before your eyes, but it was too dark to see anything.

Then I did; I saw the Egg. It seemed to be emanating a faint glow. It had slipped out of my grasp and was slowly sinking to the bottom. I took a shallow lungful of air and dived down. As my hands closed on it, I felt Minty's hand on my leg and the next thing I knew -

WHOMPF!

It was like being lurched forward, suddenly by a stationary train that is being coupled to another, except slightly more violent.

And there was light. Bright light of every colour; and then: sky.

CHAPTER NINETEEN

My ears, which had been full of water moments ago, were dry but ringing and, although my legs still felt wet, I could sense that I was standing.

You must understand that this all happened within the space of a second or so but it's difficult to get across how disorientating it really felt.

As my eyes were adjusting to the daylight and my ears were starting to pick up urban sounds of buses and children screaming, I could still hear water pouring. Then:

"'Ere! The fountain's not fer swimmin' in, yer know!"

I was staring at a policeman, dressed in a blue shirt and black tie, wearing a traditional helmet.

"I said, son, the fountain's not fer swimmin' in!"

Coming to my senses, I realised I was standing, water up to my waist, in a large fountain.

"Sorry, Officer," I said, and scrabbled out. The policeman grunted and resumed his patrol. I looked around me for a sign of Araminta.

"Chris!"

She was standing just a few feet away, at the bottom of a piece of concrete. I followed her line of sight until I found myself staring at the top of Nelson's column.

"Trafalgar Square? How did we get here?!"

"I don't know, Chris. You were the one playing with that Egg thing." She turned to look at me. "Where is it?"

"Here." I still had it in my hand.

We said nothing for at least a minute, as each of us tried to process what had just happened.

"Told you not to touch it." Apparently that's all she could think of to say. I looked around the Square at the passers by. Nothing seemed especially strange. It was as if we had simply been picked up by some great Hand and plonked right down in the fountain.

"Thought you'd be glad to be alive!" I said, feebly.

It then occurred to us that it was brighter than it should have been for early morning and that there were certainly more people about than we might expect. In fact, judging by the temperature, it felt more like midday.

"Minty, is your watch working?" I asked. Mine was very much *not* water proof.

"I didn't put it on, actually," she said.

"Oh."

I stopped a woman with a pink Mohican walking a dog and asked her what the time was.

"13.04" she said.

"Thanks."

"D'ya like it?" said the woman.

"Sorry?" I asked.

"My watch. D'ya like it?"

She rolled up her sleeve to give me a better look at a rather cheap-looking plastic, digital watch.

"Yeah. It's very nice. Very…retro," I said.

"Retro?! It's the latest – I just got it yesterday for my birthday!" she said, sounding offended.

"Oh. Sorry. Um, Happy Birthday," I said, and went back to Araminta.

We were both still only half believing the evidence of our eyes but we were forced to accept the situation for the moment. I became aware that my clothes were still saturated – as were hers – but there was nothing else to do except hope they'd dry off quickly in the sun. Perhaps walking about might help. My stomach rumbled.

"I'm hungry," I said. "Have you got any money?"

"No, Chris, I don't usually pack my purse when I go about breaking and entering."

I heard her mutter something under her breath about my always thinking about my stomach which I chose to ignore. I had wrapped the Egg up in my jumper and was carrying it in my arms. It felt warm through the wet wool and I wanted to touch it and examine it somewhere away from the crowds of people.

"Look, Chris, they're showing *Back To The Future*!" said Minty, poking me in the ribs excitedly.

"Oh, excellent. I always wanted to see that at the cinema!"

"No money, remember?" she said. "Besides, it's not showing this week. I was looking at the *coming soon* side."

We carried on walking and nearly got run over by a businessman on roller skates.

"Actually, that's a point," I said.

"What is?"

"Not having any money; how are we going to get home? Can you call your parents?"

By some miracle, Minty's phone wasn't completely water damaged.

"No signal," she said.

"What do you mean, no signal? This is the middle of London!"

"No service. Look." I did.

"Well it must have been the water then," I said.

"Guess we could use a pay phone?"

"I haven't even got enough for that, Minty. How can –"
I turned around but she had disappeared. *Great!* I thought,
and sat down on a wall as she came bounding up to me.

"Here. An old lady gave me some money for the
phone."

"That was nice of her," I said, taking a large ten pence
piece from her hand. "Hang on, what's this?"

"Money. For the payphone," said Minty, confidently.

"Right. Look it's 40p now. And this coin wouldn't
even go in the booth. You are stupid sometimes!"

"Well I'm sorry Mister I'll-just-touch-this-dangerous-
object-and-catapult-us-miles-from-our-homes, I guess I've
never had to use a payphone before."

"That, I do believe!" I said sharply and pulled her into a
red telephone box.

"That's what I like about London," I said. "They still
have the old fashioned telephone boxes." I hadn't been to
London for a while. It didn't seem as vibrant as I
remember. Then again, when you're a kid, everything
seems much more exciting.

"We can make a reverse charge call," I explained and
lifted the receiver, ready to dial. It was one of those old
fashioned ring like things where you have to put your finger
in the number and turn it clockwise. We used to have an
old one at home that Kirsty and I played with when we
were kids.

The receiver was making a strange beeping noise so I
dialled the operator but she just thought I was trying to be
funny.

"It's no good," I said. "Let's try another phone box."

We made our way down a little cobbled street and were
about to head to another payphone when Minty grabbed
my arm and gesticulated wildly.

"What?" I said.

I got no answer so had to follow her gaze. There was a white man dressed in a funny red hat and a luminous green shirt which really didn't go well and a black lady pushing a three-seater pram.

"What?!" I repeated.

Then I saw it – emblazoned in large letters:

THATCHER SNUBBED BY OXFORD DONS

You will have already guessed what had happened and you must think we were being incredibly thick, but experience sometimes makes the improbable harder to believe. At first we thought it was one of those boring headlines they use when nothing has happened recently: some political insult to the deceased "iron lady," but, as we stood in the middle of the road, we began to notice little things that weren't *quite right*:

Hair was too big and curly; no-one was plugged into white earphones; there were loads of Metros on the road.

"Are you thinking what I'm thinking?" I said, slowly.

"I'm thinking, 'I hope I'm concussed somewhere back in the Tudor House.'"

"Look, Minty, I know this is a lot to take in, but then, so is being thrown across the county. I really think we ought to check out a newspaper."

Cautiously, we wandered over to the newsagents where the large billboard with the Thatcher headline was and looked at the dates on the tops of the newspapers. It was the same on every one: a sharp chill sung in unison by broadsheets and tabloids alike:

29TH JANUARY 1985

"OK, don't panic," I said. Araminta started hyperventilating and talking at breakneck speed about nightmares and practical jokes. I took her arm and led her outside again.

"This is impossible, Chris!"

"Stop saying that; that's stupid. Clearly it's not *impossible* or we wouldn't be here," I said. "Haven't you seen any sci-fi films?" I added, unhelpfully.

"Well the ones I have all agree on one thing: you can't mess with history. So we should try to get out of here before we change anything."

"Oh, Minty, where's your sense of fun? Hey I could look up my Dad. I think he was in London before he met Mum. Aren't you a bit curious about history?"

"We need to get home and *now*."

I could tell she wasn't in an adventurous mood.

"All right," I said and looked around for somewhere fairly private.

Of course we had no idea how to operate the Egg – or whether *it* was responsible for our temporal displacement, but it seemed the most probable explanation.

"Perhaps if we went back to the fountain," suggested Araminta, "it might sort of hook onto us."

It sounded reasonable. As we turned around to head back the way we had come, I tripped on a loose stone and nearly dropped the Egg out of my jumper. Minty caught it in her left hand and instinctively grabbed my arm with her right and then...the train jolt again.

CHAPTER TWENTY

Araminta was dreading facing her father. Not only had she not followed his instructions about destroying whatever they found at the end of their trail; not only had she allowed me to touch the object, catapulting us back in time - where we might have remained for the next thirty years; not only did she risk altering the timeline, but she had not retained the device afterwards.

We had returned to 2015 in an instant. For all her years of globe trekking as a child, Araminta did not travel well. As soon as our eyes had adjusted to their new location, she felt the urge to vomit. Fortunately, we had been returned to the room with the fireplace and Araminta was just able to run outside in time.

The fireplace itself looked as it always had. The mosaic was back to its original setting and the only sign that the room had been disturbed was her father's iPad lying in the middle of the floor.

The Egg, as we were still calling it, was cool to the touch. All the same, neither Araminta nor I wanted to risk another journey and we wrapped it tightly in my jumper again. Unbeknownst to Araminta, whilst she was throwing up outside, I replaced the Egg with a large stone and hid the Device in my paper round bag; so when she got home, all Araminta could tell her father was that she was still looking for the final clue.

At least, I'm sure that is what she *would* have told her father, had he been home. As it was, Dr Stirling was nowhere to be seen. Her mother was busy writing and didn't want to be disturbed, so Araminta was able to slip upstairs into her room and change out of her wet things.

The act of changing must have given her an idea, because the next thing she did was to call out to her mother she was going for a walk and then jog round to my house.

Kirsty opened the door.

"Heya, Araminta, how're you doing?" said Kirsty, affecting a very poor American accent.

"Hey Kirsty. How are you?"

"I'm just super! Come on in!"

Araminta wasn't sure how much I'd told my sister about us spending time together so she thought it would be better if she didn't mention it.

"Would you like a coffee?"

"Oh, thanks," said Araminta, following Kirsty through to the kitchen.

"Your Mum not around?"

"No; she's at work. And my squibby little brother is on his paper round still."

"Oh."

"Great, isn't it! I have the house to myself. Hey, do you wanna help me do a make over?"

This was probably the thing Araminta least wanted to do, but she humoured Kirsty in the hope that she might stay long enough to go through my room and discover where I'd hidden the Egg.

Kirsty was one of those girls who thought that straightened hair made someone instantly attractive and a French manicure was the best use of a spare tenner. Her taste in music was predictably prosaic and the ubiquity of boy band posters made Minty's stomach heave a little. She was trying to decide whether the picture of the crow in her father's study was more disturbing than Justin Bieber's beady eyes piercing down from the ceiling or not, when she was attacked with a pair of hair straighteners.

"Ow! What are you doing?"

"Araminta, when was the last time you straightened your hair?"

"Never!"

"I thought so. Come here, it'll look much better in a minute."

"No! Thanks. I don't want to – " Araminta didn't get to finish that sentence because she found herself being chased around the bed by a mad, teenaged girl brandishing a hot pair of GHDs. Fortunately, Kirsty soon tired of this game and called a truce.

"At least let me give you some eye shadow?"

Araminta reluctantly acquiesced. This proved to be a moderate success. Apparently Mum had taught her Kirsty how to apply eye shadow subtly and she gave Araminta a discreet dusting of virgin green which complemented her red hair.

"Mmm. Not bad, though I say so myself. Now; mascara!"

"Oh, Kirsty, I'm not sure about – "

"Nonsense. Look. Max Factor!"

Just as Kirsty was applying a second coat to Araminta's left eye, the front door opened and I came up the stairs.

"Oh, it's you," I heard Kirsty say as I stomped past her room, doing a double take at the sight of Minty in my peripheral vision.

"Wow. You look…Um – " I faltered.

"She looks great, doesn't she? My handiwork, of course," said Kirsty.

"Yeah. Absolutely," I agreed.

Kirsty gave me a filthy *bugger off* look and I slunk out of the doorway and made my way down the landing to my own room.

"Oh, Kirsty, I just want to ask Christopher about that project for Mr Travis. Do you mind?" said Minty.

"I didn't think you were that keen on him."

"I think he's quite nice."

"'Nice?' Christopher is anything but nice! Vile little reptile!"

"I meant Mr Travis?"

"Oh; him. Can't comment – he hasn't taught me. Nice to look at though."

Just then, Kirsty's phone rang and she started gabbling with someone called Jasmine on the other end, giving Araminta an excuse to poke her head round my bedroom door.

"Where is it? I can't believe you did that!" she said, the mascara making her eyes seem as bright as her hair.

"Shh! Come here. There's something more important I need to show you," I said.

"What could be more important than what you've done with the – " here, she dropped her voice to a whisper, "you-know-what?"

"This." I tapped his finger on a photograph I had on my desk.

"No; sorry. I haven't the faintest idea what you're going on about."

"Look closer," I insisted, passing her a magnifying glass. It was a picture of me on my hands and knees, having fallen over on the school trip outside the Tudor House. Not one of my best moments. Trust Josh to have been at the ready with a camera.

"So what? You fell over."

"Look to the right," I said.

"The bush?"

106

"No! The coach! The coach, Minty; look!" I grabbed the photo and circled the bottom right hand corner with a red felt tip before giving it back to her.

"Look would you just spit it out? I'm obviously not getting it and I never did like 'spot the difference,'" she said.

"It's the lettering. Can you read what it says?"

"Yes. *G&H Travel Coach*. So?"

"And the colour?" I asked.

"Blue. Look, what's going on, what are you raving about, Christopher?"

"Raving about? Don't you remember?"

"Remember? Remember what?"

"The name of the bus company is *Black Orchid*. And it's supposed to be red!"

CHAPTER TWENTY-ONE

"Hands up if you read the handout," commanded Mr Travis.

We dutifully raised our hands. (Except Ryan). One thing about Mr Travis is that he's nobody's fool, so no one ever lies to him; at least, not since he embarrassed Stacey in front of the whole class for trying to get out of doing her essay by saying it was the wrong time of the month.

"Good, that's most of you. Now, keep your hands up if you understood it," he said. This was a difficult question because he was bound to admonish us for being witless if we put our hands down and tell us we were arrogant if we kept them up. Also, no-one wanted to be the only person with a hand up because then he'd quiz them to death. Unfortunately, with all this and other stuff going through my mind, I didn't put my hand down quickly enough and was immediately pounced on:

"Jones. You either think you're clever, *are* clever, or are *so* stupid you have no idea whether you're arrogant or witless. Which is it?"

"Erm…" I started.

"Don't stammer, boy. Tell us what you thought of Nietzsche."

"Um…Bit of a racist lunatic?" I said.

"That's what 98% of the world thinks. Summarise his thesis."

"His what?"

"*Thesis*, Jones! Come on, I've used the word before. I'm not going to repeat myself." He sighed: "Tell us about his notion of the good."

"Right." I *had* read it of course. In fact I'd read it about seven times because it was really confusing. I quickly flicked my exercise book open and read from the photocopy:

"'What is good? Whatever augments power. Power itself —'"

"If I wanted you to read, Jones, I would have asked Chetwind. We all know he *can't* actually read, so it would have been more amusing. *Comment* on it, Jones."

"OK. Well, I think it's interesting. I mean, it's sort of taking Darwin to extremes isn't it? But what if he's right?"

Everyone gasped.

"What if he's *right*, Jones?"

"Yes, Sir. I mean, don't get me wrong, I don't think he *is*, but it's just interesting, isn't it? I mean, why is it that we think kindness is good? Doesn't that go against evolution? It sort of suggests that we all have this built in sense of right and wrong but then there's people who have different ideas like Hitler or Stalin and we say they're bad, but aren't they just following the law of nature?" I said, speaking faster than I was really thinking.

Luke was burning to say something so Mr Travis let him put in his two pennies' worth:

"CS Lewis thinks we all have a common morality and that's why we have arguments because we're appealing to the other person, who really knows the moral law, and that what they're doing is right."

"Yes; I'd like to have seen you try appealing to Hitler, Martin. Do shut up."

Mr Travis cast his eye around the rest of the room and saw half the class had switched off through boredom, whilst the rest had switched off because they were unable to keep up with the debate. With sudden movement, Mr Travis dived into his desk and pulled out a gun. Obviously it wasn't a real gun but it looked the part. Without warning he fired a shot. We jumped out of our skins and Henni screamed. Mr Travis walked right up to Ryan and pointed the weapon in his face.

"Tell me why I shouldn't shoot you in your miserable face right now, Chetwind."

Ryan was a gibbering wreck. All of us froze. I glanced at Josh. Stacey, who had been surreptitiously texting under the desk was clearly thinking about broadcasting a message. You read about these terrible school shootings in the news and think it couldn't possibly happen over here. We don't have the right to bear arms; people would hear; people would come.

No one came.

None of us was brave enough to do something.

"P-p-please, Sir! It's not right. I haven't done anything!" cried Ryan.

"Precisely! That's precisely the point: You're weak. And, if we follow Nietzsche, I should help you to die now. This is *good*, you see: I feel empowered. The feeling of power is good, isn't it?"

"No, Sir." I stood up. My legs were quivering.

"Jones." Mr Travis turned the pistol on me.

"Look, it's never right to kill someone." I said.

"Why?"

"Because we don't know about them. We shouldn't judge. Ryan might...I don't know, he might find the cure for the common cold or something."

"Chetwind *is* the common cold! He makes my nose run and my head hurt every time I see him."

"But we don't know, do we? Sir?"

"But we do when we're historians. That's the point. We can judge Nietzsche because he's dead. People's actions are weighed by the consequences they've had. This book is outrageous. Nietzsche went clinically insane. Apparently, he looked out of his window once and saw a horse being maltreated in the street, so he rushed down and flung his arms round it. Then he realised that he'd shown compassion to another living creature and went stir crazy." Mr Travis relinquished his grip on the gun and opened the chamber. It was empty. The single bullet had, of course, been a blank. He passed the pistol to me and addressed the class:

"None of you will ever forget this lesson; so the ends justify the means. Or do they?" You could see the sweat on everyone's foreheads.

"That's the title of your next essay," he said, writing on the board: "Do the ends ever justify the means? Relate to an historical event of your choice."

At that moment the classroom door opened and the Head came in, looking anxious.

"Mr Travis? Is everything all right? Mary said she though she heard a…a…"

"Fell of me chair, sir!" said Ryan quickly.

"Ah. Good." The Head looked round the room and made to leave. A fly buzzed in my ear and made me flinch. The Head turned and saw the gun.

"Christopher Jones, isn't it? Care to explain the implement on your desk?"

"Oh. Sorry," said Mr Travis, diving forward, "better give that back, Jones. Right, has everyone had a good look at the replica, in-no-way-functional Nazi revolver? Good! Good, good."

The Head raised an eyebrow and left.

111

"I take it back, Chetwind; you're not a complete moron. Now has everyone got the essay title?"

As soon as the bell went, I ran out to the Tree to meet Araminta.

"Did you check?" she asked.

"Yeah. I asked Mr Travis after class. I said I'd lost my iPod on the coach and did he have the number of the company?"

"What did he say?"

"He just said I was a stupid boy and asked if he was my secretary. Then he told me to look the number up myself so I asked him for the name of the company and he definitely said *G&H* – not *Black Orchid*."

"Shoot. What does this mean?" she asked.

"I don't know. But if it has changed, we obviously remember it so maybe that means there haven't been any other changes or we'd have noticed?"

"Hopefully. Look, Christopher. I really think we should give this thing to Fa– to my Dad. He has...contacts that will know what to do with it."

"No way. I'm not letting it out of my sight," I said. I shouldn't have.

"You mean you've got it on you? Now? Here, at school?"

"It's in my bag," I confessed.

"That's incredibly stupid of you, Christopher!"

Quick as a flash, she grabbed the bag from my shoulders and started running.

"Hey!" I shouted, and started chasing her through the school gates and into the road, but she was much faster and I was already panting.

Fortunately my school is on a busy road which she had to wait to cross, giving me time to close on her. Araminta had clearly been keeping her athleticism a secret and she knew not to look behind her as she ran. My feet pounded against the hard tarmac of the pavement and my chest was tightening as I saw her disappear around the corner.

Summoning every ounce of energy I could muster, I sprinted into the alley she had gone down and collided with a man.

"Sorry," I said, without looking up and tried to dodge past him. It was too narrow.

"Excuse me, please?" I said, more as a command than a plea.

"Chris! Run!" Araminta's voice.

Next thing I knew, my arm had been grabbed. I looked up into the face of a tall, bald man with a scar on his left cheekbone.

"Ow! Let me go!" I said, struggling in his grip.

Araminta was standing behind him. I looked behind me but we were quite alone.

"I'll scream," I said.

"Don't be ridiculous, Christopher. I've no intention of hurting you. Or Araminta."

CHAPTER TWENTY-TWO

Everything seemed to stop at the moment the man said my name. All sorts of things raced through my mind. Mostly bad.

"Don't be afraid," said the bald man, releasing my arm slowly. "I'm a friend."

"Forgive me if I don't shake hands. I like to be introduced to my friends."

I don't know what induced me to even speak to this man after all the drilling you get as a child about not communicating with strangers, but there was something about him that did seem a little familiar. Besides, I was still out of breath from chasing Araminta and didn't fancy my chances of getting away from him any time soon.

"I'm Jeremy," he said, "and I know why you've been chasing Araminta."

Minty stepped forward and brushed herself down. She looked flushed, too.

"You have a Chronosphere and that's dangerous. You'd better come with me," he said.

"I don't know what you're talking about," said Minty. "Neither of us does."

"Araminta, I told you I'm not here to harm you. You can drop the pretence." He looked at us both and sighed.

"Would it help if I said I can explain about *Black Orchid?*"

Minty and I exchanged a glance and Jeremy smiled. "Please. Walk with me."

He led the way through the alley into a small cul de sac that Araminta evidently used as a short cut home on occasion. There was a small triangle of green turf with a bench at the end and he sat down on it.

"Still public. I don't want you two to be frightened. But we shouldn't talk loudly. It's dangerous for other people to hear."

Curiosity having very much got the better of us both, we sat down, tentatively.

"I'll give you two minutes to explain how you know our names and tell me everything you can about *Black Orchid.*" I said. It sounded good.

"I only need a few minutes to explain but you'll need more than that to understand, Christopher." He smiled again and I tried to relax.

"Firstly, I've been on your trail some time." he said. As he did so, a memory stirred from the Antechapel at Trinity College. It obviously stirred the same memory for Minty, as she muttered:

"Cambridge?"

"Yes, Araminta. Cambridge. I watched you follow the clues and you proved yourselves worthy."

"Worthy of what?" I asked.

"More of that later."

"You haven't answered my question," I said.

"Astute as ever, Christopher. How do I know you? Well there are a lot of ways a resourceful person could find out, of course, but the truth is that I've known about you for some time."

"Some time? Please! I'm a fourteen year old boy. My sister doesn't even know about me half the time."

"Don't be so disparaging about Kirsty, Christopher. You should appreciate your family. Now then, perhaps Araminta can answer your question? I can hear her brain ticking."

Araminta cleared her throat. "You're from… another… time?"

"There, that wasn't so hard, was it?" he said.

I was staring at him with my mouth open.

"It's not all that shocking is it? Not after what you've been through recently, surely?" he continued.

"How?" asked Minty.

"Same as you. The Chronosphere. The 'Egg' as you've been calling it." Araminta drew my bag tighter to her body.

"Don't worry. I've got my own. I'm from what you would call 'the future.'"

I very nearly laughed. It's one of the last things you expect anybody to actually say out loud – particularly someone as physically commanding as this Jeremy.

"And you've come here for what?" asked Minty.

"You, Araminta. You and Christopher. You see, I need your help."

"Help? Help with what?" I said.

"Well, I'll try to give you the short version: You see, in the early 26th Century, scientists invented time travel technology."

"Why are you speaking in the past tense?"

"Please don't interrupt, Christopher; you'll only get confused. And you need to open your mind beyond thinking of time as something linear." I coughed and, satisfied we were listening, Jeremy continued:

"Now, even *I* am not quite sure how the technology works; only that it *does*. Understand, of course that this was top secret research, naturally. However, as with all items of

116

power, the money behind it was political and soon, the Government – "

"American?" I interjected.

"Complicated question. You don't want to know about 26th century politics. Suffice it to say that the powers-that-be decided to immediately destroy the technology, fearing its enemies would use it to annihilate them before they were born and that sort of thing.

"Eventually, an international tribunal of philosophers, historians and scientists met. It was agreed that the technology should be used to observe history. Then, one day, someone used a Chronosphere to change something: make himself a little money on the London Stock Exchange. The problem was that nobody other than the Traveller knew the change had occurred. You see, the Chronosphere protects you from the effects of time travel – it preserves your memory of both events in case you need to alter what you've just done."

"That little egg does all that?" asked Araminta.

"Does this relate to *Black Orchid*?" I said, trying to bring the focus of the conversation back to the present problem.

"Yes, Christopher; it does. You see, the only reason we know about the man who made the money on the Stock Exchange for himself is because he also inadvertently ended up preventing his wife from being born. He hadn't made his calculations properly and so he had to come clean and ask for help in restoring the timeline.

"Well, as you can imagine, this ignited something of a debate, which became a war," said Jeremy, with some aplomb.

"A time war, like in *Doctor Who*?" I asked, interrupting him.

"No…Yes. Essentially, there arose different factions. Too many to name now, but the two that matter most are the *HIS* and *The Domino Group*."

117

"Dominos? Hey is that something to do with those murders that have been happening around here?" Minty interjected.

"Yes, Araminta. Most astute, again. I'm afraid it is. The *Domino Group* is very dangerous."

"Why?"

"I don't have time to explain that, Araminta. Only let me tell you that –"

"Hang on," I said, interrupting, "What does the *HIS* stand for?"

"*Historical Improvement Society*," he said; "think of me as a bit like Sam Beckett from *Quantum Leap* – 'striving to put right what once went wrong.'"

It was too much to take in, let alone believe.

"Look," he said, "I know you both have other questions and I *will* answer them; but not now."

Jeremy stood up, abruptly and pulled something out of his pocket. It was another Egg – *Chronosphere,* rather. Araminta was clearly thinking the same thing as me as she checked the weight of my bag.

"I'm sorry," he announced, "I should have given you a choice. But all the while we've been sat here, two things have happened – one of my greatest enemies and agents for the Other Side has been tracking me. He'll be here in under a minute and I expect him to be armed."

"What's the second thing?" I asked.

"The second thing, Christopher, is that I have been preparing our escape."

"Escape? How? Where?" I said.

"The Thirties," said Jeremy. "Hold tight, both of you. We're going to assassinate Adolf Hitler!"

Part Two

A man is compelled by fear when he does that which otherwise he would not wish to do, in order to avoid that which he fears. Now the constant differs from the inconstant man in two respects. First, in respect of the quality of the danger feared, because the constant man follows right reason, whereby he knows whether to omit this rather than that, and whether to do this rather than that. Now THE LESSER EVIL *or the greater good is always to be chosen in preference; and therefore the constant man is compelled to bear with the lesser evil through fear of the greater evil, but he is not compelled to bear with the greater evil in order to avoid the lesser.*

- *St. Thomas Aquinas, Summa Theologica, Pt 3 Q47, A2*

CHAPTER TWENTY-THREE

One of the great misconceptions we have about the Past is that it's in black and white. I shouldn't have been surprised when my eyes found their focus on a blood red flag displaying a swastika. I immediately jerked backwards in repulsion and fell over.

Jeremy took my hand and pulled me to my feet. There was something about him that made me feel both safe and petrified at the same time. I nodded my gratitude and looked for Araminta. She was behind me.

"Everyone all right?" asked Jeremy.

"Yes. No thanks to you." I hoped Araminta was directing that remark at Jeremy and not me.

"Where are we?" I asked.

"Munich. 1935. August."

"Wünderbar!" I said, "and that's the only German I know. What on earth were you thinking?"

"Keep your voice down! You're conspicuous enough as it is, wearing that school uniform!" he said, in a stage whisper.

I hadn't noticed before but Jeremy was wearing a brown three piece suit, complete with pocket watch. He pointed to a side street and dived into the satchel he was carrying and produced two shabby overcoats which he told us to put on. Araminta gave them a look of disdain and refused but the thought of being interrogated by the Gestapo was enough to make her change her mind. Mine was a little small around the middle and I said as much but Araminta just muttered something about always wanting to eat, which I ignored.

Jeremy was holding his right index finger out to us. On it were resting two black dots, each the size of a pin head.

"What are they?" asked Araminta.

"Put it behind your ear – either one. It's a translator."

"You're joking? A universal translator?"

"Not universal, Araminta. Just what you need to get by."

"Like *Star Trek*? Really?!" I said, a bit excitedly.

"Look, you already have mobiles and floppy disks went out in the 1990s. Some of *Star Trek* came true," said Jeremy.

"Don't tell me you can teleport people in the 26th century?"

"No, Araminta, that would be stupid."

Jeremy showed us how to fix the dot to our ears and we did as instructed. It was like changing the audio track on a DVD: suddenly, the cacophony of foreign voices became English. Satisfied, Jeremy indicated we should follow him.

"You should still avoid talking to people," he warned. "They might ask awkward questions. We should concentrate on our objective."

"*Our* objective? Look, I didn't ask to come here," I said, stubbornly.

"The present objective, Christopher, is to find food and shelter. If that's all right with you?"

"Food? Yeah! I could murder a McDonald's!"

"Are you trying to be funny?" said Jeremy.

"Yeah," I said, sheepishly.

"Well, don't."

"Right."

We followed our kidnapper to the door of a tall, yellow building and waited patiently for Jeremy's knock to be answered. After a minute or so, a thin, blonde woman came out and looked us up and down and asked if we were Party members.

"Do we look like Party members?" Jeremy replied curtly.

This seemed to satisfy her and the door was opened wide enough for us to be admitted.

"You'll be wanting the two rooms?"

"One will suffice, thank you."

Araminta and I exchanged a glance. I don't know if she was less happy at the prospect of having to share a room with me or with Jeremy. I did begin to feel a little sorry for her – I imagine girls like their privacy.

We were taken up a winding staircase into a room with three small iron cots, a writing desk and a chamber pot. Blue curtains framed the window and there was a distinct odour of stale tobacco.

"Thank you; this will do very nicely," said Jeremy.

The woman nodded and fished about in her apron to produce three cards and a blunt pencil. Jeremy took the cards and filled them out promptly, without hesitation and returned them to the woman who scrutinised them carefully and, satisfied nodded curtly to Jeremy and closed the door on us.

"Well, thanks a lot! Now we're in some stinking bedsit in Nazi Germany with no Colgate, no internet and no food. What do you expect us to do?"

"First of all, Christopher; how about keeping your voice down?"

"Sorry." I realised, of course, that although Jeremy was certainly not the sort of man to be trifled with, he was not our immediate enemy and the city of Nazis beyond us posed a far greater threat.

"And I'm sorry about the accommodation arrangements, Araminta, but we shan't be spending the night here," said Jeremy, apologetically.

"Oh?" said Araminta.

"This is just a stop-gap. Think of it like that scene in *The Matrix* where they load up before going on a mission."

"'So what do you need?' 'Guns. Lots of guns.'" I said, trying to affect my best Keanu Reeves impression.

"Yes, Christopher. Except, in our case, it's money."

"Money? You mean you don't have any money?" said Araminta.

"It's complicated."

"What sort of time traveller are you?" she said, raising her eyebrow. I smiled, glad not to be the one on the receiving end of her disapproval for once.

"Look, I explained about the War. Now, I didn't have time or access to a printing press so the best I could do was to come here first. I've got a plan and if you would just hear me out, that would be dandy," said Jeremy. I guffawed:

"Dandy? Who says 'dandy'?!"

Jeremy gave me a death stare and I closed my mouth.

"Have either of you noticed the wallpaper?" he continued.

We hadn't. I don't know how we hadn't, for I'd never seen anything like it: the room was covered, floor to ceiling, in bank notes. Twenty Mark notes, a Hundred Mark notes, even Thousand Mark notes lined the walls like bricks.

"If she's this minted, how come the furniture's so shabby?"

"Don't you know anything, Chris?" said Araminta, "this is the result of hyperinflation, isn't it?"

"The what?" I said, stupefied.

"Look. You know how the price of petrol is going up and, with it, bread and stuff; so the quid in your pocket becomes gradually devalued over time because you can buy less stuff with it?" she said, quickly.

"Yes, I know what inflation is, Minty."

"Well, here, after 1918, the Germans had to pay the Allies back for the First World War, except they didn't have enough gold or reserves to pay with so they ended up just printing money. Eventually, the marks became basically worthless and they started making notes with higher denominations like a billion marks was worth a penny or something ridiculous."

"It wasn't quite as little as that," interjected Jeremy.

"I still don't get it," I said.

"Well, these notes are in such small denominations, in 1935, they're literally not worth the paper they were printed on; so a lot of people used them as wallpaper – it actually worked out cheaper for them. This was probably done in 1923 or something."

"Right." I was still confused. "But how does that help us, now?"

Jeremy had been carefully peeling a note off the wall which he now passed to me.

"My dear chap," he said, "the difference between this being wallpaper and a small fortune, is simply a matter of time: all we have to do is remove this from the walls, jump back to a time when the notes were actually worth something and buy up foreign currency with it."

"Foreign currency?" I asked, still a little clueless and wishing I had read as much as Minty.

"Yes. It's no good buying German currency because it kept changing. Gold is suspicious, not to mention scarce, but the price of the Dollar didn't really change very much so that's what we'll do: we'll go back to 1919, buy up some American dollars and then, rich, go to our final destination," explained Jeremy.

"Hang on, I thought you said we weren't allowed to profit from time travel?" I said.

"When did I say that?"

"Well, on the bench. You told us about that bloke who went back and – "

"Look, Christopher, if I just wanted to make a quick buck I wouldn't have brought you two along. This is simply the most efficient way to become solvent without stealing. Well, stealing anything someone will miss. We'll need it where we're going afterwards, trust me."

Araminta muttered something about the irony of that remark and Jeremy seemed to concede the point that trust takes time – which we were now the masters of. He smiled generously and in such a way that the only way I could respond was to smile back.

"Here, let me show you how to get these notes off the wall," he said.

The thought had, naturally, occurred to me to escape back to the Present with Araminta. However, aside from the fact that neither of us had been able to work out how to control the Chronosphere, we didn't want to run the risk of returning to a 2015 we wouldn't know was changed: for, I reasoned, if the Chronosphere protected a time traveller's memory during trips made, then we would need to use Jeremy's Chronosphere to return home. This was a point on which Araminta differed.

It was all mathematical anyway: Jeremy left us alone for less than two minutes whilst he went to relieve himself in the bathroom down the hall and Minty and I spent the time arguing. Perhaps we were both secretly thrilled to be back in time and, although neither of us felt entirely unthreatened by Jeremy, we also felt safe with him.

Jeremy seemed to have everything planned down to the last detail and he made us meticulously repeat it back to him before he would allow us to make the next trip. Once he was satisfied with our education and had filled his satchel with bank notes, he told us to hold hands and prepare to say "auf wiedersehen" to 1935.

125

CHAPTER TWENTY-FOUR

I don't think there's any getting used to time travel. It's like when you've watched the same scary film over and over again: you know the jump is coming but, however hard you count down to it, you're never quite prepared. For me, the most frightening thing is that for the first half a minute or so of your materialisation in a new time period, you feel completely woozy and it takes a good forty seconds for your eyes to adjust. Appearing in the centre of the Schellingstraße as a horse drawn carriage careers down the street is not the best entrance to make. Fortunately Jeremy, being a somewhat seasoned time traveller, lunged forward and pulled me to safety in the nick of time.

"Let's try not to draw attention to ourselves, shall we?" he said, sternly.

It is, perhaps, a universal law that bankers become a lot more helpful when you have money. In fact, if I were sitting back in Miss Goring's Maths lesson, she would doubtless make us plot a graph showing the correlation between your personal wealth on the x axis, and staff-helpfulness on the y.

Furnished with enough American Dollars to buy a small sausage factory, Jeremy took us to a tailor's, where he insisted on buying us attire befitting the children of a Bavarian entrepreneur. I hadn't seen Araminta in a dress before. She looked stunning.

"Right. Now that you're respectable we can get down to business," said Jeremy.

As we left the shop, I noticed the name above the door – *Cohn*

"Sounds Jewish," I said.

"He was," said Jeremy. I sighed, and he added, "That's who all this is for, Christopher."

1919 had served its purpose well and Jeremy was eager for us to ensconce ourselves in 1923 before we made ourselves more conspicuous. I noticed the train jolt effect of the time jump wasn't so bad this time.

By now, I was beginning to enjoy walking these old, foreign streets. My Mum had never been able to afford to take us abroad, except for a day trip to Calais when I was about ten. I supposed it wasn't all that exciting to Araminta, who'd lived in at least three continents, but she told me that one of the most confusing things was hearing English voices everywhere.

"When you go abroad," she explained, "you're used to hearing native tongues. It's sort of what gives you that clue that you're in another culture. This is just odd. The signs are all in German but everyone's speaking English." She had a point.

"Hey, Jeremy, how come everything still looks like it's in German?" I asked.

"Does it?" he said, sounding surprised. "It shouldn't. Probably needs a software update. I'll try to sort it out later."

127

He was clearly looking for a particular place and there was little else to do but follow him round like proverbial lost sheep.

As we wandered the streets and squares, I really began to notice the different aromas: bread, cheese and meat hung in the air with stale beer and cigarettes. Manure, too – the inevitable pungency of a city on the cusp of motorisation.

"Here!"

Jeremy had come to a standstill at a block of apartments opposite a school. This time the door was opened by a respectable looking woman with a lime coloured feather in her hair.

"Good afternoon Madam, I should like to rent some rooms, if I may?" said Jeremy.

Again, we were scrutinised from head to toe before we were admitted.

"I have a suite of rooms available on the third floor," she said, starting up the narrow staircase. "Rates are reasonable and payable in advance."

"I trust American Dollars will be acceptable?" said Jeremy.

"Dollars?" she said.

I froze. What if she suspected us of being spies?

"Papa," said Araminta quickly, in a better American accent than I could do, "may I have first choice of the view, please?"

This seemed to satisfy the woman and I smiled at her as sweetly as I could.

"Dollars would be *most* acceptable, I'm sure."

The dimensions of our new accommodation were far greater than that of the house in 1935. Moreover, the stench of stale tobacco was replaced with lavender, and the walls were papered with a flowery pattern in off-white.

Jeremy filled out the residency cards on behalf of the three of us again, paid the woman in cash and tipped his hat as she closed the door on us. Jeremy congratulated

Araminta on her quick thinking and smiled at me. I didn't want to let him off that easily for kidnapping us, though.

"Is that why you brought us along?" I said, somewhat sulkily, "to make you seem less suspicious?"

"It's one of the reasons, yes. But I have some important work for you both – if you'll hear me out. And when we're done, I'll teach you how to operate the Chronosphere."

"Is that a threat?" I asked.

"A promise. Look, aren't we past all that yet, Christopher?" There was something about Jeremy that still made me very nervous about being in the same room as him, yet his eyes were intoxicatingly magnetic and my deeper instinct was that I could trust him more than anyone else in the whole world.

"Well, first thing's first," I said. "I'm famished."

CHAPTER TWENTY-FIVE

Food in Munich was good – there was no doubt about that. By the time we arrived back at the house we were all full and all tired. Still, I wasn't going to go to bed without discussing the reason we had been dragged into another century and I got the impression Jeremy wasn't going to leave us alone until he was satisfied we wouldn't try to give him the slip.

Araminta had said little all evening. We had mainly kept our conversation light; commenting on the peculiar dress sense or listening to Jeremy's tall tales about a tortoise and Louis XVI of France. Jeremy insisted he had funnier stories to tell but they took place beyond 2015 and he had better not say anything about our future. There was a piano in the corner of the bar we ate in and a few different people sat down at it and struck up a tune. There was something profoundly comforting in hearing a dozen voices join in a familiar tune together. Something we only tend to hear now at football matches or church, if you go. I had been to neither since well before Dad left.

Now we were back on our own, I wanted answers:

"So," I said, "you want to kill Hitler."

"Getting down to business are we, Christopher? Very well then."

Jeremy stood up and went to the window, clasping his hands behind his back and leaning out into the night. He closed the curtains and turned around to us.

"First of all," said Araminta, "why?"

Jeremy was a little taken aback.

"I should have thought that was obvious! Six million Jews, five million others murdered in the camps. Not to mention the soldiers and civilians on both sides who gave their lives."

"But, murder. It's just...just so wrong. So cold-blooded. Isn't it?" said Araminta, unconsciously touching the scar on her elbow.

"Araminta, you haven't taken a life so you don't know what it's like. You don't know what it is to see the life slipping from their eyes as they fight for one more breath; a final word; one chance to go back and undo all their mistakes that led to this final moment. But death comes to us all. Sometimes he snatches us, without warning – like a thief in the night. Sometimes he announces himself at the door and keeps company in the shadow of our homes – our bodies – for a while and then, when we're tired and too weak to turn out the light he takes us home, like an old friend. All men must die. So who is obeying the law of nature more – the one who takes life or the one who fights death?"

Jeremy's words were beginning to scare me and I said as much.

"Look, I just don't think we have the right to play jury, judge and executioner." said Araminta.

"Araminta, History has been the judge, and every soul of every Jew and every child and woman and man since, has borne witness to the evil that this man wrought upon the world. The jury of eleven million victims demand the execution."

131

He spoke calmly – without anger or violence. Yet there was a warmth in his voice, as if he had known heartbreak. As if he had been in the camps and witnessed the multitudinous murders first hand.

"But if we murder him now – if we change history, then none of those people will have died so he shan't have been guilty of anything!" said Araminta. This posed a new dilemma.

"So we either kill an innocent man or we let a genocidal maniac live?" I said.

Jeremy sat down on a wooden chair he drew up to the small table in the right corner of the double room we had rented.

"Look. I know it's confusing, but when you've been doing this as long as I have, you learn to view time a little differently. I might have taken us back to his birth or infancy and killed him then. I probably wouldn't have needed you. But I felt that would have been wrong. Everyone deserves a chance to choose their own path. And Hitler chose his. Now the wheels are in motion for the downfall of Europe and his eternal damnation. Now is the time to act!"

This spoke to Araminta more than I, and I saw a change come over her – a sort of hopefulness.

"Is Hitler truly beyond redemption?" she asked.

"What sort of question is that?" I said, angrily. "You know my great-grandparents barely escaped with their lives, thanks to this maniac!" I instantly regretted shouting and apologised. I hadn't told Minty about my own family history. I poured myself a glass of water from the carafe the landlady had left and sipped it slowly. Over the rim of the glass I saw Minty give Jeremy a quizzical look and Jeremy shake his head slightly. We kept silence for a few moments. Then, Minty stood up and said, almost cheerfully:

"What if we could change his destiny?"

"How do you mean?" said Jeremy.

"Well, I've always thought it was more nurture than nature: perhaps there's something in Hitler's past that set him on this path; something we can change?" Araminta's blue eyes flashed with a defiant hope and I began to wonder if it wouldn't be a better thing – and a greater challenge – to redeem the unredeemable. Every school boy has dreamed of killing Hitler at one point or other but when you're confronted with the very real possibility of having to take a real human life, any alternative seems preferable.

"I thought of that, too," Jeremy said. "You know, Hitler desperately wanted to be an artist. He tried three times to gain admittance to the Academy of Art in Vienna but was rejected every time."

"Nothing if not tenacious. Unfortunately for the Jews," I added, thinking of the stories my Dad told about his grand-parents' narrow escape from the Third Reich.

"Why didn't he get in to the Academy?" asked Araminta.

"He was quite good at drawing buildings but terrible at people." said Jeremy.

"Just imagine – if he'd been accepted, we might have all heard of Adolf the Artist and be queueing up in galleries to see his work," I said.

"Exactly!" said Araminta.

There was a pause for some moments whilst we considered this notion seriously.

"Couldn't we bribe the Academy?" I asked. "You've got enough cash, surely, Jeremy?"

"Possibly. But there are too many unknown factors. Those artistic types might not be open to bribes," he said.

"I thought every man has his price?" I pushed.

"They do, but it's not always money," Jeremy continued. "Besides, getting Hitler into the Academy is just the first step. Suppose he weren't any good and never made it past the first term or year? Or he was criticised and ended up back on the street?"

"What do you mean, 'back on the street?'" said Araminta.

Jeremy explained to us that Hitler spent several months down and out in Vienna and ended up in a hostel. There he met a man, Hanisch, who persuaded him to paint postcards which he would sell. It kept the pair solvent and Hitler soon became a prolific painter; yet he couldn't stay away from politics and would leap into any discussion that aroused his interest, shouting to the point of brawling when he disagreed.

"So you see," he said, "there is no guarantee that, even if Hitler *were* to graduate from the Academy, he would stay out of politics. Seems to be in his blood."

"Isn't it worth a shot, though?" I said. "No pun intended."

"Look, Christopher. There are too many unknowns. We can't change a little thing – we must change everything. The only chance we have of succeeding with the assassination – the only weapon we have is our foreknowledge of events – that is, our knowledge of history. I have meticulously researched this period and brought us to the absolute optimum juncture when it is not only most expedient, but also easiest, to kill him."

"What does expedient mean?" I asked.

"Necessary; advantageous. Look, Christopher, we might set Hitler on an art career and return to your present, only to find he started the war ten years earlier – or later – and we'd have none of the information we do now, on how it all started."

"We could go back and undo it though, couldn't we?" asked Araminta.

"You should always avoid interfering with your previous meddling with the timeline. It creates too many paradoxes," said Jeremy.

"You mean you can't touch yourself? Same matter can't occupy the same space and all of that?" I asked, thinking I was being clever.

"Rot. Am *I* telling you the rules of time travel or are you going to just believe what you've seen in a film or TV series from the 1990s? Look, first of all, the matter in our bodies is constantly changing and, second...well, it's just utter rubbish. No; the reason you shouldn't contact yourself is that it's psychologically confusing and draws too much attention. It's simply not an option," said Jeremy.

I was becoming more convinced but Araminta still had reservations.

"When you said the word 'expedient,' it reminded me of something I've read," said Araminta. "Isn't it in the Bible?"

"Yes, it's in John's Gospel – Caiaphas argues it is, 'expedient that one man should die for the people than that a nation should perish,'" said Jeremy as a matter of fact.

"It can't be right. We take a life, we become as bad as Hitler. Killing is just wrong. It's evil!" she said, sounding a little upset.

"Good and evil are arbitrary distinctions. There is only action and inaction. This is the rule of utility," said Jeremy. It sounded like a rehearsed speech.

"Utility?"

"Yes, Araminta. Usefulness. Actions are judged by their consequences. If it is necessary to murder one man to save millions, it is useful and, therefore, right."

"But isn't that the same argument Hitler would have used to justify the extermination of the Jews? There were less Jews than Germans so better get rid of them for the 'greater good' of the German people?" said Araminta, her voice raised.

Jeremy had come to the end of his arguments.

"Why don't you think on it tonight – both of you? We can discuss it in the morning. We have a few days' grace. Not more."

With that, he stood up and opened the door to the adjacent room which had twin beds.

"Now, I don't know if you'd prefer to kip in there together, or if you'd like to take this room, Araminta, and leave us chaps to the twin?"

The last thing I wanted was to be left alone with our kidnapper – however friendly and reasonable he seemed now – but I was aware that Minty might also prefer some privacy.

"We'll take the twin room, thanks," she said and smiled at me. I tried to disguise my relief as ambivalence as Jeremy nodded and bid us goodnight.

Neither of us said anything for about a minute. We stood, staring at each other, listening for any movements from the other room.

"We have to do something!" whispered Araminta as she sat down on the bed furthest from the window and patted its mattress, inviting me to join her.

She pulled out her phone and put some music on. I thought it was a good idea until the door burst open and Jeremy charged in and snatched the phone.

"Are you crazy?!" he shouted.

"Hey, what do you think you're doing?"

"What am *I* doing, Christopher? What are *you* doing? What are The Beatles doing in 1923? Oh, that's right, *nothing* – because they haven't been born! Dear Lord, are you that dim?!"

He turned on his heel, slamming the door behind him.

Araminta leant right into my ear and said, as softly as she could,

"He's dangerous, Chris. We *have* to do something."

"What?" I said, tickling her ear a bit too much so that she flinched.

"I think we should try to grab his Chronosphere and make a run for it," she said.

"Where?"

"Back home."

"But we don't know how to activate it properly. We could end up anywhere!" I said.

"It can't get much worse than pre-Nazi Germany."

"You haven't read much history, have you, Minty? At least they have running water here."

"Look, we can force him to tell us how to operate it or leave him stranded here."

"All right. We'll give it a go first thing," I said, and went over to the other bed and pulled the blanket over me.

"Chris?"

"Yeah?"

"Glad you're here."

"Me too. Night Minty."

"Night."

I stared up into the semi-darkness, watching a shadow from the faint glow of a street lamp dance over the ceiling and wondered how history would judge our choice.

CHAPTER TWENTY-SIX

"Morning! Rise and shine, you two! It's a beautiful day with an Autumnal nip in the air and a café breakfast with our names on it down the street!"

Jeremy looked transformed. He was wearing a grey suit with polished black boots and a hat that covered his bald head. The scar on his cheek seemed different – less threatening and more like a sculptor had lost his grip on his chisel. In short, he looked distinguished. He turned to the window and did battle with the casement.

Araminta nodded and I seized the opportunity to dive for his satchel. I was quick and we soon stood with our backs to the opposite wall.

Jeremy took a step forward. The light from the window made him a silhouette and he said, calmly,

"I suppose I might have expected that."

Araminta and I said nothing. I furrowed my eyebrows at her to speak but both of us were panting.

"What do you intend to do now, children?"

It was the first and last time he patronised us.

"We thought we'd abandon you to your fascist friends and make our escape," I blurted out.

He took a step forward.

"One more step and I'll do it!" I warned, grabbing Araminta's hand.

"I shouldn't touch that if I were you," said Jeremy, "you still don't know what you're doing."

"Then tell us!"

"Why should I tell you, Araminta? What could I possibly have to gain? If I do, you'll activate it, stranding me here. If I don't and you activate it, you'll be stranded in time. Constantinople 542AD, to be precise. Just in time for the bubonic plague."

"He's bluffing!" I said.

"Please; I'm not going to stop you," said Jeremy, shrugging his shoulders and gesturing towards us with open palms.

"All right," said Araminta, "just tell us how to use our Chronosphere to go home and we'll give you back your one."

"Araminta, if you travel back to your present with your Chronosphere, any changes I affect here will happen to you, and you will have no memory of the original timeline. And then, of course, I will find you and I will see to it that neither of you time travels again."

He had not needed to raise his voice. The threat was clear. I looked at Araminta and she nodded. I put down the satchel and sat down on the chair.

The clock on the mantelpiece struck eleven.

"Brunch!" he announced cheerily and stepped forward, thrusting his hand out in invitation to leave. "You know, Christopher, I am a man of my word. I shall teach you both everything once we have completed the mission. Now, who's for sausages?"

"I suppose you feel rather like a boy presented with the choice of running away from home or sticking it out with abusive parents?" said Jeremy as I tucked into my steaming hot breakfast.

"That's not quite what I'd say."

"It's important that everyone must have a choice, Christopher. Or the appearance of choice, however limited or difficult."

"Why?" asked Araminta.

"In the end, it is what defines us. When we're little, we make our choices based on what we want or from pure instinct; we can't think beyond the immediate. When we're older, we see past that – we try to see the ultimate consequences of our actions. Most of us still act selfishly, even then," said Jeremy, sounding more like a teacher than a time traveller.

"What about moral choices?" Araminta pressed.

"Well, yes. Everyone has those too. Without moral choice, there can be no judgement. Of course, it depends how you define morals, doesn't it?" Jeremy seemed to be waiting for me to answer but I had a mouth full, so he continued:

"So, you see, it would be very wrong to kill Hitler the baby, or Hitler the child. He doesn't understand his choices – he cannot be punished for them. But to kill Hitler the man – Hitler the would-be-exterminator of the Jewish people...*that* becomes permissible."

"Because we know the consequences of his choices and we can judge him better than he can?"

"In a way, Araminta; in a way."

Three men were playing Dominos on a table at my two o' clock. One of the men placed his last piece down triumphantly and cheered. The others applauded their comrade and the winner, grinning under his moustache, went to the bar.

Jeremy walked over and muttered a few words to the men, shaking their hands. He returned to our table and proceeded to line the dominos up in a spiral.

"Since the first man, we have all had a choice," he said, carefully placing the next domino. "But some of those choices are limited by the choices that others have made before us." There were now three dominos left in the box. "The trick is, to find the first cause. Then, your choices can be free."

He placed the last domino and flicked it. They capsized in turn, knocking the next down. It seemed simultaneous.

"Why does the last domino fall?" he asked.

"Because the one before it fell," said Araminta

"And why did that one fall?"

"Because the one before that fell," I said.

"And that fell because the one before that fell. And so on and so on, right?"

We both nodded.

"So what is the first cause? What causes the first domino to fall?"

"You pushed it," I said.

"Right. Something outside the dominos – that was not the domino itself, but, rather something completely alien; something other. Yet, we could go backwards: who brought these dominos here tonight? From whence were they purchased? Which factory made them? And as for me – the outside agent; am I not, myself, caused? I am here – how? Because I am able to – because I was born. We could go back through the history of the human race via my ancestors. We could talk about the person who invented the Chronosphere that enabled me to travel back to this moment, or – " Jeremy paused here for breath, as his speech had been increasing in its tempo.

"Or," he said, carefully, "we could ask 'why?' The reason I am here is because of the decisions Adolf Hitler has made and will make and the actions he will take in this city next week. So you see, my friends, sometimes the first cause is yet to come. That's what makes it so elusive."

141

I was still trying to take in everything that he had said when Araminta asked,

"You said something about the 'first man.' Did you mean Adam?"

"I don't think I believe in Adam and Eve. I think it's more of a metaphor. Given the same choices, all human beings do what they are told not to – they do it out of pride. They want to know; they think they know better than they've been told. They think theirs should be the moral authority. Perhaps there was such a moment in human history, I don't know. I haven't been there."

"Why don't you? You've got a time machine!" I said.

"Believe me, Christopher, there are plenty of fanatics whose raison d'être is to document the first human ancestors. So far they have not been successful. Possibly because their grasp exceeds their imagination."

We were silent, again for a moment.

"One other lesson from the dominos," he said, resetting them quickly. "Notice how they seemed to fall instantaneously?" We both nodded. "So it is with the ripples of our actions in time. If you're one of the dominos, standing there, you don't notice anything until you're knocked over. To the observer above, it happens, almost at once. You two and I are above time, now. We are outside. That is why we are tasked with this mission: for we alone can see what *would* happen." He stood up and removed one of the dominos, creating a space.

"The chain must be broken." He held the extracted domino up. "Adolf Hitler must be removed." He flicked the first domino over and a third of them fell, stopping at the gap.

"Now; eat up!" said Jeremy.

142

CHAPTER TWENTY-SEVEN

Jeremy spent the rest of the day familiarising Araminta and me with the City and filling us in on further biographical details of Hitler. I wished he hadn't. It is harder to hate someone when you get to know them and Jeremy painted a very human picture of him.

"I'm not trying to make you like him; obviously he's still a genocidal maniac but this will help you a little when you meet him."

"Meet him? We're going to meet Adolf Hitler?!" Araminta was horrified. Perhaps even more horrified than I.

"That's the plan. You see, one of the reasons I brought you two along was to help me infiltrate Hitler's inner circle."

"And how are we going to do that?" I asked.

"How do you feel about dogs?" asked Jeremy.

"Dogs? How are dogs going to help?" said Araminta.

"Hitler loved his dogs, didn't he?" I said, remembering something I'd read on Wikipedia.

"One in particular. Fuchsl – a little white Jack Russell terrier he had in the trenches in World War I," said Jeremy.

"Had?" said Araminta, noticing the use of the past tense.

"Yes. He just came up to him one evening in the trenches and Hitler took pity on the dog and trained him. The two were practically inseparable. Someone offered to buy him for two hundred marks. Hitler refused. Unfortunately, the dog went missing after that and Hitler never really got over it."

"Right; so you want us to go find a white terrier, train it up and present it to Hitler in the hopes that he'll be so delighted he'll welcome us – and you – into his inner sanctum, leaving you perfectly placed to assassinate him?"

"Almost, Araminta, but not quite: you see, you must not underestimate Hitler's intelligence."

"I'm not sure I like where this is going," I said.

"If it were as easy as finding a replacement dog, don't you think someone else would have bought him one already?" said Jeremy.

"Oh no. Oh no you don't!" I said.

"Don't what?" Araminta clearly wasn't quite as in tune with Jeremy's thinking as I was.

"He wants us to get the real Fuchsl!" I said.

"How?"

"How do you think, Minty?"

"Oh. Hang on – didn't you say the dog went missing in the trenches?" she said.

"Yes," said Jeremy.

"You want us to go back to the trenches of the First World War to retrieve Hitler's dog?" said Araminta.

"Yes."

"Do you have any idea how crazy that sounds?" said Araminta.

"Yes."

"Oh. Brilliant! And why don't you do it?"

"Dogs don't like me," said Jeremy, frowning quickly.

"Convenient."

"No, Araminta; it's decidedly *in*convenient. Look I thought you'd like this plan – you don't have to do any killing. In fact, you get to save a life."

"What, a dog's life?"

"Yes. I mean he was almost certainly killed, so think of it as a little rescue mission."

"What if *we're* killed?" I asked.

"Look. I'll teach you how to do an emergency retrieve on your Chronosphere. Moment you see Fuchsl – or if a shell explodes – you'll be safely back in 1923."

"You're not coming with us?" I asked.

"Like I say; dogs don't really like me."

"Why is that, exactly?" I said.

"Don't tell me," said Araminta, "it has something to do with the 26th century?"

"23rd, actually. And it's not just me. So, are you in or not?"

Araminta looked at me and I shrugged my shoulders.

"Guess so," she said.

"Good. You'll need some uniforms then and, I suggest, a pound of sausages." Jeremy stood in front of Araminta and and picked up the end of her hair.

"I'm not cutting it. Do you have any idea how long it took to grow?"

Jeremy realised it would be useless trying to press her.

"All right; you'll have to tie it up and hide it under your helmet."

"Agreed."

CHAPTER TWENTY-EIGHT

Nothing we'd seen or read could have prepared us for the horrors of war. It made *Saving Private Ryan* look like a Pixar film and turned the vivid poetry of Wilfred Owen into a nursery rhyme.

I suppose the first thing we noticed was the sound. It was utterly deafening: shells and machine guns, shouting and wailing.

And mud. Lots of mud.

The Chronosphere never seemed to pinpoint space so well as time. By some miracle we had managed to land the right side of No Man's Land – which was, of course, what we would usually have thought of as the 'wrong' or 'enemy' side. This only epitomised the folly of war: here were mothers' sons being blown to small bits by the sons of other mothers. Men who had never met; men who bore no quarrel – only a different uniform. Here, on the battlefields of Ypres, murder was not only permitted, it was the order of the day. A few miles away in the town, murder was still prohibited.

I began to understand the necessity of our mission: if we could prevent a Second World War – if there was even a chance, we *must* take it.

"Get down!" shouted an Officer. Araminta and I ducked as a shell whizzed past our ears and exploded behind us.

"Don't just stand there, damn it – put it out, solider, put it out!" I looked around for some sand or water or anything to quell the fire that had sprung up. Araminta, ever more practically minded than me, snatched up a bucket by her side and threw its yellow contents onto the flames.

The attack did not last for long.

I looked around. I had always thought of the soldiers of the War as men, but these were boys: most of them not much older than myself. I thought of Tom back at home, desperate to join the Army to 'serve his country' and wondered what purpose was ever served by war.

Someone fell into me, coughing. He splashed mud up my leg.

We had been worried we would look out of place but everyone was so busy with the business of survival, we were hardly noticed.

"I can't believe this is happening," I said. "I mean, I can't believe it happened. It doesn't make any sense at all!"

"Come on, Chris; the sooner we find that dog, the sooner we get out of here!"

I edged along the trench as best I could. The boots Jeremy had bought for us leaked. I shuddered, thinking of the photos of 'trench foot' Mr Travis had shown us and had a sudden urge to document this experience, but Jeremy had Minty's phone.

Usually, you hear a dog's bark before you see it, but the roar of battle was so thick in our ears I barely noticed the little Jack Russell making its way though the mire. Its coat was remarkably white for such a place and it seemed unperturbed by the barrage of noise and rain of bullets. I

147

tapped Araminta on the arm and reached in my pocket for the sausages we had bought from the butcher in Munich.

"Fuchsl! Here, Fuchsl!" I said. The dog seemed to take no notice.

"You're pronouncing it wrong: it's more like 'fox-ul,'" said Araminta: "Here, Fuchsl! Nice sausages, look!"

I hastily unwrapped the meat, aware that the Jack Russell was probably the least interested party. By some miracle, we seemed alone in this stretch but there was no telling who might appear around the corner. Worst case scenario was we would encounter the dog's Master.

The dog, whether obedient to our voices or his snout, came within reach.

"Now!" I said. Araminta dived into her pocket and activated the Chronosphere as I went to grab Fuchsl by his scruff. Something screeched past me and I felt a sharp pain in my thigh as my hands grasped his fur.

CHAPTER TWENTY-NINE

"Shhh! Do you want the whole City to hear you?" I heard Jeremy say.

I was writhing on the floor of the larger of our rooms, screaming in agony. Fuchsl, clearly disturbed by his sudden displacement, was growling as he cowered in the corner. Araminta was wetting a towel in the basin.

"I've been shot! Ow! I've been shot!" I moaned.

"You haven't been shot, Christopher, it's just a flesh wound." said Jeremy, standing over me.

"'Tis but a scratch!'" quoted Araminta, trying to make light of the situation.

"Look this isn't Monty Python, Minty. It bloody hurts!"

Minty pressed the damp towel against me.

"Sorry."

I smiled at her and apologised for taking it out on her. Jeremy looked at me and, almost reluctantly, went over to his satchel and retrieved a slim vial.

"Here, get this down you," he said.

"What is it?"

"It'll make you feel better." I should have been used to him not answering my questions. Another rule your

149

parents always tell you is not to eat or drink anything you don't know the ingredients of, but I was in pain.

"Good man. Now, let's see if we can't make you feel a little more at home, shall we, Fuchsl?"

At the sound of his name, the dog let out a whimper and relaxed, squatting down with his head on his paws.

"Well done, both of you. How did you find it?"

"Well, *he* sort of found *us*, really," said Minty.

"I meant the War," said Jeremy.

"If you were that interested, you might have gone yourself."

"I've been, Araminta. I have no desire to go back."

Jeremy took a step towards Fuchsl and he started growling again.

"See, I told you dogs don't like me."

"Well they're highly intelligent."

"Is that a joke, Araminta?"

"Yeah."

"Actually, Fuchsl was supposed to be highly intelligent: Hitler taught him several tricks," said Jeremy.

"Great. You know there's a website called 'catsthatlooklikehitler.com'. Suddenly, that seems a hell of a lot more appropriate than kidnapping his actual dog," I said, feeling better.

"I sent you to a few days before someone else really did dognap him so it's fine." said Jeremy.

"Right. So, what's the plan now?" asked Araminta.

"Now, we need to ingratiate ourselves with Helene Hanfstaengl. She was one of Hitler's most trusted intimates. It's probable that he fancied her. Her husband was one of his right hand men, before he defected."

"Right. So, what, we just introduce ourselves?" asked Araminta.

"Yes. 'Accidentally' of course, and, then, we make ourselves indispensable," said Jeremy.

"How do you intend to do that?" she asked.

"Araminta, how do you feel about children? Small, German children?"

I smiled. The pain in my leg had completely gone and I could tell from the expression on Araminta's face that she hated small children.

CHAPTER THIRTY

Jeremy had clearly done his research: Mrs – or, rather, Frau – Hanfstaengl lived in a small apartment two doors down the street. We practised a routine that involved Minty and I taking Fuchsl for a walk whilst Jeremy would wait around the corner. Then, upon seeing Frau Hanfstaengl, Jeremy was to bump into her, steal her handbag and run. We were to set Fuchsl after him and chase him round a few blocks until, out of sight, Jeremy would relinquish the handbag and we would return with Fuchsl to Frau Hanfstaengl. Jeremy would then get rid of his overcoat, run around the block in the opposite direction and meet us as we handed the bag back to Frau Hanfstaengl, making Jeremy out to be our father. Or Uncle. Uncle seemed a little less creepy.

Araminta and I were highly sceptical about Jeremy's latest rouse but we had forgotten that this was the twenties and, in 1923, most people left their homes several times a day to buy fresh bread and meat. Of course, the most important thing was to get the right person. The photo Jeremy had brought with him was faded and in sepia. Also, unlike the 21st century, everyone in 1923 seemed to have the same hairstyle which didn't help.

"Come on, Chris, pick up the pace!" said Araminta. She had put her red hair up in a bun and was beginning to look like she really belonged in the 1920s.

"Oh, right. Cause *you*'ve been shot in the leg."

"You weren't shot, Chris. And I thought that medicine sorted it out?"

"Yeah; well. Look, if I have to walk round this block one more time –" I was cut off by Araminta grabbing my hand.

"Look. That's her, isn't it?" We were approaching a tall brunette wrapped up in a fur coat, carrying a loaf of bread in a paper bag.

Jeremy had seen her too and burst past us, knocking me into a wall as he collided with Frau Hanfstaengl and ran on up the street with her bag.

"Stop that man, Stop that man! He's taken my bag!" shouted Frau Hanfstaengl after Jeremy.

We had just reached her and Araminta uncoupled Fuchsl's lead and told him to "give chase!" Fuchsl bolted forward and tore down the street faster than I could run.

Don't ask me how the others managed it, but by the time I had got back round the corner, Minty was handing Frau Hanfstaengl her handbag and Frau Hanfstaengl was patting Fuschl on the head.

"Hello, what's going on here?" said Jeremy, casually strolling up to her with a newspaper tucked under his arm as I stood, panting, bent over.

"We...dog...Handbag...Chased!"

"Steady on, dear boy!" said Jeremy.

Jeremy tipped his hat to Frau Hanfstaengl.

"Are these your children, sir?" she asked.

"Not mine, no. But I am in loco parentis." He extended his hand. "Jeremy Bonhoeffer." I immediately raised my eyebrow. It was not a name I was expecting but I appreciated the irony of it.

"Helene Hanfstaengl."

"Frau Hanfstaengl how do you do?" Jeremy said, charmingly as he took her hand.

"Well I really can't thank you enough. Perhaps you might drop in for tea?" she said.

"Nothing would delight us more. Now, is everything there?"

"Yes. I think so," she said, checking the contents of her handbag.

"Good."

"Did you get a description of the man?" asked Araminta.

"No. I'm afraid it all happened so quickly. Didn't you?" asked Frau Hanfstaengl.

"Only that he was wearing a coat and seemed quite short. Wolfie was the one who caught him. What a shame he can't talk!" Araminta patted the dog's head for effect and Frau Hanfstaengl smiled and presented Jeremy with her card.

"Why, we're practically neighbours!" he said.

"Well, then; more good than harm has come from the whole incident. Doesn't God move in mysterious ways?"

"He does indeed, Frau Hanfstaengl. He does indeed."

"Shall we say four o' clock tomorrow?"

"Until then." Jeremy tipped his hat to her as she walked past and disappeared into her apartment.

"Well done; Araminta that was quick thinking on your part. Just remember to call him 'Wolfie,' won't you?"

CHAPTER THIRTY-ONE

If it hadn't been for our mission, I think I would have very much enjoyed being in Schwabing: the food was fresh and the pace of life less busy. One thing I didn't miss was the internet. In fact, I had barely given it a thought. Before coming to Munich, I would have said that I would rather lose my ability to taste than the internet, but the thing is that we don't need it. We only need it because everyone else has it but if no one has it then society can function very well.

The people in the street were happy. They spoke to each other; gentlemen tipped hats and stepped aside for ladies. The children coming out of the school opposite our house seemed more contented with the books in their hands than Josh is with his iPhone. As I looked out of the window at the street below, Jeremy spoke a warning, as if he could read my mind:

"The danger of staying too long in one time period is that one becomes accustomed to it. Assimilating oneself into an era is an art and, whilst the risk of changing something you haven't come to change increases with every hour you spend in the past, the greater danger is that you

155

simply won't want to leave." I turned to face him. The scar on his cheek looked painful. We had spent the day mainly indoors, playing cards and reciting certain facts we needed to know. Jeremy had taken on the semblance of a kindly, but stern, teacher. Even Fuchsl growled less.

Dressed in a stiff collar and tie, with my hair combed back, I felt like I was auditioning for choir boy of the year. The pretty, green dress Jeremy had bought for Minty made her look as if she belonged on the cover of a contemporary magazine.

"Time," he announced.

We stepped out into the golden light of a November afternoon and walked, in convoy, down the road to the Hanfstaengls' apartment.

"Welcome! Welcome! My wife has been singing your praises!"

Our hands were firmly shaken by an imposing man with a large nose. "Ernst Hanfstaengl; how do you do?" he said, introducing himself.

Stepping inside, we saw a small boy playing with a wooden train.

"My son, Egon," explained Frau Hanfstaengl as she took our hats and coats, leading us into a small, dark room with a table piled high with neat sandwiches, hams and cheeses.

"Tea?"

"Thank you," I said. I hate tea but I was guessing there wasn't a Dr Pepper in the fridge. There wasn't even a fridge.

"Herr Bonhoeffer, perhaps something stronger?"

"Thank you," said Jeremy.

We sat down politely and helped to re-tell Herr Hanfstaengl the story of our encounter the day before.

"It sounds like we should have invited Wolfie to tea!"

"How long have you had him, Christof?" asked Frau Hanfstaengl. It took me a moment to realise she was talking to me.

"Not long. We sort of found him, actually," I said.

"He's very clever. He can do lots of tricks!" said Araminta.

After an hour or so of pleasantries, Herr Hanfstaengl invited Jeremy to join him in the other room for a brandy. This was his opportunity to persuade Hanfstaengl of his political convictions and Jeremy winked at us as he followed our host out of the dining room.

"Thank you for the tea," said Araminta. "Would you like us to help with the washing up?"

Inwardly, I groaned. I spend my life washing up.

"Thank you but I wouldn't dream of asking any guest to do dishes."

"Nonsense. You don't want it left till later," Araminta insisted. I bet she has a dishwasher at home.

Frau Hanfstaengl smiled and relented.

"Come on then, let's clear the table."

Of course, without washing up liquid, the task required a little more elbow grease, and Araminta and I stood to the side with a tea towel each, ready to pounce on the next item that Frau Hanfstaengl passed from her bowl. We kept as quiet as we could, straining to hear the snatches of conversation the two men were having.

"The problem with the economy is the Jewish problem," said Jeremy.

Araminta gave me a look and I clenched my jaw. I couldn't hear what Hanfstaengl was saying but we heard laughter a moment later.

"How old is your son, Frau Hanfstaengl?" asked Araminta.

"Egon will be three in February."

Having finished in the kitchen, we joined the boy with his train set.

"I adore children," lied Araminta.

"And I always wanted a train set!" I said, truthfully.

I watched Egon playing, blissfully unaware of the war he would fight in, should we fail our mission, and thought how important innocence was.

We were startled by a sudden rapping at the door.

Frau Hanfstaengl went to answer it and, looking up from the floor, I saw a large, unpolished boot step into the hallway.

"Uncle Dolf!" said Egon excitedly and stood up.

My eyes seemed to perform a contra zoom as I took in the figure of one of the most hated men in history.

"Hello, Master Egon! And how is my favourite boy?" Egon toddled towards him. "Has that naughty chair been attacking you again? It had better not!" Egon giggled as he was picked up, swung high and placed down again on the floor. He noticed us.

"I'm sorry, Frau Hanfstaengl. I didn't know you would have company. Should I perhaps call back at a later time?"

"Nonsense! Do come in. I'm sorry, though, we've just had tea but I can make a fresh brew for you?" He put his hand up in polite deference. Minty and I scrabbled to our feet as Herr Hanfstaengl came out of the sitting room with Jeremy.

"Sorry, didn't hear your knock my dear fellow," said Hanfstaengl, shaking his hand. "Allow me to present Jeremy Bonhoeffer – a recent acquaintance and ally of the Cause. Bonhoeffer, this is – "

"Herr Hitler. I'm honoured!" said Jeremy, accepting a warm handshake. The very thought of touching those hands made me nauseous.

"And this is my niece, Margit and nephew, Christof." Jeremy said, motioning towards us. I couldn't say anything but Araminta managed a polite curtsey and a "how do you do?" Frau Hanfstaengl took Hitler's coat and proceeded to regale her new guest with yesterday's tale (which had become somewhat embellished with each telling).

"I should like to meet this dog of yours," said Hitler.

"Well that's the thing," said Araminta. "You see he's not ours. Not really. We sort of rescued him."

"Oh?"

"Yes," I said, quickly. "You see we used to have a dog back in –"

"America," said Jeremy, interrupting.

"America?" asked Hitler, interestedly.

"Yes. My father was American, you see," said Jeremy.

"Why, you should have said so earlier!" exclaimed Hanfstaengl. "My mother was American and I was at Harvard!"

"So what brings you to Munich, Herr Bonhoeffer?" asked Hitler.

"*You* do," said Jeremy, pointedly. "You. And politics."

CHAPTER THIRTY-TWO

The genius of the American connection was twofold: firstly, it explained an absence from Munich and the reason why someone so apparently politically motivated had not become involved with the NSDAP before and, secondly, it explained why Jeremy dealt in dollars. This, coupled with the bonus of the Hanfstaengls' relationship with the United States, instantly made Jeremy an attractive candidate for a Party benefactor, and he was promptly invited to dinner the following night, to discuss "politics, economics and, of course, the Jewish question." At the mention of this third category, I noticed Herr Hanfstaengl visibly raise an eyebrow. Jeremy explained to us in private that Hanfstaengl was, himself, not all that keen on Hitler's anti-Semitic agenda which made him seem a bit better.

Araminta and I were rather pleased to have some more time to ourselves. Jeremy, seemingly more trusting of us, had returned Araminta's phone, on condition that she not use it in public. Furnishing us with a few dollars and entrusting us with the keys to the apartment, he suggested we enjoy an evening of "normality." The word might have seemed absurd days ago but we had both adjusted to our new surroundings remarkably quickly.

"I guess you're used to living in new places," I said to Araminta.

"Yeah. Not new times though!"

"It's a bit like going on holiday though, isn't it? Everything's all foreign at first and then signs become familiar. I'm sure there are loads of places in the world that are more backwards than this place, technologically?"

"Well yes, obviously," she said.

"So, what did you make of him?"

"Which 'him?'"

"Who do you think, Minty?"

"Was it me or did he have a lopsided head?"

"I think he sort of leaned it to the left a bit, yeah."

We laughed. "That's something Mr Travis hasn't taught us!" I said.

"So Jeremy's really going to...y'know."

"Looks like it." I said. Neither of us wanted to spell it out.

"Wow."

"Do you think he'll succeed?" I said, half to myself.

"He better had. He's our ticket home."

She had a point. A pretty sobering one at that.

"Hey, let's go out somewhere, Minty. How about the cinema?"

"All right."

"They're probably silent films of course."

"Of course."

We took Fuchsl for a walk as we tried to find a cinema. There were several, as it happened and there was quite a choice.

The software update on our translators had started working earlier that day but it still took a moment to adjust languages – so, looking at the title of films outside, *Der*

Mann mit der Eisernen Maske gradually became *The Man with the Iron Mask*.

"Let's see that!" I said.

"All right. I don't really fancy something heavy anyway."

We returned Fuchsl and gave him a bowl of water before heading back out.

"Well, I never did pluck up the courage to ask you to the cinema at home!" I said.

"What do you mean?"

"Oh. Nothing."

"Christopher?" I pretended I didn't hear.

"Chris?"

"Yes?"

"Do you – "

"What?"

"Do you want popcorn?" she said. We were both avoiding the issue.

"Do they *have* popcorn in 1923?" I asked.

"One way to find out."

They did, as it happened. In fact, it tasted slightly better than the usual stuff you get at our cinemas. The film itself had some terrible acting, worse special effects, appalling sets and boring music. Still, it was, as we both agreed, "an experience."

It was a cold night and we both pulled our coats about us tightly as we walked home.

"Are you worried, Chris?"

"About what?"

"Going home."

I was, of course, but didn't want to admit as much so asked instead:

"Are you?"

"Yes," she said, quietly.

We came to a halt outside a church. There was a bench in its graveyard and we sat down.

"What are you most worried about?" I asked.

"My family. Chris, what if we get back and they don't exist?" There were tears forming in her eyes. "They're all I have. I don't have anyone else. Well, apart from you."

"Well, I won't have anyone else either if it changes all that much! All either of us will have is each other!" I said, trying to make light of the situation. Then it struck me: with us being the only people protected from the changes to the timeline it was not unlikely that we might return to find out we had never been born.

"Hey, there's no use worrying about it. We can't change anything."

"But Chris, that's the whole point! We can! Or, we're going to!"

I couldn't think of anything to say. The clock on the tower of the church struck eleven.

"Come on," I said, "let's just go home."

Araminta slipped her arm in mine and we made our way back through the gas-lit streets in silence; each of us lost in private hopes and fears.

CHAPTER THIRTY-THREE

"Hitler's coming to tea," said Jeremy, calmly – as if he'd said his great aunt Mavis was popping in for a quick cuppa and a Jammie Dodger. We stared at him and burst into laughter.

"What's so funny?" he asked.

"I'm sorry! I'm sorry! It's just...that sounds so funny!" said Araminta, fighting her hysteria.

"It's like that film, *Tea With Mussolini*," I said. "It's just...*wrong!*"

"It's like a sequel," added Araminta. "It could be a trilogy: Fascist Dictator Tea Trilogy."

Even Jeremy smiled at that, before getting serious again:

"All right. But listen: this is it. This is Fuchsl's big moment. Now we've got to get him to recognise the dog and reunite with it."

"Is that what he's coming here for?" I asked.

"No. He's coming because I'm going to give him some money," said Jeremy.

"What?!" I said.

"I'm going to give him a large donation for the Party."

164

"You're going to be a benefactor to the Nazi Party?" said Araminta.

"Yes."

"That's just – horribly wrong." I said.

"Christopher, I thought we'd been over this? Stop thinking of actions as being 'right' or 'wrong' – it's about what those actions *achieve*."

I wasn't convinced.

"Look, he'll be here at about eleven, so let's do a bit of a tidy up and get rid of any anachronisms, shall we?"

I looked at him blankly.

"Anachronisms – you know, things that don't belong in this time era?"

"I'm guessing a quick photo of us and Adolf is out, then?" I said, facetiously.

Jeremy didn't dignify that one with a response.

Hitler was punctual, at least, and came armed with dog treats and an Art portfolio.

"Good day, Herr Bonhoeffer."

"Please, call me Jeremy."

This seemed to make Hitler a little uncomfortable but he tried to smile and took the seat that was offered. Fuchsl was in the other room for the time being and Minty and I brought a tray in from the kitchen.

"I brought my portfolio along because I thought it might interest the children whilst we discussed more...adult concerns."

"Thank you," said Jeremy, passing Hitler a cup and saucer.

"We had no idea you were such an artist," said Araminta.

"It used to be my dream." I thought I detected a slight note of sadness in his tone.

"But I was never good at doing people," he continued: "something about the face that's impossible to capture."

165

"Well I can't draw at all," I said, hardly believing I was engaging in polite conversation with Hitler.

"Well, shall we all have some tea, first?" said Jeremy.

"Yes. Very good," he said, in military fashion.

There was a scratch at the door and a whimpering noise.

"Is that your dog?" asked Hitler.

"Yes; that must be Wolfie," I said.

"At least – that's what we called him when we found him," added Araminta quickly.

"Well, do let him in here. I love dogs."

"Do you really?" asked Araminta.

"Yes. Some of my best friends have been dogs."

Jeremy smiled and winked at me discreetly, as Araminta got up and went to let Fucshl into the room.

It was like watching *Homeward Bound*. At the instant the door was opened, Fuchsl burst into the room, barking. His old master went white and stood up. Jeremy turned to look at him.

"I'm sorry, Herr Bonhoeffer…please, forgive my manners…I…"

"Sorry, is he too boisterous? Perhaps the children should take him for a walk?" I resented being referred to as "the children" but obediently went to look out the dog lead.

"No!" shouted Hitler, before recovering his temper. "I'm sorry. Dear me. It's…it's just that he looks so very much like my own dog."

"*Your* dog?" pressed Jeremy.

"Yes. The one I used to have. In the War."

He gingerly took a step forward.

"I lost him. One day he just…disappeared."

"What was his name?" asked Jeremy.

"Fuchsl. I called him Fuchsl."

At the sound of his name, Fuchsl darted forward wagging his tail. Sinking to his knees, he held his arms open and the dog leapt into his old master's embrace,

166

licking his face and the reunion was complete. It really was a beautiful moment.

"Fuchsl? Fuchsl? Oh it *is* you!"

We let the two enjoy a moment together and then Jeremy said: "Is it really your old dog?"

"I'd know him anywhere."

"Then, please – take him."

"Oh, but no. He's...he's your dog now."

"We've only been looking after him, really," I said.

"And he clearly loves you!" added Araminta.

"*Someone* has to!" I muttered under my breath. I forced myself to smile and as I did so, I found myself thinking *this is a human being.* Which was going to make what we were about to do all the more difficult.

CHAPTER THIRTY-FOUR

About the last thing I expected was for a red Mercedes to pull up outside our apartment the next day with a hamper the size of a small house, driven by a cheery man with a moustache who beeped the horn with such enthusiasm he might have been your favourite uncle.

"Bonhoeffer my dear man!" he called up to our open window. "Splendid day for a picnic I thought!"

It was. Despite the November chill, the sun was shining and there were no clouds in sight.

"I'm taking us all up to the mountains. Fuchsl will love it."

I peered out and saw the little Jack Russell wagging his tail.

"You can't be serious?" I said to Jeremy.

"When did Hitler go for picnics?" asked Minty.

"That's a good point, Araminta." Jeremy waved at the driver and withdrew from the window.

"Maybe we've changed something? Who knows? Maybe the pen *is* mightier than the sword and all that," I said, triumphantly.

"Don't be too hopeful, Christopher."

"Haven't you got a photo or a newspaper cutting or something we can check?" I said.

"What do you mean?" said Jeremy.

"Well, you know, like in *Back To The Future* when he checks that photo of himself and his family and they all start fading," I said.

"Haven't you listened to anything I've told you?" said Jeremy, crossly. "First of all, it's completely ludicrous how the photo fades in that scene. Surely it would either have suddenly changed or not at all? Secondly, as you have clearly forgotten, the Chronosphere creates a temporal shield around the travellers so nothing on us is affected by our time travelling."

"So there really is no way of knowing what effect we've already had?" asked Araminta.

"No," said Jeremy, dismissively.

"So maybe we've changed things already without having to use violence?" she added, hopefully.

"This isn't a naughty school boy we're talking about who just needs a pep talk and a new pet. This is a genocidal megalomaniac who has to be killed. And this presents us with a perfect opportunity."

Jeremy took a pistol out of his bag and checked the rounds.

"You're not serious. You're going to shoot him over lunch?" I said.

"What if he really *has* changed? Surely no-one's beyond redemption?" said Araminta.

"As you're both so fond of your film quotations I'll give you another one: 'some men just want to watch the world burn.' Do you know what Hitler said, just last year to a friend? He said, 'If I am ever really in power, the destruction of the Jews will be my first and most important job. As soon as I have the power, I shall have gallows after gallows erected; for example in Munich on the Marienplatz – as many of them as the traffic allows. Then the Jews will be hanged one after another, and they will stay hanging until they stink. They will stay hanging as long as hygienically possible. As soon as they are untied, then the next group will follow and that will continue until the last Jew in Munich is exterminated. Exactly the same procedure will be followed in other cities until Germany is cleansed of the last Jew!'"

Araminta and I stared at each other.

"Have you got enough bullets?" I asked, in earnest.

The horn was beeped again and Minty and I trotted down the stairs quickly.

"Hello, Christof. Good day, Margrit."

"Good day."

"Do hop in! Is your Uncle on his way?"

"Yes; yes he's just coming." I managed to say, still feeling nauseous from what Jeremy had told us.

"Good. Excellent. I take it you both like salami and so forth?"

He got out to give Araminta a hand stepping into the car. She visibly flinched but managed a smile. He handed me the hamper and we sat in the back of the car with Fuchsl between us.

"Thought we'd ask if little Egon wanted to come with us? Give our friends some time to themselves."

I nodded and he went to the Hanfstaengls' apartment to collect the boy as Jeremy came out of our building.

The drive south was pleasant enough, although we were forced to listen to some opera. Fortunately, with the wind blowing strongly, I missed half of what was being said in the front. Something about Wagner and "true German music."

Mum always says: "Give credit where it's due" – and there was no faulting the picnic preparations: there was meat of every kind, fresh bread and cheeses, potatoes and beetroot and flasks of hot tea.

"This is quite a spread, Herr Hitler. Thank you." said Jeremy.

"It's the least I could do…The least I could do," he kept repeating to himself, and stroking the dog.

"This is a beautiful spot," said Araminta. "Have you ever painted it?"

"No. I haven't. But perhaps I should. Did you like my paintings?"

"I did," I said, truthfully. "What a pity I hadn't heard of you as an artist before."

"Yes. Maybe you should do this as a scene. I bet it would sell well. You could put Fuchsl in it!" offered Araminta.

He chuckled and said: "Perhaps, years ago, but not now. Now, I have far more important things to attend to."

It was, in my mind, the saddest thing I ever heard. I turned to look at the shaft of sunlight peeking through a curtain of snow-covered trees in the distance and silently sighed for the darkness of the human heart.

CHAPTER THIRTY-FIVE

"I'm not wearing *that*," I said, pointing to the swastika arm band and field-grey windbreaker Jeremy had laid out.

"Fine. Then you can stay here. For good."

Two days had passed since the picnic. Perhaps it was because of the presence of Egon or perhaps it was because Jeremy really felt it wasn't the best time, I don't know. All I do know is that Jeremy was adamant that tonight was *the* moment we had been waiting for: the night of the Beer Hall Putsch. It was, apparently, the turning point of Hitler's career.

"On the night of November 8th, 1923 – tonight – Hitler is going to storm the Bürgerbraükeller with his troops, capture the triumvirate of 'vons' who run the Bavarian government and basically stage a coup d'etat," explained Jeremy.

"Right. I actually don't understand what any of that means," I said.

"So there are three men, all called 'Von' something: Von Kahr, Von Lossow and Von Seisser. They work under the direct supervision of Minister President von Knilling. Hitler is going to this beer hall – "

"What's a beer hall?"

"A hall where they sell and drink beer, Christopher. What do you think it is?"

"Right. Sorry."

"Hitler is going to use this to stage a coup d'etat or putsch which basically means an overthrow of the government."

"Wow. And he'll succeed?" asked Araminta.

"No," said Jeremy.

"Oh." I was confused. "So, if it's a failure, why is it so important?"

"Hitler will be arrested tonight and he will use the time in prison to write his famous autobiography and general rant about Jews, *Mein Kampf*. He will use the deaths of those who fall tonight as a catalyst for his rise to power. Sometimes, Christopher, the most dangerous man is one who thinks he has failed – for he has nothing to lose."

Jeremy then went over the plan: Hitler had kept most of his close followers in the dark, but they knew they would be converging on the Beer Hall. As history reported it, Hitler forced the three Vons into a side room where he persuaded them to go along with bringing about a new order. This would be the moment of opportunity: the Beer Hall would be crowded and emotions heightened. Hitler would say (several times) that either the revolution would come by morning, or they – and he – should be dead. Thus, reasoned Jeremy, it was the perfect moment to kill him.

Jeremy's plan was to hide in the side room where Hitler would take the triumvirate and complete the mission. We were to wait outside, dressed as Nazis, and monitor Jeremy's progress with a short range video device he had stuffed into a hollowed-out copy of HG Wells' *The Time Machine* (it seemed Jeremy had a bit of a sense of humour). If everything went well, we were to head to the river, where Jeremy would meet us. If not, we would have to make our own escape.

"How do we do that?" I asked.

"You use your Chronosphere."

"I thought you said it wouldn't protect us?" asked Minty. I was glad she was as confused as I was.

"Look. If I fail, nothing will change, will it? So the best thing you can do is make a fast getaway."

"Again, how do we do that?" I asked.

Jeremy went over to his bag and took out a small moleskin notebook.

"This will tell you everything you need to know."

I thumbed through it quickly and passed it to Araminta.

"Is this a manual?"

"Yes."

"You're giving us a manual. Does the Chronosphere come with this?"

"Yes, Christopher. When you buy one in Curry's they throw in a manual to get you started. No, of course not! I wrote this myself. I suggest you study it carefully between now and eight o'clock."

"Right," I said. I caught Minty smirking at me out of the corner of my eye and frowned at her.

"It's okay. We *will* succeed. We must," he said.

CHAPTER THIRTY-SIX

It was bitterly cold and the wind had picked up. Fog had shrouded the bridge by the Isa River and the darkness fell fast. Jeremy had underestimated his significance and Hitler insisted on giving him a seat in his car. There was little he could do about it and all we could do was wave him off cheerily, hoping he would find some other way.

"I thought the whole point was that he was going to the Beer Hall early to install himself in that little room," said Minty. I hadn't got a clue and I said as much. All we could do was watch and wait.

The street was crowded with police everywhere. I suggested we duck into a side street and tucked ourselves into a doorway. There was no-one about so I opened up the false book and we each plugged in the monitoring devices Jeremy had given us.

"Can you hear all right?" I asked Minty.

"Yeah but I can't make anything out – it's so noisy!"

"Same here."

It was like watching an episode of *Peep Show*: the camera was imbedded in a contact lens Jeremy was wearing. We kept seeing the back of Hitler's trench coat and a mob of Nazis and policemen.

Hitler spoke with the officers and persuaded them to make room for his own troops, who were expected shortly. Jeremy opened the door to the Bürgerbräukeller and they stepped inside. We recognised Herr Hanfstaengl but no one else. There was a rather striking looking woman next to Hanfstaengl, smoking and there seemed to be some argument about journalists.

The Hall was bigger than I thought it would be and they were packed in like sardines. There was a man standing on a platform droning on in a monotone about nothing in particular. The audience looked bored.

"That's Kahr," we heard Jeremy say in an undertone, for our benefit.

"I think we should get a beer. We look out of place," said Hanfstaengl, and disappeared to the bar. Hitler stood near a large pillar and surveyed the hall like a bird of prey.

"A billion marks for a beer!" said Hanfstaengl as he returned with three glasses in hand. Hitler said nothing and took a sip.

Outside, we could see trucks pulling up. There was a clock in the window of the shop we were standing by. It was a little after eight thirty. Another truck pulled, filled to bursting with armed Nazi stormtroopers in helmets. They disembarked quickly and surrounded the building. I crept along the narrow street to get a better view.

"They're doing absolutely nothing!" I whispered.

"Who?"

"The police! They're just standing there!"

Inside, we saw Hitler remove his coat. I nearly burst out laughing when I saw what he was wearing: a black frock coat and bow tie – as if he'd stopped off en route to the opera.

We heard somebody bark out an order to move out of the way and then the police did an about face and marched out of the building.

Hitler now put his glass down and took out his pistol. As if being conducted, a choir of stormtroopers chorused, "Heil Hitler" and Hitler marched forwards, into the main room, flanked by Jeremy, Hanfstaengl and four others, all wielding weapons.

The reaction was one of sheer panic. Tables were overturned. Jeremy kept turning round and the motion was beginning to disorientate me. He was clearly checking his exits: exits that had been blocked by a group of Brownshirts. A machine gun had been set up facing the audience. There would be no escape.

The man on the podium, Kahr, was clearly shocked and took several steps back as Hitler began scrabbling over a table to get to him. Suddenly, a man walked forward to Hitler with his hand in his pocket. Quick as a flash, Hitler pressed the barrel of his pistol against the man's head and ordered him to take his hand out.

"Everything will be quite all right!" he announced to the audience. "We can settle this all in just ten minutes." Hanfstaengl and the others motioned for the three men to follow Hitler into a private room. Kahr looked the most nervous and we heard one of them whisper, "put on an act" to the others.

The audience was silent as Jeremy followed Hitler into the private room with the triumvirate and another man, armed with a machine gun.

Hitler nodded at Jeremy. The illusion of the camera angle made it seem like he was staring at us and my heart began to thud. Jeremy closed the door.

"Please forgive me for proceeding in this manner but I had no other means," said Hitler.

"You gave your word you would not make a putsch!" shouted one.

"Yes, Seisser. I *did* give you my word, and I'm sorry. Sincerely. But I did it for the good of Germany – you must understand that?"

Silence. Seisser looked quickly at Kahr and the other man – who must have been Lossow.

"I am going to make ex-Police President Pöhner the new Bavarian Minister President and Ludenforff will become commander of the new national army," announced Hitler.

"A new national army?"

"Yes, Lossow: A new army based on the Battle League. They will lead the March on Berlin. Now, once we have seized power, *you,* my friends, will have even *greater* positions than those you currently enjoy!" Hitler looked around the room in excitement.

"I mean it!" he continued. "Kahr, you will be made Regent of Bavaria; Lossow, I want you to become Reich Army Minister and, Seisser?"

"Yes?"

"Siesser, I intend for you to be the Reich Police Minister!"

They were clearly unimpressed and, again, said nothing. Kahr shifted in his chair uncomfortably.

"I don't think he's military," said Araminta to me.

"Poor chap," I said, "they all think he's bonkers."

Jeremy hadn't told us if the monitor went both ways but he didn't react to anything we said so we assumed it didn't.

Hitler seemed to be sizing the three men up. He swept back his hair and nodded his head. Then, without warning, he took out his pistol and checked it.

"There are five rounds in it: four for the traitors, and, if it fails, one for me." He snapped it back and passed the weapon to his other bodyguard, who was already holding a machine gun. Hitler sounded hoarse and reached for a glass of beer on the table.

178

"To die or not to die. It's meaningless in these circumstances," said Kahr.

As if he had been been waiting for this cue, Jeremy pulled out his gun and landed a bullet in each of the five men before any of them knew what was happening. Araminta and I almost missed it: first, the bodyguard fell – slumped in his chair; Hitler's drink fell from his hand as a bullet went through his brain, and the triumvirate were executed within seconds.

Adolf Hitler was dead.

CHAPTER THIRTY-SEVEN

Araminta and I stood, transfixed to the monitor, unable to speak for what seemed an eternity. Jeremy wasn't moving either and Araminta was getting anxious, thinking someone must have heard the shots.

"He used a silencer," I said.

At last, Jeremy went over to Hitler's body. It was not a pretty sight.

"Mission accomplished," he said. "Now. Head to the river, both of you."

Jeremy went back into the the hall and closed the door to the side room behind him. The room was in uproar.

"Please, ladies and gentleman!" said Jeremy, "just another three minutes and this whole thing will be cleared up!"

"Theatre!" shouted someone.

"It's a Mexican revolution!" said another.

Jeremy squeezed his way through the crowd and caught Hanfstaengl's eye.

"Run!" he said under his breath to us.

We had been jogging for a minute or so, trying to keep one eye on the screen. We closed the book up and quickened our pace.

"Here, Bonhoeffer, what's going on?" we heard in our earpieces.

Behind us, the troops were in uproar and civilians were clamouring at the doors. We ran.

A shot rang in our earpieces.

"Keep running!" urged Jeremy's voice.

A spray of machine-gun fire.

"They're dead! They're all dead!" said a voice.

My chest was burning.

"Come, on Chris! Come on!" said Minty, rousing me from the dream-like state I was in, watching the monitor. I tripped over a stone and nearly fell over. Minty grabbed my hand and we ran together towards the bridge.

The further we got away from the din, the more fearful I became. A man started walking towards us and stared. I had forgotten we were wearing the Nazi uniforms. I tore at my sleeve with my free hand, not looking where we were going.

"Chris!"

I ran straight into a lamppost and hit my head. Minty stopped. I could see her lips saying something to me but all I heard was ringing. She pulled my hand and we started forwards again.

"Stop! Stop!" I shouted, unable to hear my own words. Minty shook her head and yanked my arm. We were nearly at the bridge.

The ringing only got worse but we made it and I sat down panting under the bridge. Minty put her hands round my face and mouthed something at me. I could feel blood on my temple, running down my ear. She pulled out the earpiece.

"Christopher. Can you hear me?"

"Yes. Yes. I can. It's ringing a bit but that's better. Thank you."

She hugged me.

"You're bleeding."

She tore off her swastika and pressed it against my head.

"It was red, anyway," she said, trying to make light of a bad situation. I snorted a laugh.

We looked around us. We were alone, for the moment.

Minty went to the water and dipped the piece of cloth in. The coolness relieved the pain a bit. Footsteps.

We recoiled under the bridge and held our breath.

"'Minta! Christopher!"

It was Jeremy. He, too, was bleeding from the shoulder and his face was pale.

"Take my hand," he said, "and let's get the hell out of here!"

The last thing I saw of Munich was the reflection of the moon in the Isa as we were, once again, jolted forwards in time.

CHAPTER THIRTY-EIGHT

We had expected there to be changes, of course. If everything had looked the same on our return to 2015, I suppose we might have thought we had failed, but it was still a shock to arrive in an empty field of dead grass with no buildings in sight.

"Where are we?" I asked.

"We should be exactly where we were," said Jeremy.

"What, Munich?"

"No, Araminta; this is England." Jeremy studied his Chronosphere. "And we are precisely at the same spot as we were when we left – in 2015."

"So where's the bench? Where are the houses?" I demanded.

"Did you really expect nothing to have changed?" said Jeremy.

"No. I suppose not. I just didn't expect *everything* to have changed."

Jeremy studied me and then nodded slowly and clenched his jaw. He walked a few paces, bent down and felt the ground, then looked at the sky and inhaled the air.

"Something's wrong," he said.

We waited for him to elaborate but nothing further was volunteered.

"No birds," said Araminta: "I don't hear any birds."

In the silence we should have heard the arrow whistle past our ears, but the first I knew of it was when my face hit the ground as Jeremy leapt on me.

"Keep down!"

Araminta immediately dropped to her knees and we began to crawl. The grass felt rough against my face and smelt charred; despite this, it was long and so it was impossible to see where we were going. I was still recovering from the run in Munich and the transit back to 2015 and each movement was painful. My head was still throbbing from the lamp post and I just wanted to stop.

A boot. Black, unpolished, dusty: it stood like the foot of a great statue, two inches from my face.

"Get up! Slowly," commanded a man's voice. We did as bidden and found we were encircled by a small, armed band, clad from head to foot in black, wearing gas masks.

A figure walked forward, past the man whose boot had been in my face, and stopped in front of Jeremy.

"Identify yourselves." It was a woman. Jeremy said nothing.

"Identify yourselves or you will be subject to summary execution," she repeated.

"Araminta Stirling," blurted out Minty.

"Christopher Jones."

"Jeremy."

The woman took a step closer and leant into Araminta's face.

"Where are your marks?"

Minty was clearly bewildered, not to mention petrified. "What marks?"

The woman straightened up and handed her crossbow to the man on the right. With both hands behind her head, she loosened something and removed the mask from her head. I couldn't help gasping. Her skin was blotched, as if someone had taken sandpaper to her face and her dark hair, long in some parts, had bald patches.

"Which generation are you?" she demanded.

I was hoping that Jeremy would think of something to say but he just stood there, dumbstruck. The woman grabbed Minty's arm and tore the sleeve.

"You clearly aren't Citizens, and you have no barcode; so you have either escaped the Breeding Centre or you are enemy spies. Either way, if you want to live, you will tell me the truth immediately."

"I don't think you would believe us," I said.

At that moment, Jeremy collapsed. Two of the soldiers (if that is what they were), pointed weapons at him and then, seeing he was unable to stand, called over to the woman.

"This one is injured."

"Please," said Araminta, "he's been shot. We're not armed and we don't mean to trespass."

The woman stared hard at Araminta. She seemed to find her intriguing. She shot a sideways glance at the man on her right and three of the others snapped into action and, the next thing I knew, a bag was put over my head.

It took a few moments for my eyes to adjust to the low light in what I can only describe as a cave. We had been bundled onto what seemed like a cart (it moved slowly enough) and had ridden for what felt like a day.

A fire was burning in front of us and, as I looked around, figures stood poised with an assortment of deadly weapons. Long shadows danced over the walls and the woman was sitting, poking the fire with a rudimentary sword.

"What have you done with Jeremy?" I asked.

"Do you know who you're talking to?"

"No. Sorry."

185

"I am General Carla: a second-generation Natural and the daughter of General Chambers and I'll ask the questions." I blinked, clearly not understanding a word she was saying.

"Sorry."

"My medic is seeing to your friend," she said, almost kindly, "so let's have some answers."

Araminta was sitting to my left and spoke calmly:

"I told you my name," she said. "I can't really tell you where I came from because I don't really understand where we are."

The General stopped poking the fire and withdrew her sword. The tip was glowing white and she pointed it in Araminta's face. She didn't flinch.

"You're not afraid?"

"I'm terrified. But I'm too confused to show it," said Araminta, bravely.

The General held her poise and considered.

"Honesty. All right. Let's start by asking what this symbol means." She pointed to the torn swastika on my arm.

"It's something we were wearing to keep us safe in the place we just came from," I said.

Araminta shook her head at me slightly.

"The Breeding Centre?" asked the General.

"Munich," I said.

We stared at each other and realised we were all completely in the dark.

"You'd better come with me," she said, standing up and taking a torch off the wall. We stood to attention and followed her through the darkness and into the light.

CHAPTER THIRTY-NINE

Nobody wins a nuclear war, and those who survive are, perhaps, the sorest losers. As we surveyed the skeletal remains of London's tall buildings, I began to feel, for the first time since our adventures began, that I was dreaming. Perhaps I just wanted, so desperately, to wake up.

"You haven't seen London before?" our captor said.

"Oh no," I said, "we've seen it before, all right. In fact, it *was* all right, before..." I trailed off, unable to find the words to express my horror and grief.

"Impossible to imagine what she was like in her glory." said the General.

I had the impression she was testing us in some way and that, if we failed, we shouldn't live very much longer.

"I don't remember St. Paul's having two domes though" said Araminta. She should have kept quiet: we were immediately surrounded by soldiers pointing crossbows at us.

"You have five seconds to explain yourselves!" shouted Cara.

I looked at Araminta.

"Four."

My heart thudded.

"Three."

My brain froze.

"Two."

I fumbled in my pocket for the Chronosphere, forgetting Minty had it.

"One."

I closed my eyes as one of her henchmen raised his weapon and then – *zing!* He fell on his back, clutching his chest. A horse whinnied and hooves thundered towards us as another of the General's men took an arrow to his chest. Cara drew a sword and charged forward. A moment later, there was another *zing!* and the sword was on the floor.

"Stand down!" commanded a voice from behind us. The horse and its rider came into view. The General stood firm.

"I am General Cara of the fourteenth legion of His Majesty's Imperial Guard. I demand that you immed– " she did not finish her sentence. The rider dismounted effortlessly and came up to her. He was wearing a gas mask and was clad in an egg blue robe.

"General, you are relieved." he said, passing her a scroll, bearing some sort of seal. She took it and, whilst keeping one eye on the stranger, perused the document.

"This is from Jerusalem!" she said.

"It is."

"You're the King's Emmisary?"

"He sent me personally to see to this matter. You are commended for your quick thinking, General, but His Imperial Majesty wants the prisoners alive until he can question them himself."

She nodded and opened her mouth as if to speak, before thinking again and closing it.

"There were just two?" asked the Emissary.

"The third was wounded," she said. "He died."

"Very well. Have you transportation?" asked the Emissary.

"I have a wagon at my disposal," said the General.

"Bring it."

She dispatched two of her men who ran off behind us and stood still. A faint breeze swept her hair and covered her face.

"You should return to your base, General. It's not good to be exposed out here for very long," said the Emissary.

"May I ask where you're taking them?"

"You may," he said. "You may always ask."

The uncomfortable silence grew to a crescendo until the men reappeared with a horse-drawn cart.

"See to it the prisoners are secure," said the Emissary.

We were taken in hand and thrown into the cart and bound with a length of rough rope, back to back. Satisfied, the men returned to their General, and the Emissary bowed in deference and walked towards the cart.

"Wait!" called out the General. The Emissary turned round. "Will you give His Imperial Majesty a message?"

"What?"

"Tell him his handwriting's improved," she said, pointedly.

The Emissary froze and the General sprang into action, snatching a crossbow from one of her men and aiming it at the Emissary's head. Before she could fire, he withdrew a gun and fired bullets into the heads of each and every soldier. Then he turned to us.

"We'd better get a move on," he said and mounted the driver's seat, cracking the reigns as we lurched forwards.

The road was rough and the bumps threw Minty and I around the back of the wagon. We seemed to be moving fairly fast, although it could not have been more than 30 miles per hour or so. The horse's hooves were kicking up dust, making me cough. The sun was burning in my face and I kept getting Minty's red hair in my mouth as our heads were flung from side to side.

We came to a stop in something of a shanty town. The Emissary leapt down from the driver's seat and came towards us with his sword outdrawn. I flinched but he simply cut our bonds in silence and sheathed his blade.

"Follow me," he said, and walked over to a ramshackle building that might have once been a church.

"Wait," he said, holding his hand up. It was silent. Everywhere seemed silent in this world. He pulled out a Geiger counter and waved it around in a circle. Satisfied, he motioned for us to continue and we stepped over what was left of a threshold.

"Watch your step," he warned. There was a set of stone steps in the far left corner, leading down to a crypt.

"We'll be warmer down there. And safer." Taking a torch out of his pocket, the Emissary led the way. It didn't quite seem to add up, but I was curious and hungry and I was hoping he might have some food.

Everything I had seen of this place had looked a little medieval, yet this crypt was filled with high-tech weaponry, computers and a fridge. It was like walking into the Bat Cave.

The Emissary motioned for us to be seated and then stood with his back to us and removed his gas mask.

"Now, then," he said, turning around, "you'll be wondering what the hell's going on."

I looked up at his face and was so shocked I was, literally, stunned into silence. Only Minty found the strength to say:

"Jeremy?"

CHAPTER FORTY

I could scarcely believe my eyes.

"No. No, I'm not Jeremy," he said. "Look closer." He pointed to his face. There was no scar. Everything else was identical.

"You're...his twin?" I asked.

"Call me Immanuel," he said, offering us each his hand. He gave a warm handshake and smiled widely. It was eerie – they were similar in so many ways.

"You'll have a lot of questions. I'll do my best to answer them. But, first things first: food!"

This was a winner in my book. Minty leaned in to me and whispered: "Do you think he's safe?"

"No, Araminta. I've poisoned the elderberry juice. Here." Immanuel took a sip from a cup of liquid he'd poured and handed it to me.

"How do you do that?" said Araminta.

"What?"

"Know everything I'm thinking?"

"If I told you…"

"Let me guess, you'd have to kill me?"

He chortled and went over to the oven that was standing in the far corner as it beeped.

"Perfect timing!" he said, opening the door. Beef casserole assailed my nostrils.

"Generator, Chris." I looked over to the right where there was a large cylindrical thing, chugging away.

"I don't know what's more impressive. Reading my mind or having electricity when no one else in the world seems to," I said.

"You mustn't judge a world by one village, Chris," said Immanuel.

He served up the casserole into three bowls and handed one to each of us with a spoon.

"Thanks." I took a slurp. It was good. Better than Mum's, actually.

"So…?" Minty wasn't going to be kept waiting.

"Right. Down to business is it? All right then. What do you want to know first?"

"Just start at the beginning," she said.

"That's not easy to pin point."

"All right. Let's start with what happened and why we're here?" pressed Araminta.

"You are here because of your choices. And because of Jeremy," said Immanuel.

"We're definitely here because of *him!*" I agreed, with a mouth full of carrots.

"Who are you?" said Araminta.

"That's more complicated than you think. For now, the most simple and accurate answer I can give you is that I'm a friend," he said.

"Funny. That's what Jeremy said."

"I'm sure he did, Araminta."

"Are you saying he's some sort of enemy?" I asked.

"I'd say we're diametrically opposed, yes. But 'enemies'…well that's a bit of a weighted word. Try to not think of it like that at all. Simply ask yourselves, *is this the sort of world I left and would want to live in?* And you will realise that Jeremy was in the wrong."

"Are you saying all this is because of – " pressed Araminta.

"Munich," finished Immanuel.

"You know about that?" I asked, surprised.

"Yes. And I know we need to correct it, too," he said.

"We?" said Araminta.

"Well, you," said Immanuel.

"Me?" I asked, confused.

"Both of you."

I chased the last carrot around my plate.

"I think you need to tell us exactly what happened," said Araminta.

"I can't," he said.

"Won't?" I said, pointedly.

"*Can't.* Not exactly – it's difficult to trace."

"But all of this – this set up here, the stunt you pulled with that Cara woman?" said Araminta.

"Parlour tricks – the apparent omniscience of a time-traveller," he said. "Really I've no idea what happened to the world. I've been trying to piece it together for months. What I *can* tell you is that this place is bad. I mean, really, really bad."

"The gas masks?" I asked.

"Fallout. I don't know when it happened exactly but there are still pockets of radiation. Seems Einstein was right," he said.

"About what?" I asked.

"When he said, 'I do not know with what kinds of weapons the Third World War will be fought, but the Fourth World War will be fought with sticks and stones.' Look around you, Araminta; this place is a graveyard: there's no electricity, no sanitised water, no government."

"What about the King you mentioned?" she asked.

"Yes. Jerusalem? Is Israel the world power now?" I said.

"From what I can tell, there is no Israel," said Immanuel.

"How is that possible?" I asked.

"No *State of* Israel, I mean. You see, in your timeline, the State of Israel was created in 1948, mostly as an international attempt to atone for the Holocaust."

It began to dawn on me.

"So, no Holocaust, no Israel?"

"I think that's been one of the effects, yes, Araminta."

"Wait a minute," I said, "are you suggesting that the Holocaust was a *good* thing?"

"No! Of course not! It was awful. Obviously. But something good came out of it: the Jews finally had a home after nearly nineteen hundred years," said Immanuel.

"It's like karma, I guess, making up for the evil that was done to them?" offered Araminta.

"Yes. Or some theologians would say that, 'all things work together for good for those that love God,'" he said.

"Do you believe in God?" I asked.

"The list of things I believe in is a lot longer than the list of things I don't."

"Such as?"

"Such as, Araminta, I do *not* believe that the *Historical Improvement Society* has the monopoly on the ethics of time travel."

"The *Historical Improvement Society?* Wasn't Jeremy from—" I started.

"That's right. You see the *HIS* believe that we should use time travel to correct past wrongs and, ultimately bring about the greatest happiness for the greatest number of people."

"That sort of makes sense," said Araminta.

"Does it?"

"Yes!" said Araminta. "Surely you believe in the greater good?"

"I do. But I wonder what you mean by that?" he said.

"Well, you know, that sometimes we have to think of the bigger picture," she said.

"Like killing one man to save the lives of millions?" said Immanuel.

"Yes."

"Like Hitler?"

There was, literally, nothing to say to that. Immanuel smiled and spoke softly:

"Let me put it like this – if there were a lunatic about to kill a room full of eleven people or a room of a hundred, which would you choose to save?"

"Well, I'd try to find an alternative," I said.

"You just killed everyone, Chris. Choose. Which room do you save?"

"The one with more in, I suppose," I said.

"What if the room with more in were all criminals – proven murderers and rapists?

"Well then I'd probably choose the room with fewer people in."

"Why?"

"Well, it would probably be in the best interests of everyone. Like you said – the 'greater good.'"

"Right. But what if one of those criminals is going to reform and discover cures for multiple forms of cancer?"

"Well you couldn't possibly know that!" said Araminta.

"Exactly!"

"Except with time travel," I said.

"Like you knew killing Hitler would cause a nuclear war wiping out most of the planet's population?" asked Immanuel.

"Is that what happened?" said Araminta.

"It's nearly impossible to trace. You two created an alternative timeline which we *have* to put right."

"But what if this *does* make things better?"

"Minty, you don't think this is better?" I said, shocked by her suggestion.

"The point is, we can't know," said Immanuel.

"Why not?" I asked.

"Because, Chris, we can't travel beyond the year 2517." said Immanuel.

"Why not?" asked Araminta.

"Because it's the future and no one has programmed the Chronospheres with the correct tempero-spatial telemetry."

I was confused.

"You've read the manual – you should know that you need to plot coordinates in space and time because the two are linked?"

I nodded and he continued:

"So we can't go to a point in space-time we haven't mapped. It's also why there haven't been any successful visits to the really distant past. It's too risky. It's too unknown."

"What are you trying to tell us?" said Araminta.

"Only this: we cannot know what the ultimate consequences will be of our actions because we can only know the outcomes of those actions along a timeline up to the 26th century. And even then, our knowledge is limited to what the time traveller can observe and remember. Some changes are so minute you might not realise. Every time someone makes a journey back in time they create an alternate timeline from that point. By now there is a multiverse of alternative timelines – or universes, if you like."

"And can you travel between them?" asked Araminta.

"No. You have to restore things to as near to how they were as possible. Sorry, perhaps 'multiverse' was misleading. There is only one universe that exists – as far as we know – but the timeline is always fracturing and being repaired – or remade."

It was all I could do not to have my brain implode.

"So you must belong to some other faction in this…this war?" said Araminta, after a pause. I had forgotten about the temporal war. Jeremy had warned us about The Domino Group but it was difficult to know who to trust. Jeremy had kidnapped us and Immanuel had saved us. Apparently.

"I belong to a group of people who believe that, as we cannot know the ultimate consequences of our actions, the only actions we can take must have intrinsic moral value: they must be good in themselves," said Immanuel.

"Well, how do you determine that?" I asked.

"We ask ourselves, *if everyone acted in this way, would I be happy with that?* If the answer is 'no,' you don't do it. So, taking a life is always wrong."

"But you killed those soldiers!" said Araminta.

"I disabled them. Besides, it gets a little hazy when you're dealing with alternate timelines. The priority has to be to restore the original timeline."

"Sounds a bit hypocritical!" said Araminta.

"So that means you would not kill someone you knew was going to murder other people? Like Hitler?" I asked.

"Yes. You're not responsible for other people's actions, Chris, just your own: everyone is his own moral agent and you can't make decisions for others. Also, you shouldn't beat yourself up about decisions others make."

"It all seems a bit naïve. Surely time travel shows you that all actions have consequences?" said Minty.

"Indeed," he said, "which is why it is so important to only act in the moment, not trying to calculate the possible outcomes of your actions. Things are right or wrong in themselves."

We considered this for a moment and then I asked,

"So, Immanuel. What's the bottom line?"

As if he were a great orator taking the podium, Immanuel stood up and said, solemnly:

"Bottom line? You have to save Adolf Hitler."

CHAPTER FORTY-ONE

We had continued the debate for some hours. Araminta argued that Immanuel was only sending us back to save Hitler because the consequences of killing him were worse than the consequences of having history run its original course. I also felt uneasy – as if we were justifying the Holocaust and making Hitler out to be some great saviour instead of an evil, genocidal maniac. Immanuel changed tactic after that and tried to convince us that the main reason for saving him was because murder was always wrong and that, had assassinating Hitler resulted in a better timeline, he would still argue he ought not be killed.

If I'm honest, the most pressing concern for me was getting back to my family and friends. Kirsty might be annoying but I didn't want to live in a world where I couldn't steal her ear phones and pretend they'd gone through the wash.

Immanuel corroborated Jeremy's take on the question of encounters with previous selves whilst time travelling. Araminta was pretty paranoid about creating a paradox that would cause the universe to implode but, according to

Immanuel, that was impossible: paradoxes just create a separate timeline.

The plan was to go back to the night of the Beer Hall Putsch and create a diversion that would get Hitler out of Jeremy's way and then kidnap Jeremy using our Chronosphere.

"You're not coming?" I asked.

"Yes. But I'll travel under my own steam," he said. "If everything works out I have to report back elsewhere. If it doesn't, I'll have to try something else. Either way, I can't afford to be bound to your 'Sphere."

"So if it doesn't work, you're just going to abandon us?" said Araminta.

"No. But enough has been asked of your two already. Look, if it all goes belly up, the best thing for you two to do is to go to a safe time and wait it out."

"A 'safe time?' What's that?" I said.

"When we first started doing this, we realised we would need somewhere safe to go in case anything went really bad. Somewhere where we wouldn't be at risk of further polluting timelines; somewhere deep in the past."

"Surely the further back you go the greater the risk of altering the timeline?" said Araminta.

"Yes and no."

"What does that mean?" I asked.

"You've heard of the butterfly effect?"

"Yeah, step on a butterfly and change the world."

"That's causality, Chris. The actual butterfly effect is the idea that a butterfly beating its wings in Africa changes the course of a river in New York."

"Right. So what are you saying?"

"It's nonsense. Look, if you complete your objective in Munich and you come back to this 2015 again – or worse, I want you to go to these coordinates and wait it out." He wrote a series of numbers on a bit of paper and passed them to me.

"Where will this take us? An abandoned forest? What are we going eat?" I said, getting a sideways look of disapproval from Araminta. Probably for mentioning food again.

"There's a community of us. You'll be well looked after," insisted Immanuel.

Araminta looked at me as if to say this all seemed too dangerous.

"Let's hope it doesn't come to that, anyway," said Immanuel.

I nodded and we returned to the business of fine tuning our plan to save the life of the man whose murder we had been plotting only days before.

CHAPTER FORTY-TWO

"I'm freezing!" I said when we materialised. Although it could only have been hours since we had been there, I had forgotten how cold Munich was.

"You'd better get running then, hadn't you?" said Immanuel. He had evidently arrived just before us, using his own Chromosphere and was clad in a long black trench coat. It still hurt my head to think about time travel. He must have changed out of his blue robes after we had left for Munich but programmed his Chromosphere to arrive some minutes before us.

"Which way?" I asked.

Immanuel's plan was to create a diversion that would call Hitler away from the Beer Hall and enable him to get to Jeremy. Minty and I were to go to the engineering barracks and start a quarrel with the engineers which would be reported to Hitler, in hopes of drawing him away. If that failed we were to go further back to the previous day and capture Jeremy. Immanuel felt that it would create less of a paradox if we allowed events to run their course for as long as possible.

"Besides," he argued, "Jeremy will be on his guard. The Beer Hall will be so crowded he won't be able to keep an eye on everything that's going on."

"How will we know if we've succeeded?" I asked.

"I'm afraid I don't have that monitoring tech that Jeremy had, so I suppose you'll just have to wait to hear from me."

Minty and I exchanged an anxious glance and Immanuel tried to reassure us by telling us it would be: "fine. Probably."

The engineering barracks were a fair trek away. Fortunately, dressed in our grey shirts and swastikas, we were soon recognised as Putchists and given a lift.

We were two of many: a great grey sea was sweeping over the Barracks like an iron wave. How easy it is to become what you despise, I thought, as we pushed our way to the front of a disassembly of Nazis.

"We've come from the Bürgerbraükeller with a message from Herr Hitler!" I announced as loudly as I could. The room went quiet.

CHAPTER FORTY-THREE

The engineers were easily angered. I didn't really know what I was talking about, but the slightest insinuation that they weren't doing their job properly created an immediate furore. The other Putchists were trying to put their oar in and someone – whether it was an engineer or a Nazi was impossible to tell – threw a punch.

Minty saw a telephone and had a brain wave to call the Beer Hall and leave a message for Hitler. We fought our way through a tsunami of sprawling engineers and Nazis and made it to the door. I narrowly dodged a fist and pulled Minty through, onto the street.

It was poorly lit and I didn't really know where we were going. All I could hope for was that Immanuel had succeeded in capturing Jeremy and he would let us know, somehow, and soon.

"I'm beginning to believe in global warming," I said.

"Say what?"

"I'm beginning to believe in global warming," I repeated, stamping my feet together and clapping my hands.

"It's bound to be colder in Munich than at home – we're much further inland." Trust Minty to come up with some nerdy explanation.

"Where to now?"

"Well, I guess we should start following the path back the way we came?" she suggested.

"Which way was that, exactly?"

"Chris! Didn't you pay attention! First rule of time travel."

"You're kidding?"

"Well, first rule of being anywhere new is to get your bearings and remember where you've been, surely?!"

"Right. So...which way?"

Minty let out a sort of whinnying sound and started off jogging down the road. I followed.

We had been at it for about a quarter of an hour when we saw the beam of a torch slicing through the mist. I put my hand up over my forehead to shield myself from the piercing knife of light and called: "Who's there?"

"Chris? Well met. Quickly, he's right on our tail. Set your 'Sphere for home and go!"

"Immanuel?"

"Yes?"

"Were we successful?"

The light was lowered and Immanuel's silhouette came into view.

"Yes. Now, take Minty home with you."

I pulled out my Chronosphere and set the coordinates. As I looked up, something shot past my head and I heard Araminta scream,

"For God's sake, Chris, do it now!"

CHAPTER FORTY-FOUR

The familiar sound of traffic in my ears told me we had at least avoided a nuclear apocalypse. Yet, as my eyes adjusted to the new conditions, I could sense there was something very wrong with the scene: there was no Araminta.

It was possible, of course that we had simply been separated by a few metres – even a street; but in my heart, I knew she wasn't there. Neither was Immanuel.

I was standing in the middle of Verity Close – a small cul de sac that runs off the main bus route back to my house.

One winter, not long after my Dad left, Kirsty was taking me to the shops whilst Mum was at work. We shouldn't have been left by ourselves of course but Mum couldn't afford child care all the time. It must have been school holidays. I remember our bus hit a sheet of ice and we were hurled against the windows with a jolt as we skidded into the kerb. Our driver was experienced and we avoided a collision, but a tyre was blown out and we all had to get off. Several of the other passengers chose to stay, huddled, at the side of the road, waiting a replacement service but Kirsty decided we should start walking and, taking my hand, led me down a side street. I remember the cold biting my feet through the wellies as snow began to fall. Soon enough, it had covered the pavements like a dusting of fine icing sugar. We wandered, aimlessly, through the side streets as the pale yellow sky darkened. My sister was never one to admit she was in the wrong and, without the aid of sat nav or maps we were soon well and truly lost.

I remember sitting down on a wall, wanting to give up: to go to sleep and never have to wake up and be warm. The next thing I knew was feeling a cold, wet punch in the face as a snow ball hit me. My fatigue left me in an instant and we abandoned despair for childhood games. Kirsty clearly had the advantage, being older and bigger than me but I knew how to pack my snow balls tightly and I aimed a winner right at Kirsty's back whilst she was bending down. Caught off guard, she slipped and careered into a street sign, denting it in the process.

That dent was still there.

Perhaps everything was going to be all right.

I put my hand in the dented sign and looked up at the sky. It was the same sky – the same lid of the same earth as five years ago and five minutes ago, in an earlier decade, eight hundred miles away.

I started running for home.

CHAPTER FORTY-FIVE

I had a terrible dream that night: For some reason, my arms were being amputated. I had some disease and they needed to stop it spreading throughout the rest of my body. They were going to give me prosthetic limbs. I remember asking if I'd be able to play the piano again and they said, "no."

Time is very funny in dreams. In an instant, I seemed to be transported several years in the future. I was trying my luck at internet dating, creating a profile and deciding whether or not to mention the fact that I was an amputee. For the first time, perhaps, I was able to truly empathise with someone else. My conscious mind tried to steer its way through the fog of my dream and tell me this was symbolic – that there was a lesson to be learned.

Almost as suddenly, the scene changed again and I was lying in a hospital bed, paralysed. Mum came in and told me that my spine was crumbling and I would be dead very soon and I should think about making preparations. There was the oddest feeling of failure. I wasn't angry, I wasn't even particularly upset. I just felt that I had failed in some way. Any resentment I bore my mother or sister vanished.

I tried to divide up my CDs and DVDs to my friends. I said I wanted everyone to wear white at the funeral and I wanted to be buried. And then I realised: the only person who wasn't there – who didn't know – was Araminta. Why would anyone have thought to tell her? I pleaded with Mum to find Minty's number in my phone and call her and ask her to come. I started shouting and I could hear the nurses telling Mum I wasn't going to make it and then – mercifully – I woke up. I felt like a death row inmate must feel when his sentence is reprieved and I knew what I must do.

CHAPTER FORTY-SIX

No one was answering. It had taken me ten minutes to pluck up the courage to walk up the Stirlings' drive and at least another minute to lift my hand to the knocker. I stared up at the imposing infrastructure and imagined a time when the house was lived in by an old, wealthy family with servants and a mad wife in the attic.

Now that such times were within my grasp, their sense of intrigue only increased. I lifted the knocker a second time as the door was opened by Mrs Stirling.

"Hello Christopher. Do come in."

"Thank you," I said, stepping into the hallway.

"Would you like some tea? I've just made a pot."

"Yes, thank you." I strained my ears, listening out for any sign of Minty's voice. Her green scarf was hanging on the banister. Perhaps I was worrying over nothing.

"Is Araminta still sleeping over at your sister's?"

My heart skipped a beat. "Um. I don't know."

"I'm assuming you came to see me about my book?"

"Right!" I said, as convincingly as I could. "Actually, I was sort of hoping I might be able to see Dr Stirling about something?"

"Oh yes? It's not to ask for our daughter's hand or anything, I hope?" she said, a little too seriously.

"Pardon? Oh, no. Nothing like that."

"Well he's just gone down to the Post Office. I expect he'll be back presently. Meanwhile, you can tell me how you're getting on my with my novel. Where are you up to?"

I was, genuinely, enjoying the book but I'm a bit of a slow reader and with everything that had been happening, I had barely read past the first ten chapters.

"Well, to be honest I've only just started chapter eleven. I'm a bit of a slow reader, you see."

"Right."

"But I was going to ask you – why can't Thomas ask Mary out? I mean I thought they were part of the same social thingy?"

"They're both part of the nobility, of course, but neither is free to marry whom they wish: Thomas is betrothed to an Earl's daughter."

"I see."

"What do you make of the King?" she asked.

"Henry? You see I wasn't sure which King it was supposed to be at first, which is clever. He actually seems a pretty funny guy," I said.

"Funny?" said Mrs Stirling a little sharply.

"Yes, that line about the sausage, for instance."

"I liked that bit too."

She handed me a cup and saucer and invited me to sit down. The armchair was covered in newspapers; the Domino Killer was all over the headlines again, having claimed his fourth victim. This time, in Yorkshire. I had read all about it, doing my paper round.

"Mrs Stirling, may I ask you a question?"

"Christopher, you strike me as a fairly intelligent young man; surely you know that asking such a question is redundant? I can hardly stop you asking a question and I don't have to answer if I would prefer not to; but your asking permission to ask the question makes me think I won't like the question – which gives me time to consider dismissing it, whereas, if you simply asked the question straight out, I might be put on the spot and would be more likely to answer it. However, the fact that you have the manners to ask in the first instance means you are aware of others' feelings, and so I find it unlikely that any question you might put to me would be rude. So. Go ahead."

This completely baffled me and I forgot the question so I just sat there, bumbling, as a key was put into the lock and the heavy oak front door sighed open.

"Darling! Christopher Jones has come round to see you." called out Mrs Stirling.

"Has he, by Jove? Well, then, let us see." Dr Stirling marched into the room we were sitting in and stood over me, bending his head down and peering over his glasses at me.

"Mr Jones."

I fumbled with my teacup, swapping it to my left hand so I could shake hands but he withdrew, stiffly, and pecked his wife on the cheek.

"You were gone a long time," she said.

"Unbelievable queues. The man behind the counter seems to get slower every week."

"Yes," I said, "he does my papers in the morning and it's such a slow process! I've taken to loading them in my bag myself as I know the round pretty well by now."

"Cup of tea, Darling?" said Mrs Stirling, ignoring me.

"Please. In fact, perhaps I'll take it in my Study. Christopher, would you care to join me?"

"Thank you."

I slurped the rest of my tea down (trying to hide my disgust for the taste) and smiled my appreciation at Mrs Stirling before following the Dr Stirling up the stairs.

I had not been inside this room before but I liked it immediately. It felt like stepping back in time; without the train jolt and the misty eyes. If not for the computer on the desk this might have been the 1920s. The same brown colours from the wooden desk to the wallpaper reminded me of that first room in Munich we visited. A sort of dankness that appealed to my childhood sense of adventure. I felt like Peter from *The Lion, The Witch and The Wardrobe*, standing in front of Professor Kirke. Actually I was probably more like Edmund, having abandoned a girl somewhere alien and lied about it. Or at least, omitted the truth.

"Has something gone wrong?" he said, sternly.

"Wrong?"

"Christopher, there are many things I don't know but one thing I have always been fairly sure about is my daughter. And without being rude about your sister, I am certain that Araminta would not choose to spend a night with her talking about boy bands and make up."

I snorted a laugh and said: "Well you're not wrong there. Minty is too sophisticated for that." It was too much for Dr Stirling; he stood up from his chair, suddenly, and placed his enormous hands the desk.

"Christopher, why don't you please tell me what the hell is going on?" I took a deep breath and averted his gaze to gather my wits and was about to tell him everything when I saw it: the cufflinks he was wearing were dominos. A five and a six. I took a step backwards and tripped on a stack of papers.

"Christopher?"

"Sir?"

"Something the matter?"

"No. Nothing." My mind was racing. There had always been something slightly sinister about him. The murders could not be a coincidence. He was away a lot with his job. This whole trail he had Minty go on, lying to his wife. I couldn't risk telling him the truth. I just hoped he wouldn't kill me next. I gulped.

"Araminta's still in Canterbury," I lied. "We realised we needed to go back and we thought I could explain it to you and you'd smooth things over whereas my Mum would go ape if I went missing."

"And what have you found?"

"Well, actually we found this poem and it all pointed to this chapel in the Cathedral. Minty managed to persuade the Guide to take her up the bell tower today which we think the last clue is pointing to. I'm afraid of heights anyway." At least the last part was true.

"So where is she staying?"

"Oh, a hotel called the Farringdon Arms. It seems nice. She said you'd given her some money?"

"I had. So should I expect her back this evening?"

"Or tomorrow I suppose. You could always call her. I sent her a message earlier but I think she was out of signal."

"I'll do that. Thank you Christopher."

"Thank you."

I turned to leave and reached my hand out for the door when Dr Stirling's large paw took hold of the handle before I could.

"Oh and Christopher?"

"Yes?"

"Let's keep this little chat between us, shall we? No need to trouble my wife with it all."

"Of course."

I walked as calmly and slowly as I could out of the room, down the winding staircase and across the gravel drive before I started sprinting.

The thought occurred to me to simply travel back to Munich and watch out for Minty but, with two versions of ourselves already running about there I didn't want to risk another jump. Besides, I might easily miss her.

I increased my pace as I turned the corner of her street and, not watching where I was going, bumped into someone.

"Sorry," I muttered. I was grasped about the scruff of the neck.

"Chris! What are you doing?" It was Immanuel.

Trying to catch my breath, I stood, back arched, panting at the ground.

"Come on, let's sit down," he said.

There was a bench a few houses up. I knew it to be a place where the druggies go to do their dodgy dealings so, normally, I wouldn't sit there, but I was sure Immanuel could handle a few chavs, should any show up.

"Why are you here?" I asked.

"Isn't that obvious? I'm here to help you find Araminta."

"You know where she is?"

"No, Chris, that's why I said I'm here to help you *find* her."

"Oh. So how did you know she was missing?"

"I've been following you since Munich. I just got a little delayed. You did well, there."

"Thanks. Look, do you have any idea where she is or what happened to her?"

"Not exactly."

"What does that mean?" I asked.

"I have a gut feeling…but you're not going to like it."

Part Three

For there is nothing either good or bad, but THINKING MAKES IT SO.

- Shakespeare, *Hamlet* II.2

CHAPTER FORTY-SEVEN

Araminta's eyes adjusted slowly to her new surroundings. She thought she would have become accustomed to the jolting and the accompanying dizziness by now but this time trip seemed to have been the worst so far.

"It's OK; you're safe. Don't fight it, just let yourself adjust normally," she could hear, murkily – as if she were underwater.

She could sense light – blues and reds. And it was loud. She inhaled: a cool, crisp air. She was outside. She could see now. A vast city of tall skyscrapers and flashing lights. Something whistled overhead. A car?

Araminta fainted.

When she came to, she was inside what she took to be a high rise apartment, laying on a white chaise lounge with a glass of water on a metal table at its side. Jeremy was playing a brown grand piano opposite her. She recoiled instinctively and he stopped playing.

"It's all right. You're safe." Araminta clearly didn't trust him.

"I'm not going to hurt you," he insisted.

Araminta sat up.

"Where am I?"

"My apartment. Well the one I have here, at least."

"And where is, 'here?'"

"Perhaps the better question to ask would be 'when.'"

Araminta might have expected such a retort. She looked out of the window – or, rather, the sheet of glass that served as one of the walls. This was like no city she knew.

"The future?"

"I told you we can't travel into the future."

"You don't have to be so pedantic," she said.

Jeremy grunted a laugh. "I think that's the first time somebody has accused me of pedantry. You are right, I suppose. Time is a matter of perspective."

"What year is this?" she asked.

"2517. The Present. This is the last stop on the Chronosphere. Beyond it, everything is unknown."

"You see I don't understand that. Surely people from, say 2527 could travel back to now?" said Araminta.

"They could. Possibly. But all the Chronospheres we have, have been manufactured in the past fifteen or so years. And since the temporal war started, we have developed technology to prevent unauthorised spheres from materialising here."

"And who, exactly, is 'we?'"

Jeremy pointed to a tower block to the left side of the city. Araminta could make out the letters *HIS* on the side.

"*The Historical Improvement Society* headquarters," said Jeremy, proudly.

"I thought it was a faction. That looks more like a corporate or government building."

"It's probably a little of both."

Araminta looked down at the street. People were moving about, close enough to see their expressions. They could only be about –

"Ten storeys high. Yes." Araminta hated it when Jeremy did that.

"They look happy," she said.

"Why shouldn't they?"

"Is this a good place?"

"I like it."

"So why did you bring me here?"

"Better get some rest, Araminta. There's a lot I have to show you in the morning."

"That's not an answer."

"No." he said. "It isn't."

CHAPTER FORTY-EIGHT

"Well?" I asked Immanuel.

"First things first, Chris – we need to go somewhere safe where we're not wasting time."

"What do you mean?"

"I mean that every second we spend in your present isn't one we can return to without causing a small paradox. Here; hold on."

Immanuel took out his Chronosphere and held it out to me. I touched it and held my breath for the train jolt.

The air smelled good and it was warm. Summer. We had materialised in a copse by a great lake and the sun was reflecting off the surface of the water like a Christmas tree, bouncing light off the tinsel; or, rather, I supposed, it was the Christmas tree that was like the lake; for as sunlight kissed the surface of the water I felt as though this were the first example of such a thing – the purest form of light being reflected. I could feel a Magic stirring there, as Poseidon and the river gods of folklore came to life. And it was quiet.

"'An impulse from a vernal wood may teach you more of man, Of moral evil and of good than all the sages can.'" Immanuel recited, and inhaled deeply.

"I love this place!" he said and ran down to the water's edge. I wanted to press him about Araminta, but there was something about the place that made me want to be very still and to rest. The surface of the lake was smooth and tight like the skin of a drum. A swan stood and beat its wings, sending vibrations across the timpani. I closed my eyes listened for the music and then watched the ripples spread wider until they had disappeared.

"Should we be here?" I asked at last.

"How do you mean?"

"Ripples. Won't we change something? When are we?"

"Chris, just enjoy it. Do you see anyone about?"

"No."

"We're far too early for that. The Lake District never really seems to change though."

"What about Ara–?"

"Just...just relax, Chris. Take in the view. This is where Wordsworth will come to write and the Novum Treaty be signed."

"But time is –" I pleaded.

"No. We have all the time in the world, Chris. This is what the 'Spheres give us. Wherever Araminta is, we'll get to her precisely when we need to."

CHAPTER FORTY-NINE

They were standing at the bottom of the *HIS* building. Businessmen in suits passed, looking as if they were walking down Oxford Street on their way to work.

"Some fashions stick longer than others," said Jeremy, again seeming to read Araminta's mind. "Shall we?" He motioned to a large revolving door at the foot of the building which looked like something from the 1960s. He paused and looked up at a beam of light above the door which scanned him as he stepped inside.

Five armed guards stood sentinel and silent. A silver reception desk was positioned slightly to the right. Behind it, stood a young brunette, holding a thin piece of glass which she seemed to fold in half as she looked up at us.

"Good morning, Assistant Director."

"Good morning Lisa," said Jeremy.

Araminta raised her eyebrow in surprise at hearing Jeremy's title and followed him across the hallway into the lift at the end.

"Still using lifts, then?"

"My office," Jeremy instructed. The doors closed and Araminta felt them move sideways and up.

"Some improvements," he said curtly as the doors reopened into a bright, blue room, where a young man stood, dressed in a navy pinstripe suit, complete with red tie; hands clasped behind his back.

"This is Mr Rains. He'll give you a tour, whilst I attend to a few matters," said Jeremy.

Araminta still felt displaced but the man smiled at her warmly and shook her hand.

"If you'd care to follow me, Miss?" Araminta looked back at Jeremy who nodded and then sat down behind a desk in the corner of the room. She did as she was told.

"I know – it's pretty daunting at first, isn't it?" said Mr Rains, sweeping back a mop of unruly blond hair.

"What is?"

"Coming here. First time I took a trip to this century I passed out!" he said, cheerfully as they turned a corner.

"You're not from this time?" asked Araminta.

"No. I'm from yours, I think? I was born in 1985."

"So what are you doing here?"

"Well, you see, the *HIS* has been in existence for far longer than the technology it utilises. We recruit across the last five centuries," he said.

"What does that mean?"

"It means, in practice, that I work, for the most part, back in the 21st Century. I come here about once a month now to check in with head office."

"So there are people, back at home, working for the *HIS*, now?" asked Araminta.

"Yes. And before then."

"*Before?*"

"You've heard of Area 51?"

Araminta scarcely believed what she was hearing. It sounded too fantastic – like science fiction.

"Do you want to see bottom up or top down?" he asked.

"Which would you recommend?"

224

"Well, as we say in the business, it's all relative." He paused, as if awaiting some applause. Araminta realised he had meant to make a joke and laughed, politely.

"Let's start with the manufacturing chamber." He led Araminta into a lift and said, "Assembly."

A moment later, the doors opened on a large workshop area. About half a dozen people in white overalls were stood over different benches, fiddling with intricate equipment. Mr Rains patted one on the shoulder who switched off the machine she was using and removed a pair of goggles.

"This is Amelia. She's in charge up here. Amelia, would you mind explaining to Miss Stirling what we do here?"

"Not at all." She had a sweet, high voice, and Araminta liked her immediately.

"This is where we build the 'Spheres. Each agent has his or her own Chronosphere, programmed accordingly."

"There aren't many of you making them," Araminta observed.

"That's because we don't make many: only as necessity arises. Most of the 'Spheres are disposable, you see. Not that we don't trust our operatives, but we don't want them falling into the wrong hands – so it's more efficient to customise them," said Amelia.

Araminta was about to blurt out about her own Chronosphere but managed to hold her tongue and instead, pointed out that Jeremy's 'Sphere seemed able to take him anywhere.

"Indeed. But then he is the Assistant Director. You could hardly expect him to have to come down here every time he needed to travel somewhere!" Amelia stopped at a workbench where a thin sheet of glass was being pasted onto the inside of a 'Sphere.

"Is that glass I keep seeing everyone use?" asked Araminta.

"It's a sort of synthetic, partially organic, translucent digital paper we've developed. A bit like a microchip I suppose only much more efficient. And flexible. This is, essentially, the computer component of the 'Sphere," she explained. They moved to the right where another worker was painting something onto the outer shell.

"DNA recognition technology. We can't afford it to be highjacked by an outsider. Jing here is an expert at genetic coding." Jing smiled through her mask.

"The other stages are pretty technical and fairly boring. But, essentially, if you're a regular agent, or even if you're in RA, you have to come here to get your passport to the past!" said Amelia.

"RA?" asked Araminta. She hated it when people spoke in jargon.

"I'll explain that in a moment," said Mr Rains. "Amelia, thanks."

"Any time," she said and shook Araminta's hand.
"NEXT STOP: RA."

CHAPTER FIFTY

Immanuel was right. After everything that had happened, I needed some respite. The magical quality of the Lake seemed to heal the very weariness of my soul. It stood outside of all time and yet seemed to be all times. *This is where Arthur claimed Excalibur*, I found myself thinking, *and where Ophelia drowned.*

"A little too far North for King Arthur, I think," said Immanuel, as if he had read my thoughts.

"It feels enchanted," I said.

"'There are more things in heaven and earth, Horatio, than are dreamt of in your philosophy.'"

"What do you mean?"

Immanuel picked up a pebble and skimmed it across the water.

"I mean that what you call 'magic', and others, 'technology' and others, 'supernatural,' might be more like all of those things. When you've been time travelling as long as I have, you realise that the difference between myth and history is partly to do with memory and partly to do with something else that we haven't quite understood yet, and perhaps never will. You know, there is a faction in the

26th Century who call themselves the De-Mythologers. Their mission is to find the historical basis of legends such as Robin Hood and King Arthur and Jesus and take out all the poetry. So far, all they've done is have one of their members burned as a witch in 1083 – which I find somewhat ironic."

There was a far-off look in his eye and I began to sense a great weariness within him. There was a mist on the water now, and it seemed as if heaven itself had come to settle on the earth. I could have believed in gods and giants and dragons all at once. My mind was frantically searching through my memory to recall whatever it was that I had forgotten which was giving me the strangest feeling of déjà vu.

"The wood between the worlds," said Immanuel, wistfully. And that was it, precisely – that in-between place in *The Magician's Nephew* that Digory's uncle sends them to when they first put on the rings. A timeless place.

Re-acquainted with the memory of a childhood book and the thought of Digory's friend, Polly, I sprang to my feet and said, rather sharply: "Now look – we can't hang around here forever! What about Minty?"

CHAPTER FIFTY-ONE

"This is my department," said Mr Rains as the lift opened into a large, open plan room bustling with people sat at desks, pouring over sheets of glass. A sign hanging from the ceiling opposite read RISK ASSESSMENT.

"What do you do?" asked Araminta.

"OK, so, basically, the Board meets to decide what trips they want to run. They do some preliminary homework and then they send it down to us. Our job is to research the era and find out if there are any potential risks to time travellers."

"What sort of risks?" she asked.

"Well, risks like language barriers or mad emperors; an unknown plague or a natural disaster that hasn't been recorded. Sometimes it's because there's a witch hunt going on, or it might be that there are members of other factions already present in that era."

"And how do you assess these risks?"

"Well, we have to go back. But we're not allowed to interact, only observe. Then we report our findings, calculate the risks and submit our findings to the Probability Department."

"Do you ever get it wrong?" asked Araminta.

"Sometimes. That's the risk, obviously. An experienced risk assessor will err on the side of caution. There are some eras considered so high risk we won't even send Assessors back. The only time you can be sure is when you get an ANR," said Mr Rains, as if that were meant to mean something to Araminta.

"What's that?"

"Assessor Not Returned. You see, the 'Spheres are programmed to transport you back after a certain amount of time and they can withstand pretty much anything. So if a 'Sphere returns without its Assessor you can be sure it's not safe."

"So you just abandon her?"

Mr Rains looked at the floor sheepishly, which Araminta took as an ashamed affirmation.

"So it's actually a pretty dangerous job?" she said.

"Sometimes. Mostly it's just pretty dull. The boys upstairs have all the real fun."

"Upstairs?"

"Alternative Futures. Probability."

"Well, Mr Rains," said Araminta, deliberately fluttering her eyelashes. "What are we waiting for?"

CHAPTER FIFTY-TWO

"Araminta could be anywhen, Chris – that's the truth of it; it is imperative that we find her in the right era."

"What does that mean?"

"You know by now that time is not exactly linear – we fold it, change it. This point in time is, for you, after last January 2015, yet it is thousands of years ago."

"Right," I said, still confused.

"So the only way in which time is at all linear, is in the way in which we experience it: every person on the planet has their own personal timeline. Most people's are straightforward – they are born in one era, they live and die. Yours and mine are more complicated. Now, if we were to find Araminta in a point, halfway through her timeline and pick her up, it might change everything else for her, so it is important that we figure out where she went directly after Munich and, if possible, retrieve her from thence or her next port of call."

"Now I'm totally confused: wouldn't it be better to do the opposite? Surely we need to pick her up at the end of her trail otherwise we'd change her timeline?" I said.

"Yes, Chris, but as I suspect that Jeremy's lot have recruited her to change the past, we need to prevent that from happening."

I was confused. One of the main problems with this whole experience was knowing whom I should trust, for everyone seemed to be serving their own purposes. I had the distinct feeling that Immanuel was trying to use me as a pawn in his game of temporal chess with Jeremy. Still, I reasoned, perhaps it didn't matter if I were aware of it. The important thing was to find Araminta and find her safe. Once reunited we could deal with the rest.

"So, what leads do we have?"

Immanuel took something out of his pocket which looked like a small sheet of glass. He unfolded it and passed it to me.

"It seems Araminta has a fair few adventures ahead of her."

I looked at the glass which began to flicker with a series of dates and pictures of documents, like watching the opening title sequence of *Quantum Leap: 1859, 1895, 1942, 1985* were amongst the numbers that flashed.

"How did you get these?"

"It doesn't matter. But do you notice how several are clumped together?"

"Around the nineteenth century?"

"Yes. Now what do you make of that?"

I tried to rack my brains but drew a blank.

"If we work from the assumption that the *Historical Improvement Society* is behind Araminta's disappearance, then we should concentrate on what we know of their mission," he said.

"Which is?"

"Well, what did Jeremy have you do last time?"

CHAPTER FIFTY-THREE

The Probability Boys, as they called themselves, were the heart of the *Historical Improvement Society:* they had the onerous, yet essential, task of calculating the possible causal outcomes of changing past events. According to Mr Rains, this required expertise in the fields of maths, history, philosophy and temporal mechanics.

"Did you make up that last field?" asked Araminta.

"Temporal mechanics? Certainly not. I've got a first class degree in it from Oxford."

"Oh. Sorry."

Araminta looked around the room. It was circular in dimensions. Something resembling a timeline ran like an Arthurian table in the centre and the men (for they were all men) were busying themselves pointing at places on the map, arguing and furiously scribbling on sheets of glass. Two men over in the far left seemed to be in the middle of a fierce argument:

"I'm telling you – he had it coming. I mean I literally could have predicted it. He forgot Jackson's Fourth Law!" said one.

"It wasn't Robert's fault – the Assistant Director insisted! He – " The second man looked up as he noticed the two visitors.

"Excuse me," he said, apologetically, "my colleague and I were having a professional disagreement." He was tall, with a mop of grey hair and green eyes.

"I'm just showing Miss Stirling around on a little tour. She's a guest of the AD," said Mr Rains.

"Oh, well, look; I…" the man faltered, clearly worried his erstwhile mutinous allusions had been overheard.

"It's all right. I have no idea what's going on here. I'm from 2015," said Araminta cheerily.

"Oh. Oh I see. Well, would you like me to explain what we're doing? Rains is all right but he's only RA and they don't really know one line of a temporal equation from the other!" Mr Rains tried to hide his disdain with a wry smile and Araminta affirmed her interest.

"Well this is a sort of time-line simulator. We programme in scenarios and we should be able to see the ripple effect that the change has on the timeline. Now, the further back in time, the greater the ripple. For example, if we were to go back to yesterday and warn Malcolm not to cross the road until he had looked left again, he wouldn't be in sick bay. Not a big deal. If we went back to 2340 and persuaded Lucy Jackson to join the a cappella group instead of the Temporal Mechanics club at University we wouldn't have the Four Laws. That would lead to all kinds of calculation disasters and we would probably have destroyed the entire human story. Do you see?" The details were lost on Araminta, but she was beginning to understand, although one thing confused her:

"Well, obviously I have no clue what you are actually talking about, but I think I get the gist. One thing that confuses me is how you can track changes to the timeline – I thought without the protection of the Chronosphere you travel with, you can't remember what should have happened?"

A third man who had, evidently, been eavesdropping butted in: "Well, you see this entire building is protected with a sort of temporal shielding which makes everyone in it impervious to changes in the timestream."

"Timeline," corrected the grey-haired man. "Do try to use standard terminology. It avoids confusion." The third man scowled and turned his back on Araminta.

"David's quite right, of course," he continued; "there could be a nuclear apocalypse and we would remain unharmed. In fact, I believe you witnessed that little miscalculation first hand?"

Mr Rains took something out of his pocket and checked it.

"Excuse us," he said, "the AD wants to see us."

Araminta muttered a "thank you" to the Probability Boys and followed Mr Rains into the lift once more, thinking that little had changed for gender equality in five hundred years.

CHAPTER FIFTY-FOUR

"I thought we proved killing Hitler only made things worse. What makes you think Jeremy's lot are still obsessed with all that?" I asked.

"I think the *HIS* believe that if they go back far enough they can prevent the ideas behind Nazism which might, in turn, prevent World War Two *and* that horrific nuclear apocalypse," said Immanuel.

"Well, how far back is 'far enough?'"

"That, Chris, is the million dollar question. You see, the fallacy that the *HIS* operate from is that time travellers know more about the past than historians. In fact, the opposite is probably truer because historians are only slightly less arrogant than time travellers and use a greater variety of sources."

"I'm not sure I'm following you," I said. My stomach rumbled and I realised it must have been hours since I last ate. No good asking for a Mars bar or a Jammie Dodger. The only thing edible in sight was a prickly looking bush with dubious fruit growing on it.

"The Historical Improvement Society employs a number of people to calculate the possible causal outcomes of tampering with past events. They believe that by understanding the effects of these causes, they can alter the timeline for the better."

"Yes, I understand all that." I paused, waiting for him to say something new.

"Well, the problem is, when you look at Nazism, the ideas aren't all that new: so the dates 1895 and 1859 should have set off alarm bells," said Immanuel.

"Why?"

"They're the publication dates of two rather inflammatory books – Nietzsche's *The Anti-Christ* and –"

"*Origin Of Species*," I interjected, suddenly remembering Mr Travis' lesson. "So, what you're saying is that these books influenced Hitler?"

"Possibly. I'm not sure, but I think *Jeremy* believes they did, and that's the key."

"So he's sent Araminta back to kill Darwin now?"

"I don't think it's quite like that. Also, they do tend to work backwards, so 1895 would probably be an earlier trip."

"Right. So is that where we're going?" I asked.

"No."

"Then where?"

"We need to return to your present, Chris. It's the only way to determine what's been changed."

CHAPTER FIFTY-FIVE

The lift opened into the Board Room. It was very much like a 21st century Board Room.

Jeremy was sat in an old-fashioned leather chair at the head of a glass table. Five others were sat around the table and each turned to look at Araminta as she stepped forward. Jeremy nodded slightly to Rains who smiled and stepped back inside the lift. Jeremy extended an open palm, inviting Araminta to sit down which she did, silently. Jeremy cocked his head and she realised she was supposed to say something.

"It's quite an impressive place," she said.

Jeremy laughed. "I suppose that is *quite* a compliment." He stood and went over to one of the windows on his left.

"Do you see that man being escorted out of the building?" Araminta stood to join him. They were too high up for her to see with any definition. Jeremy tapped on the glass and a live camera feed appeared on display. A blond man wearing a brown suit with a blue shirt was having something attached to his arm by two security guards. He looked up at the camera and nodded. Without warning, the man suddenly vanished into thin air.

"So long, Robert Barrington Junior," said Jeremy. "Enjoy your retirement in Auschwitz."

Araminta tried to hide her horror.

"It seemed fitting. After all, it was his error that probably caused – or re-caused the Holocaust," said Jeremy.

"How can you be so callous?" asked Araminta.

"Look, I don't write the contracts, I just follow them. That's something to take up with the Director himself. Only I shouldn't recommend it." He sat down in his chair and waited for Araminta to follow suit. The other ten pairs of eyes were boring into her; she could feel their gaze permeating the very fibres of her being, judging her. She felt as if she were on trial in a foreign country. She didn't understand what she was accused of. She didn't understand the language. She just wanted to go home.

"We'd like to offer you a job, Araminta," said Jeremy at length. She laughed, involuntarily.

"Something amuses you?"

"It's just that that was, like, the thing I *least* expected you to say! I'm not sure what that even means!" she said. One of the women sitting opposite Araminta cleared her throat and began to speak, not unkindly:

"It means, Miss Stirling, being looked after. For all possible contingencies. Our operatives have an excellent Ensurance Package."

"Look, I won't even be fifteen till next May, I'm not really interested in life insurance. Or any other insurance come to that."

"I didn't say *in*surance, my dear, I said *en*surance." Araminta looked confused. The woman smiled – a saccharine smile, through bright blue lipstick that made Araminta feel slightly nauseous.

"Let me ask you this: what disturbed you most about your little visit to Alternative Future 416?" said the woman.

"She means the post-apocalyptic 2015 you experienced," interjected Jeremy.

"What do you mean? The entire experience was disturbing, Jeremy. No thanks to you. And that's another thing: just how *did* you manage to escape?"

"Because I think," continued the woman, ignoring the exchange between Araminta and Jeremy, "that what should disturb me most, is the thought that I might have been born into that god-forsaken world and know no difference. Or, that I might not have been born at all."

"Well," said Araminta slowly, "I think you're wrong actually. Isn't ignorance bliss? Surely it's worse to know there's a better alternative that you can't return to?" She saw Jeremy smirk in her peripheral vision.

"The *Historical Improvement Society* can ensure that you are never thrust into an alternative timeline in which you were not born or should not want to live: working for us would protect you from the usual vulnerabilities of temporal warfare." The woman had clearly given this sales pitch a dozen times before.

"And all I have to do is...what exactly?" said Araminta, unimpressed.

"All you have to do, Miss Stirling, is help us catch a killer." The blue lips pursed. Jeremy nodded at an older man with a streak of floppy white hair. He pressed the glass table and activated a display. News stories covered the table from the past. Mutilated bodies lay sprawled across pavements, desks and fields. On each of the victims, a different domino piece.

"The Domino Killer? But that's from my own time," said Araminta.

"Precisely," said Jeremy. "You see, we usually like to recruit members who can work, predominantly in their own era. We find they're better at spotting anachronisms and it also reduces the risk of displacement."

"I still don't understand what you want from me?" said Araminta.

"We would like you to be our eyes and ears in 2015: track this killer down and help us to bring him to justice." said Jeremy.

"Why are you so interested in this case? Surely it's just some lunatic going around stabbing people. He probably wants to be famous."

"This was sent in by one of our Risk Assessors yesterday," said the white-haired man, bringing up an image of a woman laying on a cobbled street; her throat slit and a domino in her mouth with three dots visible. She was wearing a Victorian hoop dress.

"What year was this, Hendry?" asked Jeremy.

"1844," said the white-haired man.

"1844!" repeated Jeremy emphatically. "Now are you beginning to see, Araminta?"

Araminta looked at the evidence on the table and considered the burden of responsibility. After everything she had gone through – after everything Jeremy had put her through, she could scarcely believe he had the audacity to ask her for this. She summoned her courage and took a deep breath.

"You've coerced me, kidnapped me, done all manner of unspeakable things and withheld basic truths from me and now you expect me to help you hunt down – what, a member of this Domino Group? You know the only person that seemed to show us any real kindness was that Immanuel? And what's the story there? Are you, like, his evil twin or what?"

Jeremy put his hand up in resignation. "I'm sorry. Minty, please –"

"Don't call me that," warned Araminta.

"Sorry. Again."

The woman with blue lips took up Jeremy's mantle now:

"The Domino Group aren't responsible for the murders, Miss Stirling; they are the victims."

Araminta looked back at Jeremy who nodded his assent.

"But I don't understand: I thought you were at war with The Domino Group? I would have thought you had ordered these...*hits*, if that's what they are?"

The aspersion was visibly repugnant to Jeremy.

"Just who do you think we are, exactly? We're not savages!"

Araminta remained unflinching; she was clearly bemused, if not perturbed by the whole prospect. Jeremy considered for a moment.

"We do not kill agents from other factions unless it is absolutely necessary, Araminta. The Domino Group tries to foil our plans but we have superior technology. They have better agents. I suppose you might say there is a sort of truce between us. Since this war started, the *HIS* has only ordered nine kills. None of those were other time travellers."

"Who, then?" she asked.

"Men you have not heard of. Men like Adolf Hitler. Men who do not now exist. You see, we prefer to discipline time travellers in our own time. We are quite civilised. There's a court of law and due process."

"What about that man you just sent to Auschwitz?"

"Oh he won't die there. Just a little disciplinary procedure. A fortnight. No more," said Hendry, in defence.

"So you think this Domino Killer is another time traveller but not an *HIS* agent or a member of The Domino Group?" asked Araminta.

The woman with blue lipstick started to hypothesise:

"He – or she, I suppose – is targeting Domino Group members – sometimes even before they have been recruited; so it has to be someone who has access to The Domino Group database. Which makes me think it's an inside job."

A murmur went around the table indicating a general consensus.

"Forgive me, but I don't see what this has to do with you, on the opposite side of the so-called war? And I'm pretty sure it has nothing to do with me. Frankly, I'm tired. I haven't been to school in a month and I'm probably really behind – and I know you'll say that time is relative but it's not to me – I've forgotten all the German vocab I was meant to learn for a test tomorrow. Or three weeks ago. Or whenever. I just want to go home and have a bath. All right?"

Hendry smiled at her. It seemed genuine.

"Firstly, Araminta, I explained to you that 26th Century politics were convoluted, but you should think of us as the peace keepers: or at least the regulators of time travel," said Jeremy. "There are many factions: some of them violent and many of them using time travel in what we consider the 'wrong' way but we know who they are and, to an extent, they are sanctioned by governments or corporations. Think of the First World War and imagine what would have happened if, in the middle of the Somme, a renegade Korean started taking pot shots at the Germans and the Allies. Secondly, of course; if that's what you want. What you *really* want." It sounded like a loaded question.

"To go home? You know it is."

"Very well," said Jeremy, standing. He motioned towards the lift. "Of course," he said suddenly, as if he had just changed his mind, "I understand you not wanting to help people you don't know. Why should you? All these Domino Group members – these potential targets – they're nobodies. Anonymous." The lift doors opened.

"I only have one other question." Araminta turned as he said, softly: "Do you know who your Father works for?"

CHAPTER FIFTY-SIX

I was beginning to feel like a tennis ball, being knocked back and forth by two players of equal skill, who bore no regard for the feelings of their racquets. We materialised metres from where we had been – a stone's throw from the bench (even by the way I throw stones). Nothing seemed out of the ordinary; in fact the same Asda bag was being blown across the road as it had a minute (or, rather, several hours) before.

"Appearances can be deceptive," warned Immanuel. The thought then occurred to me that events might have been changed before I arrived back in 2015 from Munich – after all, if I hadn't travelled with Araminta, I would not be protected from those changes. Immanuel reassured me that the very fact I was thinking that meant that nothing really had changed in that period.

"Of course," he added, "that might just be because you are about to go back to all those time periods and prevent the *HIS* from changing them." He laughed and I hoped he was joking.

"I think I should go home now," I said, tentatively. The truth of the matter was that I was ravenous, shattered and befuddled. I just wanted to have a Big Mac and go to sleep and discover this was all a dream."

"Agreed."

It wasn't too far to walk and we spent most of it in silence. As we approached the house I turned to say to Immanuel that it might be better if he didn't come inside but he anticipated this and volunteered to remain around the corner whilst I ascertained who was in.

As I'd thought, Mum was at work and Kirsty was obviously still at her boyfriend's house, so I came out to let Immanuel in and we went up to my room.

"Do houses look very different in the future?" I asked, trying to make small talk.

"Well, you know you shouldn't know too much about the future."

"Fine; don't tell me." That usually did the trick with my friends.

"People still need something to sleep on, sit on and eat off." he said.

"Fair enough."

Immanuel was looking round my room with either suspicion or awe (it was difficult to tell). He picked up a snow globe of the Eiffel Tower I kept as a paper weight. It was the last present my Dad ever gave me. He'd been there on a trip with his girlfriend. I had always wanted to go.

"Have you been to Paris?" I asked him.

"It was me who picked out the paint for the Eiffel Tower. They were going to use white, would you believe?"

"Really?"

"No. I'm kidding. Although I have been. A few times. My favourite time to visit is the 1920s. Although about now is pretty good too. There's a man who sells violet ice cream in the Latin Quarter."

"You must be a frequent visitor to know that," I said.

"Part of the job is noticing the little details. It makes it easier to spot changes. Now, have a careful look round your room and tell me if anything is different."

The problem with my room is that it's pretty small and usually untidy. I scanned around. "Everything seems to be in order. Well, disorder I suppose. You'll have to excuse the mess."

"Good. That makes things better, although not necessarily easier."

"How do you mean?"

"If something obvious were different then it would give us a clue as to where to look," said Immanuel.

"Right."

I heard the front door open and Immanuel shot to attention like a scared rabbit. Heels clumped noisily up the stairs. I popped my head out of my room to see Kirsty, dressed in a pink hoodie and short skirt, taking her earphones out.

"Tea ready?" she said.

"Dunno. I just got in myself," I said, as casually as I could.

Kirsty stopped and scowled at me.

"Chris! It's your turn to cook!"

"Sorry! Like I say, I just got in."

"From where?"

The floorboard creaked in my room. Kirsty tried to look past me.

"You got someone here?" she asked.

"Um..."

"Chris, have you got a *girl* in your room?!"

At this, Immanuel came out and stood behind me.

"Chris, why is there a strange man in the house?"

"Um...Freecycle?" I said, quickly.

"Freecycle?"

"Yeah. This is Immanuel. He's come to see if he wants that book case I've been trying to get rid of."

Awkward silence.

"So are you going to cook tea or not?" she asked.

"Yes. All right! Just give me a minute, ok?"

Kirsty's phone beeped.

"Oh. Well I've gotta go out again actually. But I'll be back by Seven so you can leave mine in the microwave, ok?"

"Sure," I said, smiling. Immanuel stood there, staring at Kirsty who dashed into her room, changed her heels for trainers and ran down the stairs again and out the door.

"I know!" I said: "I can't believe we're related, either!"

CHAPTER FIFTY-SEVEN

Araminta was still trying to process what Jeremy meant when the floor started to shake. She had experienced several quakes from her years living abroad and resisted the urge to scream, although she was certainly caught off guard. The lift doors were still open and, as she peered into it, a ball of fire erupted. Jeremy dived on top of her.

"Get down!"

The fireball engulfed the ceiling. A sound of shattering glass filled her ears and a cold blast of wind entered in place of the windows. Then the floor gave way. Now she screamed.

It was as if they were on a large ship pitching on the waves in a terrible storm. Araminta felt herself sliding towards the broken window. A hand was on her foot. She looked behind her. It was Hendry. He had his own legs wrapped around the legs of the table and was trying to prevent her from falling to her death. A creaking sound and a steel beam crashed through the ceiling and sliced through the floor beneath them, pinning Hendry's torso underneath. He let go of her leg.

Araminta fell.

It was black and cold. She felt the wind rush by her and imagined angels struggling to bear her up to heaven, pitted against a stronger, darker force that dragged her down.

If she could have seen the *HIS* building, she would have thought she were watching old footage of the terrorist attacks on the World Trade Centre. A huge explosion had cut a hole right out of the centre, where the *I* of *Improvement* ran down and the whole building was leaning like a domino before it falls.

Something glinted in the corner of her eye like a sliver of moon, white and smooth. She thought how beautiful it was. How near and far away. She thought of her parents and felt a solitary tear form in her right eye. It began to fall down her face, slower than she was falling.

The sliver of moon shone brighter and Araminta smiled. It was the last thing she saw.

She hit the ground.

CHAPTER FIFTY-EIGHT

A shiver went down my spine.

"Chris?" asked Immanuel.

"Yeah?"

"You ok?"

"Think so."

We were still in my room, trying to figure our next move.

"Do you still have the parchment you found at the Tudor House?" said Immanuel.

"Yes," I said, not thinking to ask how he knew about that. I had managed to get it off Minty without her noticing and now thought how pathetic I was to mistrust her.

It was in my Dictionary. Kirsty had a nasty habit of going through my stuff so if I wanted to keep anything safe I had to hide it in plain sight, in something she wouldn't be interested in. Generally, reference books were pretty safe.

I took it off the shelf and opened it to *anachronism* which had seemed an appropriate place to stuff the parchment. Immanuel picked it up carefully and examined it.

"Have you got a match handy?" he asked.

"A match? What do you want a match for?" Immanuel didn't wait for my response. He wandered out of my room, down the stairs and began rummaging about in the drawers of the sideboard that stood in the dining room.

"Eureka!" he said, rattling a box of matches triumphantly.

"What are you doing?"

"Here, hold this," he instructed, passing me the parchment. "Nice and tight." He struck a match and held it behind the parchment. Slowly, some letters began to form.

"Really? Invisible ink?" I almost laughed.

"How do you think things become clichés, Chris?"

I watched in wonder as the letters formed words: *Chris. Come get me. 51.40330.3375-15412310A.* I grabbed the parchment from Immanuel's hand and stood, staring at it.

"What does it mean?"

Immanuel withdrew the sheet of folded glass from his pocket again and placed it on top of the parchment. It seemed to scan it and he pressed a few buttons. The suspense was killing me.

"Coordinates. Space-time coordinates!" he announced.

"For where?"

"Don't you mean for whom?"

I furrowed my eyebrows in confusion.

"For Araminta, Chris! This must have been the reading on her 'Sphere."

"'Sphere? Immanuel, tell me what's going on."

"What's going on, is that we're going to get a change of clothes," he announced, cheerily. "And, then, we're going to pay a little visit to Henry VIII!"

CHAPTER FIFTY-NINE

Her first thought was that she was dead. In a way, this comforted her; Araminta had always hoped there would be an afterlife and part of her was disappointed when her eyes opened to a blue, cloudless sky and a pain in her back. She let out a short, involuntary whimper.

"You're awake!" said a man's voice. It was soft, with a slight Welsh lilt. She could hear the cracking of wood burning and smelt something cooking.

"Where am I?" she murmured.

"Oh about twenty miles from Court now," said the voice.

"Court?"

The voice's owner came into view: a kindly, bearded face with deep set brown eyes and earthy hair. He smiled with blackened teeth. Araminta tried to move.

"Don't. You've had quite a fall," he cautioned.

"You saw me?"

"My man saw you hit the ground – although he couldn't ascertain from whence you fell. Pray, tell me the villainous tree that shook you from its boughs and I will cut it down and burn its treacherous branches limb by limb."

Araminta tried to laugh but it hurt too much.

"Tell me, my lady, where is your horse? Might I fetch it for you?" he said.

She looked closer and noticed her rescuer was wearing a ruff – the sort that the Tudors wore in her history books. Two questions presented themselves: where was the Chronosphere and how could she use it to get home? She sensed that the man was waiting for an answer.

"I...he must have bolted when we were attacked," she said.

"Attacked?"

"Bandits. I was with my...Father and...now we're separated and we're lost," said Araminta, hoping it sounded plausible enough.

"There's not much we can do for you here, my lady. If you think you have the strength to make it to Court, there are fine physicians there. I'm sure the King would be gracious to one so young and beautiful."

Araminta smiled and another man passed her rescuer a bowl.

"This is some soup of my own making," he said. "You should eat, if you can, and regain a little strength."

Araminta moved her head forward and he took it gently and guided a spoon of hot liquid into her mouth. It tasted good and she allowed him to feed her. If she believed in such things, Araminta would have said the soup were enchanted, for with each mouthful, she felt her strength return and her pain numb, although she could still not sit up.

"That really is a marvel," she said, trying to sound as Tudor-like as she could.

"Well, it has a little of my own remedy in."

"Are you a physician?"

"No, no. I'm an academic. But I dabble in herbs now and then," he said, modestly.

"And whose name should I mention in my prayers this evening when I thank the Lord for my rescue?" said Araminta, enjoying the role play.

"Wygan. Guy Wygan." He bowed low. "Your humble servant."

CHAPTER SIXTY

"I look ridiculous. Why did people wear this? Seriously!"

Immanuel had momentarily disappeared in time and returned with an assortment of ill-fitting garments which he forced me to put on.

"This collar's killing me!" I said, trying to adjust a starched ruff that was digging into the back of my neck.

"The collar is better than an executioner's block, Chris; and if you want to keep that head of yours you're going to have to look the part."

"Why does it have to be green? I hate wearing green! It clashes with my hair!" I said.

"It was in fashion. We can't very well go dressed as peasants or we won't get into Court."

"Which court would that be?"

"Hampton court. Now, are you ready? Taken off your watch? Good."

I didn't really get a chance to protest; I braced myself for the jolt.

Books don't have smells. They might have a scent about them – musty old books with yellowing pages, full of dust, or shiny new books whose pages are imbued with an alpine scent of fresh promise – but they don't prepare you for the sort of stench that 16th Century England had. It was all I could do not to vomit right onto the street. Mind you, if I had done, I doubt anyone would have noticed: I was very nearly hit in the face by some human waste as someone flung open a window and chucked the contents of a chamber pot over our heads. Fortunately, Immanuel pushed me forward and all I got was a bit of excrement on my boot, which I tried to wipe off as we shuffled along the dusty street.

"Quicken your pace, Chris; he who hesitates is usually robbed!"

There was a market directly ahead. Live animals baying, and merchants with linens and assorted foods stood haggling with customers. Immanuel went up to a stall selling relics. A man with a great ginger beard, dressed in a simple white linen shirt was trying to persuade a punter to part with some silver for some "wood of the True Cross." He looked up at Immanuel and frowned, as if trying to remember his patronage. Immanuel picked up an icon bearing the Madonna and Child with the letters *IHS* on and traced his finger slowly from the H to the I and then S. The bearded man looked about him quickly and then beckoned Immanuel closer.

"Come with me," he whispered.

We went behind the curtain of his stall and followed him down a narrow street to a great oak door. Again, looking about him first, the man opened it and bade us follow him inside.

There was not much light: only a high window facing north which let in little of the low sun. "Treuga Tempus." said the man.

"Treuga Tempus," repeated Immanuel, adding, "tempora mutantur et nos mutamur in illis."

The man looked at me, as if to utter some secret Latin password. I shrugged.

"He's not one of us," said Immanuel.

"*Us* or *you*?" asked the bearded man.

The two of them remained silent, as if sizing the other up for some moments, until the stranger invited us to sit and we found ourselves two wooden stools to perch on. They weren't comfortable.

"Well, firstly, perhaps I should tell you that I'm not quite who you think. I'm not *HIS* for starters," said Immanuel.

"It doesn't matter. You know we don't take sides," said the man.

"Perhaps. But I also know you're more sympathetic to our cause," said Immanuel.

"And what might that be?"

Immanuel withdrew something from inside his clothes and placed it in his hand. Being careful only to reveal half of the object, he held a golden domino piece out to the man. It had six dots on one side.

"You'd better put that away," he warned. "So; how may I help?"

Immanuel related to him the circumstances of our arrival in Tudor England, leaving out as much detail as he could about the Munich endeavour. On hearing of a damsel in distress, the man's tone changed and he became more helpful.

"As Time would have it, I did hear of a maiden pass through these parts not two days hence."

"You've been here too long old man," said Immanuel.

The man chortled and replied that it was a nicer way to talk.

"I'll see if I can find out more through our network. In the meantime, I suggest you stay here awhile; I'll see to the necessary documents and so forth." He nodded slightly at me and left us.

"He might have offered us some food!" I said.

CHAPTER SIXTY-ONE

Araminta grimaced as she tried to bear the pain of being jolted about in the back of a carriage as they made their way through woodland and onto the London road. Mr Wygan did his best to make polite conversation but he could see that she was clearly in distress. Every now and then he would make some comment about the weather or ask her opinion on some passage of scripture (evidently he was a theologian). Not being particularly religious, Araminta was a bit stumped but found if she let out a little moan of anguish, Mr Wygan would hold his tongue for two minutes at least.

On arriving at court, Mr Wygan was taken to be presented to the King, whilst Araminta was taken on a make-shift stretcher, into some sort of vestibule. All she could see were the ceilings.

She must have passed out because the next thing Araminta knew was that she was lying in a bed, being prodded in the ribs with a cold piece of metal by a man with appalling breath.

"Will she live?" said a disembodied voice.

"Oh, certainly, certainly," muttered the man peering over her. He leered through his toothless mouth at her and then shook his head: "Although she may not walk again."

CHAPTER SIXTY-TWO

"Want to tell me what's going on?" I asked Immanuel as soon as I was sure we were alone. "And what was all that Latin?"

"Treuga Tempus: Truce of Time. It's their motto," said Immanuel.

"Whose?"

Immanuel sighed. He didn't like telling me things about the future. Even though, according to him, 2015 is the past.

"Look, I told you there are several factions," he said.

"I remember."

"Well, the Tissot are a neutral faction. They've existed for some time now and their purpose is to ensure temporal warfare is conducted within the bounds of the London Treaty. They know some of our 'hot spots' – particular eras that attract a lot of time travel – and they imbed themselves into society and act as a sort of neutral embassy for time travellers. Some eras are pretty dangerous and the last thing anyone wants is for someone born in a thousand years' time to be burned as a witch or a heretic by some medieval lunatic."

"So how did you know he was one of them – the Tissot?"

"They publish a list of their 'embassies' in case we need them. And they tend to be ginger."

"Oh. Are they Scottish?" I asked.

"Swiss, actually."

"Oh, that's typical."

"Typical?"

"The Swiss are always neutral. At least that's the impression we get in my century. Swiss people are famous for chocolate, the alps, remaining neutral in every major conflict, cheese, euthanasia and Roger Federer," I said.

"Federer?"

"Tennis player."

"Right. I remember. You forgot watches," said Immanuel.

"Watches?"

"Yes. In fact, Tissot makes watches in your time."

"They do?"

"Yes. Not inexpensive ones."

There was a squeak as the door opened and the Tissot operative entered. Immanuel, who had risen to his feet in poised anxiety, sat down again.

"Do you want the good news or the bad?" he said.

"Why do people always say that?" I asked.

"It's a test of character."

"Right. What's the test?"

"People who want the good news first are hoping that it will sweeten the bad news; invariably they are so busy worrying what the bad news is, they don't enjoy the good news. They are essentially pessimistic. People who choose the bad news first are leaving the good news till later because they are hoping it will make the bad news bearable – they are essentially optimistic."

"Well," I said, "I'm essentially optimistic but I think it depends on your perspective as to whether the news is good or bad anyway."

"You're beginning to sound like Jeremy," Immanuel muttered. Then he said, aloud, "Just tell us what you know."

"Your friend is in the Palace, being attended to by one of the Court physicians."

I looked quickly at Immanuel and then asked: "Is that the good news or the bad?"

"Both," said the Tissot operative.

"Look, I think *21st* Century medicine is barbarism, Chris. You don't want to be ill in this century!" said Immanuel, by means of explanation.

"What's wrong with her?" I asked the Tissot operative.

"I believe she suffered some form of back injury."

"Her back?! Is she all right?!" I was suddenly struck with a sense of guilt. It was all my fault. She might be paralysed and it would all be my fault.

"She was found by the newly appointed Regius Professor of Divinity at Cambridge – a Mr Wygan. She's in good hands and no harm should come to her."

"We need to get to Court then," said Immanuel.

The operative inhaled sharply, marking his reticence.

"We cannot be party to any changes in the timeline or any actions that might lead to such changes," he said, parrot-fashion.

"I know that. We just want to extract her. If anything, it's her that is polluting the timeline. The longer she's here, the larger the ripples," said Immanuel. It seemed to satisfy the Tissot operative.

"Very well. You'll be needing these." He passed Immanuel some papers. "It says you're father and son. A noble family from Italy. Don't worry about the accents. Araminta is your daughter. She went missing when you were attacked by bandits, bringing a gift to His Majesty.

Now, pay attention and I'll tell you how to recognise my colleague who stands guard at the Palace entrance."

"Is he ginger, too?" I asked, and got a foul look from the two men.

CHAPTER SIXTY-THREE

If I ever made it home one of the things I intended to do was to write to the producers of *The Tudors* and say that Henry Tudor looked nothing like Jonathan Rhys Meyers. Neither was he like those famous portraits which just look a little ridiculous to us. What all images fail to capture is the sense of presence a person commands. In the same way that Hitler had seemed almost gentler – and perhaps the more vile, and dangerous for it – so Henry seemed more kingly. Perhaps I was simply in awe of the costumes and the sounds and smells of the court; certainly I was aware that if I put a foot wrong I very well might lose my head but something in the way he sat, enthroned and statesman-like in euphoric serenity – like a god watching his creatures, knowing they feared his whim – made me half believe in the Divine Right of Kings.

As in the 21st Century, the quiet efficiency of the Swiss was unimpeachable. We had been positively welcomed into the Palace and had waited behind a queue of other noblemen and dignitaries to be introduced to the King.

I bowed as low as I could and uttered a feeble, "Your Majesty." Immanuel did likewise; the King stared at us for a moment and nodded his head slightly. I had the distinct impression that he was waiting for something and I'd seen enough old *Blackadder* episodes to suspect he was expecting some sort of gift.

"I think he wants us to give him something," I whispered to Immanuel.

"Well, all I have is an apple and my Chronosphere," said Immanuel through gritted teeth as he tried to keep his smile fixed.

"Your Majesty," I said, as confidently as I could; "we are not so blessed as to be endowed with worldly riches to bestow upon thy Grace. Though had I all the kingdoms in the world and all thy riches it would not be enough for the love we bear thee. Yet, in our land, tis said that music be the food of love. Wherefore, O Majesty, permit me to perform a composition of my own making which, if it falls on kind ears shall outshine the wealth of a thousand suns and be remembered ever in thy honour as the King's piece."

In honesty I had not the foggiest idea what I was saying but I hoped it sounded Tudor-ish. To my embarrassment the King simply stared at me and burst into laughter. I looked sheepishly at Immanuel who shrugged and we stood there looking as out of place as a pair of lemons in a sausage factory.

"By all means," said the King.

"Is there a keyboard I might play, Majesty? I regret, we were unable to transport such an instrument."

I was sure I sounded like a complete idiot. My music history wasn't very good either and I wasn't even sure I'd be able to play the clavichord or whatever it was they had but, fortunately, when they brought up a virginal it seemed to have the basic keyboard layout.

A hush fell over the court as a chair was brought to me and I sat down, anxiously. The King leaned forward. I breathed in deeply and rested my thumb on E, and my second finger on G. My hand was shaking and I was worried I wouldn't be able to remember the tune. Then again, if no one had heard it then they wouldn't know if I played it right. This gave me confidence and I counted myself in a bar of 6/8 and began to play.

CHAPTER SIXTY-FOUR

Mr Wygan had been more than attentive and did not like to leave Araminta alone. He had spent the last few days sat by her bed reading to her from the Great Bible. Frankly, Araminta wasn't sure how much more she could stand of the Song of Solomon and began to suspect he had a somewhat ulterior motive.

"Read me the story of Jesus healing the lame man?" She said, half remembering something from Sunday school. Mr Wygan smiled and obliged. There was something comforting in the story: the faith of the man's friends, their dedication in bringing him to this healer. Her mind wandered as Wygan described them lowering their friend through the roof. Did the guy who owned the house sue them? Was it even an open top roof? Then she remembered she didn't believe any of the story anyway. The pain came back and she closed her eyes for a moment but every time she did she began to see herself falling again. She thought of her Mother, shut away in her Study, writing away about some future past. As Jesus talked to the lame man, Wygan read to her, her Father lectured in Cambridge,

Hitler spoke in the Beer Hall and Jeremy shouted for her to take cover.

All times converged.

CHAPTER SIXTY-FIVE

As I finished the last note, I felt I had made a terrible mistake and an utter fool of myself. I hardly dared to look up from the keyboard and started exhaling loudly.

"Again!" said the King. "Again, again! Come, musicians let's have some strings with it!"

I faltered slightly and began the melody once more. This time I was joined by a lute, plucking chords softly and a recorder playing some harmony. The King started waving his arms about and then roared, "Stop! No, no; that certainly shall not do! Too melancholy, too melancholy!" I froze, certain I was about to lose my head – or at least, hand – over some stupid piece of music I learned to play when I was seven.

"Add a C#," whispered Immanuel. I suddenly realised what the King meant – I was playing the minor version of the melody and quickly did as Immanuel suggested. The King sat back in his throne with a look of satisfaction.

"What do you call this melody?"

"Whatever pleases Your Majesty," I said.

He arose from his throne and the Court fell silent. Sweat dripped from my forehead and I wiped it with my arm.

"Then I shall name it in your honour, boy with the green sleeves," he said.

"Your Majesty," I said, bowing low.

"Now, come, pray tell me what brings you to my Court."

I stepped forward and muttered something about Araminta. The King immediately signalled an aide and bade him make the necessary enquiries and we were invited to take some refreshment.

It seemed an eternity before the aide returned and spoke softly in the King's ear. Immanuel and I were drinking some wine and trying to remain as inconspicuous as possible. One of the musicians was asking me awkward questions about my "composition" which made me feel rather a fraud. I could tell that Immanuel had heartily disapproved of my rendition and I was expecting a ticking off as soon as we were alone.

"Your daughter is taking her rest in one of the guest chambers," said the aide to Immanuel. "If you would care to follow me, my lord, I shall take you to her." Immanuel and I exchanged an anxious glance and obeyed.

CHAPTER SIXTY-SIX

My heart leapt and sank at the same time to see Minty lying as still as a corpse or a Sleeping Beauty in the narrow bed of the chamber. Her eyes were closed and a man sat by her side. He stood, as we entered and bowed to us.

"Guy Wygan, my lord. Your most humble servant."

Immanuel took his hand and thanked him:

"It was you, I believe, who came to her aid on the road?"

"It was, sir. A most pleasant duty. I am only sorry I did not arrive sooner, or my men might have dispatched your attackers."

Minty opened her eyes and I rushed to her side.

"Chris?"

"Minty! Thank God you're safe!" Without thinking, I embraced her and she winced. I apologised.

"No. It's the pain, I'm sorry. It's so good to see you!" she said, and smiled. I couldn't tell her how much I had missed that smile.

"I shall leave you alone," said Mr Wygan and started out the door, slowly. I could tell he had formed some attachment to Minty and our reunion displaced him. He faltered slightly before muttering some prayer or good wish and closed the door.

"What on earth happened to you?" asked Immanuel.

Minty tried to relate everything as clearly and as fast as she could. The news of the attack on the *HIS* building troubled Immanuel.

"We've got to get you out of here as fast as we can and back to civilisation," he said. "Can you move?"

Minty tried but the pain was too much. I hated seeing her like this. Immanuel examined her briefly.

"I can't see any lasting damage," he said; "I should be able to fix you up with a bit of modern medicine. I suggest we make a fast exit."

"We can't," said Minty. "Not yet, at least. I've lost my Chronosphere!"

CHAPTER SIXTY-SEVEN

It was impossible to tell if Immanuel was more cross or concerned with this last bit of news.

"This could literally unravel the whole chronoverse as we know it, Araminta. It really is *the* most serious thing! Supposing some idiot finds it, presents it to the King and he disappears? Or a peasant who will one day have an important descendent? Or someone clever who works out how to use it properly and becomes the first time traveller? Think of the untold damage it might do! But you didn't think, did you?" Immanuel's voice was getting louder and faster; he didn't notice that Minty was sobbing.

"Stop it! All right? Stop it! Can't you see she's distressed enough already?" I shouted at Immanuel, who took a breath and muttered an apology and no one said anything for a minute.

"Look," he continued, "I didn't really mean to tell you off but this is extremely serious. For all we know the person who finds it could be your Domino killer, or the person who bombed the *HIS* headquarters, so it is *absolutely imperative* that we recover it. Now, where do you think you last had it?"

"Well that's the loopiest thing I've heard all day!" said Minty.

"What did you say?"

"I *said*, Chris, that that was the loopiest thing I've heard all day. I mean, first off I have no idea where I was. There was an attack. I started to fall. I think I felt a Chronosphere. I must have grabbed it or something. But why did it bring me here? Second –"

"Sshh!" I said, interrupting her. "I've thought of something."

"What?"

"It was what you said – that word you used," I said.

"Which word?"

"'Loop'. You said: 'loop.'"

"I said 'loopiest.'"

"It doesn't matter – *that's* the answer; don't you see?" I exclaimed, as everything fell into place. The others stared back at me, vacuously.

"The whole thing is a big loop! All this time! To think – the answer was just staring us in the face!"

"Chris, what *are* you jabbering about?" asked Immanuel.

"This whole thing is a time loop. Think about it. What brought us back here?" The penny dropped and Immanuel beamed.

"Of course!"

"Of course? Of course *what?*" demanded Araminta.

Immanuel explained about the final clue we had found in invisible ink on the parchment from the Tudor House and how we had followed its instructions to return to this time.

"What does that mean?" she asked.

"It means, Araminta, that we *shall* find the 'Sphere and then we shall bury it," said Immanuel.

"But how do you propose we go about finding it? It's not like there's a 'find my Chronosphere app' is there? And, in case you haven't noticed, I'm not exactly in a condition to go gallivanting across the county in search of the place I might or might not have dropped it."

"No," said Immanuel slowly, "then I suppose we shall have to enlist someone who can."

Almost on cue there was a knock at the door and Mr Wygan returned with another bowl of soup.

"Ah, Mr Wygan," said Immanuel, "we were just talking about you."

CHAPTER SIXTY-EIGHT

Having never ridden a horse, the last thing I felt like doing was saddling up and going on a Medieval scavenger hunt. Immanuel had obviously considered this as well and suggested I remain behind to look after my "sister," whilst he and Wygan went off in search of the Chronosphere. Wygan, upon hearing that Araminta had dropped a valuable item in the forest which he had failed to retrieve, positively jumped at the opportunity to play the proverbial knight in shining armour and vowed under a most solemn oath that he should neither sleep nor drink, nor eat, nor talk – save to pray – until he had discovered and recovered the missing artefact. In fact, he was so eager to venture forth on this "quest", it took some persuading before Immanuel was set to accompany him. Only when Immanuel pointed out that only he would be able to verify the artefact did Wygan insist upon them both setting out at first light.

We spent the night slumped in chairs that were brought in for us. The King insisted on us having separate guest quarters but we declined, as politely as possible, in favour of being able to attend Araminta though the night.

The King's magnanimity was beginning to make me a little nervous. Just after dark, he sent a messenger to summon me back to the throne room to perform once more. I could see that Araminta was impressed but Immanuel, ever the party pooper, began to tear me off a strip about altering the timeline until I pointed out that it had always been legend that Henry VIII composed Greensleeves and, for all we know, he *had* – and it was just another example of a time loop: the only reason I knew it in the first instance was because I had taught it to Henry VIII who had left it to posterity, enabling me to learn it in the 21st Century. This argument seemed to appease Immanuel, if not quite satisfy him.

"You will be careful out there, won't you?" said Araminta as Immanuel fastened his collar. The second-to-worst thing about this century was the lack of hot showers. The worst thing was that no one seemed to mind going about the place unwashed.

"Araminta, I've been riding horses since before you were born, long after you'd have died and in several universes in which you might never have existed. I think I'll be all right. But, thanks." There was something slightly wistful in Immanuel's voice which I couldn't place but he gave a lingering look at the bed before he exited, leaving the two of us alone.

"So..." I started, unsure what it was I wanted to say.

"So?"

"Come here often?"

She laughed and I sat down, tentatively, at the edge of the bed.

"I'm glad to see you, Chris."

"And I, you. What...what was it like? Falling like that?"

"What was it like? I thought I was going to die, Chris! That's the honest truth. I know we came a little close in Munich but this was very different. For this one moment I felt as though I were flying; then the panic set in, the regrets, fears, loss and, as I was seconds away – though I suppose the whole fall was only seconds – I found a strange sort of acceptance."

"Wow." It was a useless thing to say but all I could think of.

"Let's not dwell on all that, though, it's not very cheery is it?"

"No. What then?" I asked.

"Fancy helping me with my vocab? I've got a test when – if – we get back," she said.

"French?" I asked.

"German."

"Bum. Sorry, Minty, my German is shocking. Didn't you notice in Munich?" I instinctively touched behind my ear. The translator was still there.

"Then again, who needs to learn it now?"

The dawn was beginning to seep in through the window, casting a soft orange glow on the bed, as if to remind me of the constancy of seasons and days. The world still turned in the same direction; all those living now, were dead and all those yet to come are unborn. I fell silent. Araminta noticed and said, quietly:

"I noticed it too, here; it's funny you know – just laying still. Time seems very different now, doesn't it?"

I nodded and listened to the birds of ages past singing outside.

CHAPTER SIXTY-NINE

"We had better get going right away!" said Immanuel as he burst through the room some hours later. He was accompanied by a ruddy-faced Wygan who was still recovering his breath.

"Triumph, my lady!" he said, bowing at Minty's bedside.

"You really found it?" she said.

"Wygan was a complete brick," said Immanuel.

"A brick, my lord?"

"It means you were a great help," I said.

"Simply could not have done it without you. You really are a marvel," said Immanuel.

"Oh, too kind, my lord."

"Nonsense. Now then, we really should be —"

Immanuel looked round but Wygan had already taken several steps forward and was poised at Minty's side.

"How are your ailments, my lady?"

"I'm doing very well, thank you. I'm just eager to return home now, I think." Wygan's face fell ten miles.

"After all, it would be terrible bad manners to impose further upon His Majesty's hospitality," she said.

"Why, then, allow me to accommodate you, my lady! I shall be returning to Cambridge within the week and I have a small dwelling not far from there where you could take recuperation. Indeed, there has recently been some work done on the ground level and I have commissioned a great carving for the main fireplace and shall incorporate some text from The Great Bible, whereof I read to you these past days."

The mention of the fireplace clinched it for me and I immediately blurted out:

"Mr Wygan, there is a great and secret favour we might petition you to undertake for us."

Immanuel shot me a glare but Araminta seemed to cotton on.

"There is none other I would entrust this sacred task to," she said.

"Why, then, my lady, I do entreat thee to speak on! Pray tell me the particulars."

"Have you parchment and quill? Also, you shall need some ink and, later some lemon juice," said Immanuel, curtly.

"I shall dispatch myself this instant."

Wygan smiled and, with a slight bow left us alone.

"Are you sure about this, Araminta?" asked Immanuel.

"Come on!" I said, "you heard him – he's obviously the owner of that Tudor house we broke into. All we have to do is get him to write out the poem we found and the other message with these space-time coordinates and have him hide them in his house where we can find them again. Or did find them."

"How can we be sure he'll do it?" asked Immanuel.

"Well, surely if it's a time loop, then the fact that we're here now proves that he did?" I said.

"Not necessarily. You're creating a causal loop here, Chris, not closing it. There are other ways that piece of paper might have found its way with the 'Sphere into that compartment. One of you might be trapped here and hide it yourselves," said Immanuel.

This thought had not occurred to me. I shuddered.

"What we need to do," continued Immanuel, "is see to it that Wygan guards the 'Sphere and its secret with his life."

"How do we accomplish that?" asked Araminta.

"By putting the fear of God into him."

At that moment, there was a sharp rap on the door and Wygan entered, armed with an assortment of stationery.

"Ah! my dear fellow! Now, take this down, will you?" Immanuel nodded at Araminta and Minty and I managed to recite the sonnet, as we had read it from the parchment, perfectly. Wygan took it down without so much as a raised eyebrow and blotted the ink carefully when he had finished.

"Now then, listen very carefully," commanded Immanuel. "What I'm about to tell you is strictly confidential, do you understand?" Wygan affirmed that he did.

"What date is it today?" asked Immanuel.

"The first of November, I believe."

"Indeed it is. And on this first day of November, in the Year of our Lord 1541, Archbishop Cranmer, recently arrived at this Court, is composing a letter. This letter he will leave in place after Mass tomorrow for His Majesty to read. Its content is of the most sensitive nature and refers to the Queen."

"To Queen Catherine?" asked Wygan, nervously.

"The very same," Immanuel said, pausing for both breath and effect. "Its contents are particularly inflammatory and, within a week, the Queen shall, herself confess to several indiscretions. Forthwith she shall be imprisoned in the Tower and duly executed next year."

"This is remarkable! Truly beyond reason. What pernicious accusations are these?"

"It is neither iniquity, nor sorcery," said Immanuel, sternly. "We are no more spies than we are dogs, and our loyalty is to the King. I tell you these things only that you might believe my words and, in believing my words, will adhere to the strict letter of instruction I am about to give you concerning the parchment you have written on and are about to further mark, and the object you and I recovered not three hours hence."

Wygan considered for a moment and flared his large nostrils. My heart started thudding. I half envisaged him screaming for the guards and us being rounded and burned as seers or spies. Wygan did nothing hastily. He closed his eyes for a moment and interlocked his fingers.

"Very well," he said at last, "I shall put these aspersions on the Queen to one side until I am able to verify their particulars. If events transpire as you say, I shall be obedient to the very iota of your instructions and keep them secret until my last breath. If not, I shall be duty bound to report this parchment, the artefact and a record of your testimonies to His Majesty. Are we agreed?" He offered Immanuel his hand.

"We are."

The men looked at each other carefully and clasped each other's arms.

"Very good. Now, then, as to what we would like you to do with the…Egg?"

CHAPTER SEVENTY

Wygan was certainly a discreet man. Once he had listened to Immanuel's instructions, he wrapped the Chronosphere carefully in a piece of silk, took the parchment, shook our hands solemnly and departed.

"Stroke of luck finding him," I said.

"That remains to be seen." said Immanuel, gravely.

"I don't think it was luck," said Minty, "more like destiny."

"There's no such thing as destiny, Araminta. You're a time traveller now – not only do you make your future, but also the past," said Immanuel.

"But everything we've done – the very reason for being here, now, was because of the poem in the fireplace. A poem we were destined to ask Wygan to put there. It's Fate, or Time, or Something," said Minty.

"So you're saying we weren't free to choose to give Wygan the poem? You're saying we were pre-determined to do it?" I said, not much liking the idea of not being free.

"Well, over the past few days, as Wygan has been reading to me, he's talked a lot about pre-destination. In fact he said there's a double pre-destination."

"Codswallop! He would. He's just the sort of man who would believe in double predestination," scoffed Immanuel.

"What do you mean? What are you two talking about?!" I asked.

"Double predestination is the idea that God has already decided who's in heaven and hell and you're going to one of those places no matter what," said Immanuel, quickly.

"Oh. I thought we had free will?" I said.

"We have the illusion of it. All our choices are limited aren't they, by birth, wealth and experience. For example, Chris, you *could* rob a bank, but in your society you'd get caught and put in jail," said Immanuel.

"No I wouldn't – I'd time travel out of there!" I said, facetiously.

"Talking of getting caught and time travel, oughtn't we be going about now?" said Minty.

"Araminta's right, we should leave at once." Immanuel peered out of the window. No one was in sight. He took out his 'Sphere and we all laid hands on it and said goodbye to Hampton Court.

We materialised back at the Lake. It smelt the same, but this time there was a thick mist near the water, seeping like the breath of a great dragon, steadily towards us. Araminta had been flung a few feet away and Immanuel was dusting himself off. Immediately, he went over to a bush and retrieved a satchel. I couldn't help but laugh – it was a *Blue Peter* moment.

"One you made earlier?" I called out. Immanuel ignored the comment and walked over to Araminta,

"Here, this won't hurt. I promise." He placed his hands beneath her back and seemed to inject some instrument into her. Araminta didn't make a sound. I walked up and stood over her.

"How do you feel?"

"Incredible. The pain's completely gone!" she said.

Immanuel gave her his hand and she stood up easily.

"Good as new! What was that you gave me?"

"I didn't give you anything as such, actually. I just put you back into shape. Marvels of modern medicine."

"Well, thank you."

"Don't thank me. It was probably my fault you fell out of that window in the first place, if you think about it," said Immanuel.

Araminta smiled and walked a few paces towards the edge of the mist.

"It's beautiful here! Where are we?"

"The Lake District," I said.

"Wow! Well I've seen some amazing places - some exotic places in Africa and South America but this is so unspoiled – so mysterious and intense!"

"The world before we ravaged it. The Garden of Eden. Shangri-La. Paradise," said Immanuel.

We stood in silence for some minutes, as a hallowed quiet fell on us. There was something truly spine-tingling about being here, near the beginning of the world.

"What now?" I asked.

"Now, Chris, it's time for you to go home."

"Home?" I said. The word sounded alien. I had almost forgotten I had one.

"Yes," he said.

"Oh." I heard the disappointment in my voice.

"We can't very well bounce around in time forever, Chris! Aren't you forgetting we've got families and friends and school?" said Minty. She was right, of course.

I turned to Immanuel and asked, rather uselessly, if he were coming with us.

"No," said Immanuel. "I've got to go see what's happening in the Present. If there's been an attack on the *HIS*, I need to find the party responsible; it's incredibly likely we might be next on their hit list."

I nodded, slowly.

"What should we do when we get back?" I asked.

"Go to school. Do your vocab test, Araminta. And, both of you, stay out of trouble!"

"You expect us to just go back to our normal lives?" said Araminta. I hadn't imagined she'd want to continue time travelling after her recent experiences but I understood her trepidation in having to return to anything we had before.

"Look, you've proved yourselves already; that's not in question. But you need a break and I need to evaluate what's going on in the Present. Besides, you both need to think about which side you're on," said Immanuel.

"Side?" I asked.

"The attack on the *Historical Improvement Society* changes everything. Whoever did it – and I hope to goodness it wasn't anything to do with us – has just turned the heat up on what *was* a cold war. There will be casualties now. Real casualties. I only hope I can work out who they are and what they want before they kill more people. Or, worse, eradicate us from the timeline. So, you see, the most use you can be right now, is *safe*. Think of yourselves as sleeping agents. Be ready but don't wait your lives away." Immanuel came to the end of his speech and gave us a half-smile.

I stepped forward and shook his hand, which seemed about the most appropriate thing to do.

"You have your home coordinates?" he asked. I nodded.

"Then Time be with you," he said, as the train-jolt hurled us back to 2015.

287

Part Four

Do I dare
Disturb the universe?
In a minute there is time
For DECISIONS AND REVISIONS
which a minute will reverse.

- TS Eliot, *The Lovesong of J Alfred Prufrock*

289

CHAPTER SEVENTY-ONE

As soon as we got back, there were mundane things we had to think about – like calling parents and sorting out clothes. We had both managed to materialise inside my bedroom – which was probably better than being a mile apart from each other, but potentially rather awkward to explain. I had often wondered if our time travelling generated any noticeable light or noise but apparently not.

Minty and I were stood face to face, almost touching. I couldn't help but stare.

"Chris! You in?" called a voice.

Kirsty! Of all the moments, she had to pick right then. Of course she also didn't wait for a response, she just stormed into the room without knocking and caught us standing in a near embrace; me dressed in my ridiculous green-sleeved doublet and Minty in something they'd given her at the Palace.

"Oh. What's going on here? Romeo and Juliet?"

"Bugger off Kirsty! Don't you ever knock?" I said.

"Mum's still at work. And it's still your turn to cook!"

"All right. I'll do it in a bit; just let me finish this – " I faltered for an excuse.

"This costume fitting for the Tudor day," said Minty, quickly.

"Right. Whatever. Araminta, I'm surprised Chris dragged you into this. Not very cool. Anyway. Laters!"

With that, Kirsty flounced out of the room.

"Look, I can't really go home dressed like this. Have you got anything I can change into?" said Minty, tugging at her Tudor dress.

"Well, just borrow some of Kirsty's jeans or something?"

"She's a fair bit thinner than me."

"My Mum's stuff any good?"

"Chris!"

"All right! Sorry, I don't know, do I?"

Araminta folded her arms and gave me a scathing look.

"You know, Kirsty keeps a few of her older clothes in the cupboard still; worth a look?" I said.

Araminta nodded and went off to investigate while I sat down on my bed and loosened my collar. I was still holding the Chronosphere.

She came back clutching a pair of jeans and a top.

"Think she'll mind me borrowing these?"

"Haven't seen her wear them for years. You'll be fine. Want to change in the bathroom or something?"

"Sure."

As soon as I heard the door close I also divested myself of the Tudor garb and slung on a pair of jeans and a T-shirt. Catching my reflection in the mirror, I noted, with some irony, that I didn't look as good.

The bathroom door opened and the transformation was complete. It was as if we were both Cinderellas, being returned to our pre-ball state at the stroke of midnight. There would be no princes or ball gown, no carriage nor glass slipper. We smiled at each other in the way that people do when they've shared a life changing experience and know they must put it behind them for a time.

"I'd better get back," she said, touching her left elbow. "My parents will be worried."

"Yes, of course," I said and then, remembering: "Oh, yes, I think your Father was going to call you."

Minty's face went pale.

"Chris. My phone's missing."

"You're joking."

"No."

A thousand possibilities went through my mind and a hundred science fiction films.

"You realise if someone were to find that…" I started.

"I know."

"I mean, supposing Hitler finds it in Munich and wins the War? Supposing Wygan recovers it and does some weird thing with it and –"

"But we're still here. Nothing's changed," said Minty.

"But we're protected by the 'Sphere," I said.

"Our memories are in tact but this universe is the same as when we left it."

"Right. So what does that mean?"

"I must have lost it in the fall."

"When, though?" I asked.

"In the future, I suppose."

"Well how are you going to explain it at home?"

"I haven't thought about that yet."

She sat down on the edge of my bed and I realised I had been a bit harsh with her.

"Sorry, Minty. It must have been horrible, being caught in that explosion."

She nodded and we said nothing for a few moments.

"Are you going to tell your Father the truth?" I said, breaking the silence.

"I'm not sure." There was something she wasn't telling me, but I didn't press her.

"Well, I would say let me know how it goes, but I suppose you won't be able to without a phone. Meet me at the Tree at break tomorrow?"

"Sure," she said, quietly.

"Good luck," I said, and showed her out.

I couldn't have known how nervous Minty was feeling about going home. She was still in inner turmoil, reeling from what Jeremy had said to her before she had stepped into the *HIS* lift. Could it be that her Father was a member of The Domino Group? If so, should she trust him with her secret or keep it from him? She wasn't even sure which side *she* was on, let alone her Father.

As she walked up the gravel drive Araminta felt incredibly alone. *I should have confided in Chris,* she thought. Having secrets was divisive. The best thing about having a secret is being able to share it, after all. Sharing the secret of the Chronosphere with me – of all our adventures – had helped her forget her loneliness. Now it seemed all over she didn't know how to feel.

Her Mother saw her approaching and ran out to meet her.

"Araminta! Oh my darling! We were beginning to worry!" She embraced her tightly. Her mother did not usually show such affection and it was rather overwhelming.

"I'm sorry. So sorry. I lost my phone and I had no money to call you. I only just managed to make it home," said Araminta, sobbing.

Her Mother seemed satisfied with this answer, happy to have her daughter returned safely. Minty crossed the threshold and looked up at the staircase where she could make out the shadow of her Father standing sentinel.

"You must be famished! Let's get you something to eat," said Mrs Stirling.

Araminta followed her Mother into the kitchen where a hob was lit and some pasta put on the boil.

"Araminta."

She turned round to see her Father standing with his hands clasped behind his back. He was wearing a tweed jacket and had not shaved for a few days which meant he was not in a good mood. She would have to eat slowly; clearly she had some explaining to do.

CHAPTER SEVENTY-TWO

I had missed school. Much as I hated to admit it, I enjoyed the structure. School was safe; boring at times and restrictive, but easy. Walking into the classroom was like having the weight of the world lifted from my shoulders. No one was going to die if I got a question wrong, no apocalypse would result from my failure to hand in my homework on time. Mr Travis had other ideas:

"Jones, where have you been?"

"Been, Sir?"

"I can only surmise, from your lack of homework, that you've taken a little trip to pre-historic Britain or a concentration camp or somewhere else where you had no access to pen and paper."

"I...um..."

Mr Travis reached into his desk and took out a pink detention slip.

"Wednesday," he said, shortly.

"After school, sir?"

"Precisely."

I almost smiled. Josh frowned at me and drew a cartoon of me writing lines. I had missed him, too, though I couldn't say as much. For him it had been hours; for me, weeks had passed.

The morning seemed incredibly long. I hadn't been able to contact Minty the night before and I was beginning to imagine all kinds of things.

As soon as the bell went for break I ran out to the Tree. I knew Minty had German so I wasn't expecting her to be straight out, but, as the seconds turned into minutes, my heart was beating furiously in anticipation.

After what seemed an eternity, I saw her walking towards me, carrying a satchel on her right shoulder. I breathed a sigh of relief and bounded up to her.

"Everything all right?" I asked.

"Yes. Fine."

"You don't sound fine," I said.

"Really. I'm fine. It's just...odd to be back."

"Yeah; yeah, it is."

We sat down and Minty told me that she had managed to avoid too many questions with her Mother and she told her Father that she had been found by Jeremy and had lost the poem to him, along with her phone. Although he admonished her at first for not telling him what they had found earlier, his concern for his child's safety was, apparently, slightly greater than his penchant for solving mysteries. Once Araminta had described Jeremy to her Father, he told her he had encountered a man fitting his description in Cambridge and, all things adding up, the matter was dropped.

"So that's an end to it, then?" I asked.

"I guess so. At least where they're concerned."

"At least," I said wistfully, not a little sorry that there wasn't some immediate threat or danger we had to tackle.

"Hey, how did the vocab test go?" I asked.

"Alles gut. Then again, of course it was fine."

She touched behind her ear.

"Yeah, I guess we'll both get good grades in German now."

"Feels a bit like cheating but I don't know how to switch it off."

And that was it. Mrs Collins blew the whistle signalling the end of break and we made our way back into the building for Maths and English respectively.

The days became weeks all too quickly and I adjusted to the life of a twenty-first century school-boy all too soon. Minty and I still spoke occasionally but, with little happening and no sign of Immanuel or any other time traveller, we started to drift apart.

It was time to choose GCSE options, so I was thinking about that. History had seemed an obvious choice but part of me wondered if I would ever truly learn anything about the past from books, when I could visit there at the touch of a button. On the other hand, if I were to start time travelling again, it might be good to read up about it first.

Josh wanted to do History, but Mr Travis said if his latest essay wasn't good enough, he wouldn't recommend him to the Head and he'd have to do Geography instead. The other thing that seemed an obvious choice was Music. I had started to practise a lot since getting back. Once you've played for a King, the old upright in your front room doesn't really seem that exciting, I'll grant you, but it seemed a useful skill to have in most time periods.

CHAPTER SEVENTY-THREE

It happened on a Thursday: Kirsty had invited Minty to dinner so she could show off the new hair straighteners she'd got for her birthday and we were walking home. This close to the end of term it started getting dark pretty early and Mum always made us promise to keep to the main roads but neither Kirsty nor I managed to stick to that rule. I wished we had.

Perhaps it was my fault; we were just at the kerb when I noticed my shoelaces were undone and I bent down to re-tie them. Minty waited for me but Kirsty just walked on. She was halfway across the road when she noticed I wasn't with her and turned to face me. I didn't even see it:

A screech of brakes. A thud. Minty screamed. I saw her legs first – those stupid pink and black tights that she insisted on wearing, even though she'd been warned twice by her Head of House not to.

It was one of those unnecessary, petrol-guzzling four by fours. The driver was a woman; possibly mid-thirties, with blonde hair streaked back in a pony tail. She was standing over my sister, looking completely aghast.

"Get out of the way! Get out of the way!" I screamed at her.

Kirsty's face was covered in blood and the tears welled up in my eyes as the ambulance sirens got louder. I knelt down beside her and took her hand. The driver was trying to tell me she was sorry. I swore at her and she moved away.

"It's all right, Kirsty. You're going to be all right," I told her.

No response. I felt my hand being squeezed and smiled in hope. It was Minty; she had made her way to kneel beside me.

"Kirsty, can you hear me? It's Araminta. Hold on. The ambulance will be here any moment. They'll fix you up all right."

Still no response.

I grabbed her wrist, desperately searching for a pulse but there was none. Blood seeped from her wounds like the promises of time ebbing away. I could almost see the scene from an extreme high angle shot, slowly moving out. The sirens were getting closer but I knew they would only confirm that she was dead.

I looked at her. All the petty squabbles of sibling rivalry vanished. I wanted to embrace her, to tell her I loved her. I wanted to sit on her bed again and talk about the boys she fancied; to be left at home to cook and watch TV together while Mum was out, and argue over the channel. I wanted to be annoyed by her, I wanted to buy Christmas presents for her. I wanted to see the woman she would become. Her eyes stared back, empty.

"Chris? Chris…I'm so sorry."

I could barely hear Araminta. Something was playing over in my head; something I had half forgotten and could not quite remember. It was a sort of nagging feeling. I stood up and looked around me, as if I were a complete stranger.

It was a peculiar scene: The car was stopped, slightly at an angle and, I thought, a little over to the right hand side of the road. I memorised the number plate. To its left, an old woman with a Golden Retriever stood, looking on. A football was stuck on the roof of one of the houses next to the dog walker and there were faces at the net curtain of its front windows. A teenaged boy plodded along, plugged into his white earphones; he passed, oblivious to the tragedy. A carrier bag swept across the road and, as I turned to complete the scene, Araminta's blue eyes, teeming with life: with promise and despair, looked into mine and read what I was thinking.

"No, Chris."

"This is not supposed to happen. It's a mistake, Minty and I'm going to fix it."

The siren stopped and a door was opened. I didn't dare to look. Minty and I gazed at each other for a short eternity and then she nodded as I started running with one word on my mind: *Chronosphere*.

CHAPTER SEVENTY-FOUR

I had left the Chronosphere under a floorboard of my bedroom. I visualised grabbing a hammer and tearing up the nails, as I willed my legs to move faster. The pavement was already becoming slippery with frost and my shoes were not well designed. I could hear Minty close on my heel; she was calling my name. I ignored her and tried to run faster, my chest pounding.

I was only a few streets away. I kept chanting to myself, "If I can just get home she will be safe."

I felt a hand grab my arm and I tried to shake it off but slipped and fell over.

"Chris! You all right?"

"Minty? What are you doing? Get off me!"

Minty bent down and pulled me to my feet.

"You can't do this!" she said.

"Do what?"

"Use time travel to alter your own past."

"It's not my past, it's my present – it just happened, Minty!"

"You can't play God with people's lives like that. I won't let you!" Her voice sounded frightened.

"What are you going to do, report me to the police?"

We were both still panting and I was sobbing through the shortness of breath. I sniffled. In truth, I was exhausted – physically and emotionally.

"Otherwise, what's all this for, Minty? Surely we're meant to use it for good? We've been running round, doing whatever those twins told us to do and neither of us stopped to ask why we had ended up with the 'Sphere in the first place did we? Well maybe it was for this."

"And maybe not," she said.

"And maybe not, but I'm going to do it anyway and if you're my friend you'll accept that."

For the slightest of moments I do believe Minty was considering coshing me on the head, breaking into my house and burying the 'Sphere where I'd never find it ever again.

"All right," she said, "we'll go together." I nodded and we started jogging again, hand in hand.

Mum was at work, of course. I was such a nervous wreck though, it took me about five attempts to fit the key in the lock and, in the end, I had to let Minty do it. I led the way upstairs and into my bedroom, where I attacked the floorboards with the nearest heavy object I could find.

"Careful!" Minty cautioned.

I was too desperate to heed any advice and stabbed my finger trying to rip the nail out.

"Let me help."

Minty found a proper hammer and finished the job. I put my hand into the crevice and felt around.

Nothing. It wasn't there.

CHAPTER SEVENTY-FIVE

"Are you sure it was here?" asked Minty.

"Of course I'm sure! I put in there and bashed the nails in myself the day we got back!"

"And you haven't touched it since?"

I flashed her a filthy look.

"Sorry; just making sure," she said.

I sat down forcefully on the end of my bed and buried my head in my hands. It was all just too much.

"Hey. It's all right. We'll figure it out. We always do, don't we?" She rubbed my shoulders and I tried to nod my head.

A clang resonated in the street outside and startled me. Minty went to the window.

"Chris! Look!"

"What? What is it?" She was standing in my way and I couldn't see.

"Over there – by the tree!"

I squinted my eyes and made out a shape moving by the palm tree in our neighbour's garden. I leapt over the bed and ran down the stairs and out into the cold, shouting something. The figure, who had his back to me, turned around. It was Immanuel.

"Immanuel! You bast–" I never finished the insult as something knocked him to the floor. Minty was outside by now. I hadn't even noticed it had been snowing for some time. I could just make out Immanuel and started to cross the road.

"Careful, Chris."

I ignored Minty and walked over to where Immanuel was laying, flat on his back, writhing in agony.

"Look out!" he warned as something flashed past me and hit the ground by Immanuel, hissing in a cloud of smoke. Immanuel sprang up and lunged forward – I thought, at me but he was going for someone behind me who was pointing a weapon. Before they could fire again, Immanuel had them pinned to the ground and they rolled over and over in a fierce grip. Minty looked at me. There was nothing either of us could do. Immanuel wrestled the weapon free of his opponent and aimed to fire it. A fist struck him and the weapon was thrown to the ground. Minty nimbly dived in and retrieved it and, taking a few steps back, aimed it at the two of them.

"I'll shoot." It was not a threat.

"Don't! Araminta!" I shouted.

The two figures stopped their wrestling, immediately frozen like stone statues.

"Get up. Both of you. Slowly."

They obeyed her: first Immanuel and then the other, so that they were both standing with their backs to us.

"Now, turn around," she commanded.

I should have anticipated what happened next – it seemed so obvious – but something still made me gasp when the other turned his face and I saw that it was Jeremy.

CHAPTER SEVENTY-SIX

"Now then," said Jeremy softly, "we don't want to make a scene, do we? Let's all just calm down and we can talk this through."

"What have you done with my 'Sphere?" I demanded.

"If you shout, your neighbours will hear and you won't get the answers you want, or the 'Sphere; to say nothing of Kirsty, Christopher," said Jeremy.

"Give it back! Give it back now!" I said.

"I don't have it."

I looked hard at Jeremy. Immanuel had been silent until now, and I noticed he was fiddling with something behind his back.

"Hands where I can see them!" demanded Minty, tightening her grip on the weapon.

Immanuel took his hands out slowly. He was holding a Chronosphere.

"Is that –?" I started.

"Yes; it's yours. I took it, Chris. I had to."

"Don't believe a word he tells you!" shouted Jeremy. I told him to be quiet and walked closer to them.

"Give me the 'Sphere back and tell us what you're doing here: both of you." I held out my hand but Immanuel did not move.

"Tell him," said Jeremy. "Or I will!"

"Tell me? Tell me what?" I said, as a deep sense of panic started to set in.

"The truth, Christopher. You deserve to know the truth!" said Jeremy, loudly.

I looked back and forth between the two of them and saw the same fear in their eyes. Minty had lowered her weapon. We stood there, hearts racing, butterflies in stomachs, wondering which would speak next.

"What truth?" I asked.

Jeremy took a step closer to me and bent down, into the light of the street lamp.

"That I am you," he said.

"And so am I," said Immanuel.

I literally didn't know what to think, let alone say. I looked at Minty but she just furrowed her brow in astonishment.

"Explain," I managed to utter.

"This is the moment that changes everything, Chris," said Immanuel. "This is why I had to take the 'Sphere from you."

"And why you knew I had to stop you," said Jeremy.

"Please!" I said, "this is too much! One at a time! Immanuel; you first."

He started, slowly and softly, telling me how much he had suffered since losing Kirsty; how everyday was wrought with grief and regret but that he knew he had to endure it – that changing the past was never right. Kirsty was simply meant to die and I had to accept it. He had come back in time to prevent me from altering the past.

"I thought you were from the future?" I managed to say, at last.

"I work in the future. I'm about fifty years old now. Thereabouts. It's difficult to keep track of age when you're a time traveller."

"And you?" I asked of Jeremy.

"I am the you that you are about to become, Christopher. I won't accept his argument: you *must* save your sister. Power like this is given to very few. I admit I was wrong about Hitler: I couldn't see far enough. But this is different. This is your sister! How can you just let her die? It's wrong!"

"It's like you've swapped arguments! I thought you always argued about the consequences of our actions. I thought you said there was no such thing as right and wrong, just action and inaction?" I said, confused with grief and time.

"It's *Kirsty*, Christopher." appealed Jeremy.

"Don't listen, Chris! You can't afford to be led by your emotions. You must act out of duty. You don't know what the consequences of your actions will be: supposing you save Kirsty and she grows up to do something terrible? Or something else terrible happens to someone else because you saved her?" said Immanuel.

"That's rubbish and he knows it: he's right, we can't know the ultimate consequences. That's where I was wrong before, I see that now but you have to right this wrong," said Jeremy.

"No! Chris! Listen to me! Listen to me: the driver: The driver was on her phone at the time. That's why she hit Kirsty. There was an eye witness. She's going to be prosecuted and will go to prison for several years. If you save Kirsty, she'll be free! She might do it again and someone else will die!" Immanuel was shouting.

"You can't know that!" I said.

"That's why you have to do what's right, Chris. You must act out of duty," Immanuel pleaded. Jeremy picked up on this last word and tried to convince me my first duty was to my family – that I couldn't put the lives of possible strangers in front of my own sister or Mum. He sounded genuinely upset but Immanuel turned on him:

"Jeremy I've hunted you across the chronoverse and I have never harmed you but if you keep twisting his mind like this I will have no choice but to – "

"'But to' – what?" asked Jeremy.

I did not hear Immanuel's answer. As they were arguing I saw my window of opportunity and I took it, diving forward and grabbing the Chronosphere from Immanuel's hands, I skidded along the pavement and punched in the co-ordinates as fast as I could.

They didn't have a chance.

CHAPTER SEVENTY-SEVEN

I hadn't had time to calibrate the space variables so I materialised back at the house. It wasn't dark yet and there was no snow on the ground. I peered in through the window of my neighbours to read their kitchen clock. It was was only just gone three. I started sprinting towards School.

I didn't really know what I was doing. I was being fuelled by adrenaline but still reeling from the shock of the double revelation I had received. Several things about time travel still confused me and I wasn't sure if this would even work. I ran faster.

The wind was biting at my neck. I noticed I still had my coat and bag on. I was beginning to feel the weight of my school books. I had half a mind to ditch the bag but I didn't dare stop for a moment to deviate from my rescue attempt.

I reached the road where the accident happened. It was quiet enough. I checked my watch. No good, of course. I looked around for someone to ask the time from but it occurred to me that it would do no good as I hadn't thought to note the time when Kirsty was hit. I closed my eyes and tried to remember.

I saw the teenager, the dog and the ball in my mind's eye. I looked around. No Golden Retriever in sight. The only pedestrian was a man, mid-thirties, on his phone. The ball was still on the roof of the house. I waited.

A car shot down the road past me. It was going too fast. Most people drove too fast down here. I didn't know whether to wait or to move. I took a step forward and immediately back. The temperature was dropping. Still no sign of a dog. No sign of the three of us either.

I began to worry that, feeling so cold and standing so still, I would freeze to the spot and be unable to do anything when it happened. I paced up and down a few times and then the thought occurred to me to walk up the road in the direction that the car came from and flag it down when I saw it approaching.

I could only have gone a few hundred yards when I saw it, parked outside someone's house, round the corner. I did a double take. It was definitely the car. I looked at the bumper, half expecting to see Kirsty's blood splattered all over it. It was clean as a whistle. I repeated the number plate to myself and began frantically looking for a clue as to the whereabouts of the owner. *Then again,* I thought to myself, *what would I say? "Hello, you're about to murder my sister. Please don't drive?"* In the distance I could see a dog being walked and I panicked: without a second thought, I took out the pen knife I had in my bag for DT and stabbed at the tyres. It was much harder than I thought but I was, eventually, rewarded with a hissing sound. I immediately repeated this action on the remaining wheels and scuttled back, hoping to avoid detection.

Was is it enough? Something in my head played over and over – what Immanuel had said about it being 'meant' that Kirsty should die?

"No," I said, out loud, and started running back to the spot where she was hit.

It began to happen: the Golden Retriever came into view and the teenager came out of his house and plugged in his earphones. Over in the far corner, on the opposite side of the road, three school children were approaching. Us.

I held my breath. Everyone was converging on the scene like a carefully orchestrated and over-rehearsed piece of theatre or dance. I saw myself bend down to tie my lace as Kirsty neared the kerb and started to cross.

She was meant to die.

Out of nowhere, a car. I shouted and ran into its path, knocking Kirsty out of the way just in time as I felt the impact.

Everything went black.

CHAPTER SEVENTY-EIGHT

The darkness only lasted a moment. I heard Kirsty screaming my name and then Minty. I opened my eyes, slowly.

"He's all right, he's all right!" A pain shot through my face. I put my hand to my cheek. It was bleeding profusely. An older man was bending over me.

"I'm so sorry. I'm so sorry. I don't know why I didn't see you. Are you all right?"

I looked at him.

"You were driving?" I asked.

"Yes. Yes I was. Look, let me call you an ambulance."

"I'm fine. My sister. How's my sister?"

"I'm fine, Chris. I'm right here. Thanks to you. You saved my life." Kirsty smiled at me and kissed my head.

"How on earth did you get across the road like that, Chris? One minute you were tying your lace, the next you dove right across the road and pushed Kirsty out of way of the car! It was like you were Superman or something!" said Minty, clearly impressed. I turned to look at her. She had no memory of Kirsty dying, of course. I strained my head, looking for the other me but there was no one there. The pain became excruciating.

"Don't move, Chris. Just wait for the ambulance," said Kirsty.

I laid my head back in Kirsty's lap and looked up. The ball was still on the roof. A snowflake fell.

CHAPTER SEVENTY-NINE

If I'm honest, I rather enjoyed being a hero. Kirsty had not mentioned the iPod for a week and Mum had even taken a day off work to be home for us. When I went into school, Josh yelled out, "Three cheers for Christopher Jones!" and at least four people joined in. I choose to think of that as a victory.

Minty and I kept quiet. We spent a few breaks and lunches together. After a week of keeping the whole truth from her, I couldn't handle the burden of secrecy anymore and decided to tell her everything. It had taken me some time to work it all out, anyway.

Finally, I had come to terms with the truth: the men we knew as Jeremy and Immanuel were really me – albeit different versions of my future selves, from alternative timelines, or reality: Immanuel had grown up in a timeline in which Kirsty had died; Jeremy, in which she had not: the reality I had just created. It seemed my destiny was sealed. I recoiled involuntarily to think I could ever become Jeremy. Perhaps he wasn't so bad, after all. Had he remembered everything? Would *I* remember everything that happened? If so, I wondered why I would kidnap my younger self and attempt to assassinate Hitler, if I knew it would be futile.

For all the revelations, I was left with only further questions – questions I asked Araminta.

She sat there, under the snow-covered Tree, wrapped up in a deep blue coat and scarf; a white bobbly hat on her head, and listened, completely non-judgmentally. Once I had finished she simply asked,

"Did I really point a gun at them? At you?"

"Yes."

"Sorry."

"I'm afraid, Minty – afraid of what I'll become, what I'll do. That means all that time I knew what was going to happen? How could I become like that? How could I forget?"

"I suppose even *we* don't know what the future holds."

"It just seems that it was always going to happen." I touched my cheek. The stitches were due out next week but I didn't need the nurse to tell me there would be a lasting scar. I had seen it already.

"I just feel like I'm not free any more, Minty."

"But you chose to go back – to save her. You will choose again, in the future. And Immanuel – that's the other you – an alternative you?"

"I think so."

"Explains why neither of them wanted to harm us," she said. I agreed and we sat for some time in private contemplation until a snowball narrowly missed us. Year Eights were playing around the Tree. It made me think of something:

"What about the other me that was tying the laces?"

"I don't know. I told you, Chris – from my perspective, you simply appeared in the middle of the road and pushed Kirsty out of the way of that Corsa – or whatever it was."

"That's another thing. In the original timeline she was hit with a four by four – a female driver. What if…what if it was meant?"

"'Meant' – by whom? Chris, surely if we've learned anything, it's that we *don't* know the future – even if we've been there?"

"You're the one that's been there." I muttered. If I'm honest, I was a little jealous. I've always wanted to see the future. Perhaps it was better, now, that I didn't.

"So we should bury the Chronosphere? Bury it deep and forget about it?" I asked.

I looked at her and knew she wanted to – too much power had already cost us dearly, but both of us knew it was impossible. She touched her elbow and looked into my eyes.

"You're forgetting something, Chris: *he's* still out there. We can't stop until we've found him. You're not safe. None of us is safe."

For a moment I thought Minty was talking about her Father. There was something about Dr Stirling that made my blood run cold. Perhaps the Domino cufflinks had been a coincidence. Perhaps he was working with Immanuel's lot. Either way, there was something menacing about him. I hated that I couldn't share my feelings with his daughter.

"You mean the Domino Killer?" I said.

Araminta brushed her finger gently across the stitches on my cheek.

"Yes. No version of you is safe until we find him and put an end to it."

I had the feeling there was something more that she wanted to say, but she just smiled at me.

"You know, we're forgetting the enormous fun we can have with a Chronosphere," I said, cheerily.

"Like what?"

"Like stopping by 20th century France for a decent pastry, or watching some vintage Wimbledon. When was the last year before Murray that a British player won the singles title?"

"I think it was Fred Perry for the men – before the Second World War!"

"Or we could see if Murray wins next year? Place a bet…" I said, goading her.

"No, Chris; *no!*"

"Just a little iddy-biddy one?"

She poked me in the stomach and we laughed.

"So I'm guessing using it to win the lottery is out?" I tried.

"Neither of us is even old enough to play it."

"Good point."

"Besides, how would we explain it to our parents?"

"Intuition?"

"You're also forgetting we're not the only one with the ability to time travel, Chris. I think the plan should be to lay low for a while. Not draw attention to ourselves. Or *your*selves," she corrected herself.

"I think it's too late for that."

"Maybe. But I'd just like to be able to concentrate on school for a bit, if that's ok? I know I'm sort of used to being bounced around from pillar to post by my father, but when you add time into the mix –"

"You just want a bit of break from the travelling?"

"Yeah. I want to, y'know, make some friends. Be a teenager. Even if we are a bit older, I guess, now."

It hadn't occurred to me that our biological ages were more than our official ones in our present, thanks to all the time we'd spent time travelling. I wondered if I had changed much.

"Do you think of me differently, now?" I asked, nervously.

"Yes."

I looked down, ashamedly.

"Not because of *that*, Chris," she said, pointing to my cheek. "I mean, because of everything. Besides, we only need to start worrying if you go bald."

That made me laugh.

"And I'll be there to keep you in check," she added.

"Promise?"
"Promise. Till the end of time. Or times," she said.

We held each other's gaze for a moment and knew we were bound by more than time or friendship now. Some might call it Fate or Destiny. Perhaps it was duty, perhaps a choice. Like I said, there was no reason that we should have met, but we made the reason now:

"I don't think there *are* any ends, Minty; not anymore. Now, there are only beginnings."

CHRISTOPHER JONES AND ARAMINTA STIRLING
WILL RETURN IN

TIME'S FICKLE GLASS - BOOK II:
THE GOLDEN RULE

ABOUT THE AUTHOR

Born the elder of non-identical twins, Tristan Stone trained as a classical pianist and violinist at the Royal College of Music, where he was a Junior Exhibitioner for seven years. He then read Theology and Religious Studies at Cambridge University, where he began to develop an idea of *Imaginal Theology* –that in order to speak meaningfully of what is otherwise beyond our epistemology, we must use our imaginal faculty. This will be the focus of his forthcoming doctoral research on philosophical and theological method.

Upon graduation, Tristan trained as a Secondary School teacher, teaching English, Music and RS in schools and colleges around Kent. He is delighted to be currently teaching Philosophy, Theology and Ethics at Harris Westminster Sixth Form, London (which opened in September 2014).

Over the past decade, Tristan has written and produced several plays and published Study Guides for topics in Philosophy of Religion.

When he is not writing, teaching or working on independent films, Tristan occasionally sleeps, and enjoys living in Surrey with his wife, Laura, and their imaginary pets.